D1541249

THE WIDOW FILE

THE WIDOW FILE

A THRILLER BY

S.G. REDLING

PUBLISHED BY

THOMAS & MERCER

Text copyright © 2013 S.G. Redling

Printed in the United States of America.

Published by Thomas & Mercer, Seattle

www.apub.com

ISBN-13: 9781477808610
ISBN-10: 1477808612

Back cover photo by: Stewart A. Williams

Library of Congress Number: 2013906096

This book is for the Hitches—
Gina, Debra, Tenna, Christy, and Angela—
I wouldn't trade one of you for hard black shoes.

BOSTON

Shooting people is so boring, Booker thought as Mazan dropped to the floor. Or maybe it was Jusef. He hadn't paid much attention when they'd introduced themselves. The little one in the kitchen had been a fighter, nearly making enough noise to alert his friends before the garrote finished him. Now *that* was a job. That's why he made the money he did and had the reputation he had—hands-on craftsmanship. Shooting goat-eyed fools who didn't have the sense to run? Beneath him. They weren't even armed. Yet.

Booker unpacked the case the students had thought was research material from the university and began assembling the weapons. The calfskin gloves barely slowed him down at all. He shook his head.

"Wouldn't you think," he said to the dead boy flipped over in the chair, "that you'd notice something like a man not taking off his gloves? You're from Syria, for crying out loud. Aren't you guys born knowing stuff like this?" He slid two AK-47s underneath the couch and rose to hide the smaller guns in the kitchen. Stepping over the bent boy on the floor, he tossed a 9mm into a junk drawer and then taped another under the kitchen table. From where he knelt, he could look into the young man's bloodshot eyes.

"But hey, maybe I'm just jaded. It's good that people trust." He laughed. "And for all I know, you may not really be from Syria. See?

1

I trust too. What are you going to do?" He tapped the boy's cheek and realized what he most disliked about jobs like this—the lack of conversation. It was worse than cold. It was uncivilized. He pulled out his phone and was happy to see a message waiting for him from his previous client. Why did he know he'd be hearing from them again? One job at a time, however. He hit redial.

The current client answered with a terse "Yes?"

"I've put the groceries away." He rolled his eyes at the ridiculous code phrase the client had chosen. Why they made these things so complicated was beyond him. His last client had insisted he recite "Hey Diddle Diddle" so he supposed it could be worse.

"Yes." The client sounded like he was smiling. There was something off about the volume. He must have someone in the room with him. In trying to sound natural, he sounded to Booker as if he was twirling his mustache while kicking a puppy. "Why don't you go ahead and finish the paperwork? Oh and thanks for calling. Uh-huh."

Booker tossed the phone in the open case. There were two laptops on the table. Unfortunately the one closest to him had been open during the hit and the keys were a mess. It was unlikely law enforcement officials would believe the young men had roused themselves from their death throes long enough to check their Facebook. Wiping the fingertips of his gloves inside his jacket pocket to remove any traces of blood, he lifted the lid of the other laptop carefully. The blood spattered across the top had already congealed enough to not run.

The computer glowed to life and once again Booker shook his head. Not even password protected. "It's a good thing you guys really aren't terrorists," he muttered to himself, clicking on the Facebook shortcut. "You would be terrible at it." Like the computer itself, the social media opened with no need to enter the password he had memorized. He typed in the message he had also memorized and posted it as Jusef's status. Before closing the page, he scrolled through the newsfeed. Most of it was in Syrian, in which Booker wasn't fluent, but there was a video link of a baby penguin squealing as a zookeeper tickled it.

"That's adorable." Booker clicked the "like" button.

CHAPTER ONE

Choo-Choo looked hung over. He threw down his headphones. "You know, if we're going to get paid to sit around and do nothing, we should at least get to do it in our underwear."

Dani gnawed her thumbnail and prayed the blond analyst wouldn't turn around and see the blush warming her face. She'd spent far too much time imagining those long, pale limbs sprawled and bared. Fay described Choo-Choo as "an obsessive compulsive nerd underwear model." Dani just thought of him as Viking Porn.

"Your underwear would be a damn sight more appealing than that mess you're sporting now." Fay dropped her bright orange Kate Spade bag on the desk across from Dani. She squinted at the blue shirt he'd wrapped himself in. "What is that? Flannel? Are you even allowed to wear flannel? I thought you'd burst into flames or get kicked off the society register."

Choo-Choo graced Fay with one perfectly arched brow. "Well we can't all dress like escapees from a Caribbean brothel, can we?"

"You wish you could pull this off," Fay said with a laugh. She ran her long nails through the mountain of curls piled on top of her head, a chartreuse elastic band struggling to contain it. "I make this mess look sexy."

Dani giggled and Choo-Choo snorted. Everything about Fay was larger than life. Every inch of her nearly six-foot frame was draped in a rainbow of brilliant colors. And despite a profound lisp, Fay nonetheless peppered every sentence with as many S words as she could manage. After working together for five years, Fay was the best friend Dani had ever had.

"Seriously," Fay said, sprawling in her chair, "the way you two dress. You've got teeny tiny Dani curled up in her teeny tiny black clothes. What are you supposed to be? A comma?" Dani laughed out loud at her friend's teasing. "And then you," she waved at the blond man smirking at her. "I bet you sported something sexier than that last night for whoever she was. Or he was. Or *they* were."

Choo-Choo feigned offense. "What are you implying, Fay? That I'm a th-lut?" Fay threw her head back, letting out a loud barking laugh. Dani settled in. They could go back and forth like this all day, getting funnier and funnier and never getting offended. She never tired of the show. Then she saw Choo-Choo turn his pale eyes toward her. She shrunk down in her chair.

His voice was a purr. "Why are we always talking about my sex life? How come Dani never tells us of her exploits with her latest conquest? Bob? Ben?"

Fay snorted. "Ben's a dick."

"Ben? A dick?"

"Ben-a-dick!" Fay laughed at her own joke. "Ben-a-dick Arnold— 'I regret that I have but one small penis to give to my girlfriend.'"

"Fail." Choo-Choo threw a pen at her. "Patrick Henry had but one small penis to give."

Dani spoke up. "That's Nathan Hale."

"Nathan Hale had a small dick?" Fay asked.

"No, he had but one life to give for . . ." She saw them both laughing at her and she buried her hot face in her hands. "I hate you guys. I really do."

"You adore us. Well, me, at least," Choo-Choo said. "Fay is take it or leave it." He dodged the pen Fay hurled back. "In any event, you're stuck with us since you're unfit to work anywhere but here. Just like us."

Here was Rasmund, a private security firm specializing in corporate espionage, extortion, and threat assessment. Many of Rasmund's clients could be recognized by their well-known NASDAQ codes; the rest operated at a much lower profile and a much higher profit margin. Rasmund didn't advertise in trade magazines. The people who needed their unique services operated within an information network that needed and desired no publicity.

Dani and Fay made up a small part of the team currently working on assignment for their latest client, Swan Technologies. Internally, their crew went by the designation Paint, so called for their ability to cover every inch of a scene without being noticed, blending into the background. Choo-Choo was their audio analyst. They waited in the well-appointed room for another part of the assigned team, the part known as Faces.

Faces were just that—the public face of Rasmund, or as public as such services demanded. The Faces went into the businesses and situations being investigated with cover stories and artificial backgrounds. They were operatives trained at information retrieval and, due to the high-end lifestyle of most of their clients, their personal styles had to reflect the same. Faces got to go to parties and galas and travel in private jets and on yachts. Faces also risked personal safety, often finding themselves on-site when questionable situations turned dangerous. Dani couldn't think of anything she would want to do less than be a Face.

Not that there was much chance of that had she so desired. Coming in at five feet tall and showing a distinct lack of fashion sense, Dani didn't mind that she fit perfectly the company's stereotype of Paint. Her short black hair stuck up in erratic tufts, trained in an unruly pattern by her habit of wrapping rubber bands around random locks while lost in the data. She spent more evenings than she liked to admit untangling the tiny hair prisons before heading out into public. As for her habit of doodling on the insides of her wrists, all she could hope for at this point was that people assumed they were tattoos.

The door swung open and a perfectly dressed couple strolled into the room. Fay let her head loll on the back of her chair, stage-whispering to Dani, "Thank God the Faces have made it. We're saved."

Todd Hickman ignored her. He slouched into his chair and sighed, picking nonexistent lint off of a blue cashmere sweater that Dani knew cost more than Fay's shoes. (She'd run some background on a previous client's shopping preferences last year.)

Evelyn Carr had slithered into her seat beside him, followed by her ever-present cloud of Chanel No. 5 perfume. Dani didn't know how the bony redhead managed to saturate herself so thoroughly with the fragrance but the result was an eye-watering funk that lingered long after the Face had left the room. Between that and Evelyn's permanent sneer, it was a wonder to Dani that Hickman could stand working with her. When Fay had learned that Evelyn's birth name was actually Twyla Dawn Cruickshank, Dani had sworn her to secrecy. That was the sort of tasty morsel that could come in handy should the arrogant team member need a touch of mortifying.

"Anyone else coming in?" Hickman asked.

Choo-Choo said, "Phelps is supposed to be on the golf course with a couple of Swan's VPs. I sent out the call. Don't know if he'll make it. Eddie's transfer came through. I don't want to say he was anxious to get out of here but his office was cleaned out when I got here."

"Wow, tough gig for both of them," Fay said. "Golfing at the Greenbrier or picking your office in Miami. They'll miss all the excitement of going through another megaton of intercepted e-mail that says absolutely nothing. Does anyone else think this job is weird?"

"You mean sitting in a dark room and listening in on half a dozen conversations you don't care about?" Choo-Choo asked.

"No, I mean this job. The Swan job. Nothing seems to be adding up to any kind of tech leak or industrial espionage. And now that that guy is dead. . . ."

"Marcher," Hickman said, twirling his gold signet ring. "His name was Eduard Marcher. He was my contact. He was a good man."

Evelyn made a show of examining her nails. "That remains up for debate."

"He's dead, Ev. How about a little respect?"

Dani sat still in her chair, watching the two teammates. This wasn't the easy bickering she enjoyed with Fay. Todd's and Evelyn's body language spoke of a long-running argument even while their well-modulated tones sounded casual. At Rasmund, few people worked together long. Faces paired up and switched out job by job, the nature of their tasks requiring them to be fluid and adaptable. Paints tended to work alone—Fay and Dani being a notable exception.

"There's definitely something going on in that lab." Hickman kept spinning that ring. Dani knew that gesture. It was as close to fretting as the man ever got in public. "We don't know any more than you guys do. Swan's convinced someone in his organization is leaking information, maybe selling their tech, and I'm inclined to agree."

"Well you'd know," Ev said. "You've spent enough time in that lab."

This wasn't the first case with an uncertain directive. Despite Rasmund's reputation for complete discretion, many clients' operations were so covert in nature that the teams often worked with a minimum of information. This served not only to protect the privacy of the clients but also to minimize the legal implications for Rasmund itself. Mrs. O'Donnell and her superiors held plausible deniability at a premium. But Dani agreed with Fay and could tell the rest of the team did as well. Something about the Swan case felt off.

"We know they're gearing up for a big announcement on some new tech," Fay said, twisting the end of her hot pink scarf through her fingers. "Standard R&D gag order is in place. It doesn't appear that Marcher's death has slowed anything down." This last bit of information seemed to irk Dani's partner. "All communications suggest that the lab is operating at situation normal."

"Hmm," Ev said, crossing her legs, "maybe Marcher's death brought everything back to situation normal."

When Hickman spoke, the edges of his lips whitened. "I thought you were the one who kept insisting the police were correct, that the wreck was an accident. Completely coincidental."

She shrugged. "There are coincidences and there are coincidences. I'm just saying there was suspicion that someone was stealing research from Swan and selling it. Swan has several defense contracts. It would be safe to assume whoever wanted to steal from them would be dealing with dangerous people—people who would know how to fake a car accident. Maybe the situation straightened itself out without our interference."

Hickman's voice rose, control abandoned. "So you're saying that his death convicts him of industrial espionage?"

"There really isn't any sign," Dani spoke up, making everyone in the room turn to look at her. Dani rarely jumped into conversations but she liked Hickman. She did more jobs with him than with any other Face at Rasmund. More important, she trusted his instincts. "Nothing in the materials suggests there was any information leak from the lab, much less from Marcher. He spearheaded the team; they seemed to really like him."

"Like he's going to leave a receipt of sale," Ev said. "Maybe you should look in his garbage disposal, Dani. Maybe he chewed up the evidence."

"There are signs," Dani said, ignoring Ev's dig at her unconventional analysis style. "People who are trying to cover something up leave trails; they make mistakes. That's what Fay and I look for. That's what we get paid to do."

"You have to excuse Ev," Fay said. "It's hard for her to imagine actually working, not spending all day dashing around in designer clothes hobnobbing with the elite."

Choo-Choo let out a long, exaggerated sigh. Nobody could express exhaustion quite like Choo-Choo. "Why don't we save the class warfare until our reigning monarch has held forth? She called us in for a reason. Let's save the bloodletting until we know how long we'll be on the killing field, all right?" He draped himself across the silk chaise like a cat.

The room they occupied looked more like an aristocratic drawing room than the conference room for an information retrieval company. Sprawling across the second floor of a graceful antebellum estate in Falls Church, Virginia, nothing about the room or even the building itself suggested any security measures were in place, much less the state-of-the-art shielding and monitoring that secured the perimeter. The gates that opened onto the long, curving driveway in the front and the narrow, rutted service road in the back only looked antique. The closed-circuit monitors and electronic keypads hidden among the filigree ensured that nobody wandered onto the premises. A helicopter pad took up the southern edge of the roof and a tunnel ran from beneath the four-car carriage-style garage to a private airstrip two miles down the river. Rasmund's clientele expected efficiency and discretion, all wrapped in an elegant facade of luxury. Rasmund delivered.

Choo-Choo and several other audio analysts had a bank of rooms on the third floor beneath a squat turret lined with listening equipment of every variety. Fay, Dani, and other Paints in data analysis sequestered themselves in suites of rooms across from Audio. Some Paints preferred desks, some rooms with long tables and file cabinets. Dani and Fay had furnished their room in a combination of styles that included dorm room, head shop, and rabbit warren. Mrs. O'Donnell and the powers of Rasmund didn't care how the Paints chose to work. All that mattered were results, and Fay and Dani had an impeccable track record.

Unscheduled team meetings like this one meant one of two things: either the client had information that had to be disseminated immediately and in one go or, as was more often the case, the job was being terminated. Dani hoped it was the former. Even though she could find no signs of the suspected thievery, something about the materials gathered from Swan niggled at her. She'd been infected by Hickman's determination to stay on the job. Dani didn't know what she thought she might find but she hoped she'd have a chance to keep looking.

The hope died a quick death when Mrs. O'Donnell strode through the door from the front hallway. All Rasmund employees, even Faces, used the back hallways and rear entrances at all times. Only Mrs. O'Donnell and the very top brass at Rasmund used the front. Clients used the front and the less they saw of the teams that would be infiltrating them, the better. Mrs. O'Donnell was dressed in her customary palette of black and gray, the gray streaks in her swept-back hair making her look to Dani exactly like Anne Bancroft. She even had the same low voice and wry smile.

"I hope no one was expecting a champagne party." She wrapped the edges of her long gray cardigan around her slender waist. Dani could see, even from the back of the room, that the cashmere in Mrs. O'Donnell's sweater made Hickman's look like low-thread-count sheets.

Choo-Choo put his headphones on as if to block out the news he knew was coming. Hickman and Fay sighed at the same time and Evelyn made a *tsk* noise before she spoke. "Do we even know why—"

"No, we do not." Mrs. O'Donnell folded her arms as Hickman looked up at her.

"Is there any word what the job—"

"No there is not. Our client has pulled the line on the job. He made no move to explain to us why and we made no move to inquire. Patrick Swan has no further need of our services and so this is a wrap." Her dark eyes showed nothing but their usual icy grace. Mrs. O'Donnell exuded a combination of elegance and iron. Like all members of the team, Dani had every intention of staying on her good side. That anyone wielded authority over her stretched the limits of Dani's comprehension.

Hickman made a move as if to speak and Mrs. O'Donnell arched her brow, silencing him. "Mr. Swan's liaison will be on-site in two hours to collect any and all materials. Usual protocols in place. Purge, burn, block, and black out. Choo-Choo, call in the Stringers. Fay, Dani, try to pack your materials in some semblance of adult order. We don't need a repeat of the Raisinet incident." Fay and Dani looked away at the mention of their recent blunder, spilling a whole bag of candy into a client's case box. "Mr. Hickman, you will oversee the sign-off. Ms. Carr, come see me in my office when you've finished wrapping up your end. Understood?" Evelyn turned a tight smile her way. Hickman nodded and Dani wondered if his pinkie was sore from the twisting of his ring.

Everyone rose from their seats to begin the standard post-job shutdown. All surveillance data and accumulated information would be boxed and tagged and electronic files loaded onto portable drives and double-erased from Rasmund's hard drives. These materials would then be turned over to the liaison in person, signed off on, and released as soon as proper payments had been wired into the proper accounts. The absence of any trail or evidence was a Rasmund trademark. Which was exactly the reason Dani felt herself sinking into her chair, hoping to render herself invisible.

Mrs. O'Donnell pushed off from the desk she'd been leaning against and strolled through the room toward the door to Dani's left. For one beautiful moment, Dani thought she would leave without another word but, like her hope to keep the case open, her optimism was short-lived. The older woman barely paused in her long stride, slowing only long enough to murmur as she passed. "All materials, Dani. Two hours. I suggest you take a pouch."

"Yes ma'am." Dani tried not to cringe. She didn't know why she was surprised that her boss knew everything that went on in the house. It was her business to know everything. And it wasn't as if Dani had broken any serious rules by taking nonsensitive materials home. Most Paints loaded documents and audio files onto their Rasmund-issued laptops; data files and bugged phone calls were the starting points for most investigations. But Dani tended to operate differently. It was one of the reasons she had worked so well and so long with Hickman and Fay.

Fay wagged her finger at Dani as the door closed behind the administrator and Choo-Choo covered his mouth in fake shock, whispering. "Dani B. busted again!"

"How was I supposed to know they were going to call it?"

Evelyn didn't join in on the teasing. Instead, she slithered from her chair and patted her undisturbed hair. "Maybe you should consider being prepared for all eventualities. After all, isn't scenario prediction supposed to be your specialty? Why don't you make a note of it and put it on one of your state-of-the-art cork boards?"

"Good idea, Evelyn," Dani coughed and waved the perfume funk away as the redhead strolled past her. "Maybe I can fasten it to the wall using that stick you've got up your ass."

Hickman let Ev walk out in front of him, pausing by Dani. "I won't let you get busted for my materials." He leaned in close so only Dani could hear him. "Get them to me on the side. I'll make sure they get in the box before it's sealed, okay?"

"Thanks, Todd. I think I'm running out of good graces with Mrs. O'Donnell."

X X X

Ten minutes later, Dani was gripping the wheel of her '97 Accord, muttering "Shit shit shit" as she threaded her way through Beltway traffic to her apartment. Even at midday on a Saturday, the Embassy Row neighborhood had no parking spaces available, so Dani parked in a loading zone and fished around under her seat. A sign for Big Wong's Thai Delivery in the windshield and a flick of her hazards and Dani figured she had at least thirty minutes before anyone decided to ticket her.

Thankfully Ben had headed off to work. They didn't technically live together but he spent as many days working from home at her place as he did his own Capitol Hill apartment. She peeked into the bedroom. The space didn't have room for anyone to hide, but Dani wanted to be sure. Ben didn't really know what she did for a living. He thought she worked the information desk for the Rasmund Historical Society because that's what her badge said, that's what she said whenever anyone asked, and that's what the Web site linked to her e-mail said. They had been together four months and Dani had never felt the urge to unburden her secret to him.

She moved down the narrow hallway to the utility room. It was really more of a cubby created when the original building had been broken down into smaller units. A compact washer and dryer filled in a corner beside a folding table surrounded by shelves of detergent and paper products. Ben teased her about her need to squirrel away supplies in every available corner. He had no idea what she had hidden. She pulled open the accordion doors across from the washer, revealing an ironing board piled with clothes in a shallow closet.

Ben had left a pile of shirts to be ironed. "You really are a dick," Dani muttered. She pitched the shirts onto the table and reached under the ironing board for the catch. One press and she unlocked the board from its latch, lifting it and locking it in place against the side wall. A batik sheet of Tibetan prayer symbols covered the back wall of the cabinet and Dani pulled out the little step stool in the lower corner, still having to stretch to her full length to grab the upper corner of the fabric. A quick pull and the sheet separated from the Velcro that held it in place. Dani bumped the sides of her fists against the bare wall and it separated along a barely visible seam.

Dani had built the hidden cubby into the wall not long after taking the apartment. It hadn't taken much—some light plywood, interior hinges, magnet clasps, all assembled with enough care to be easily hidden behind the wall cloth. She had a similar cubby in the floor of her bedroom beneath the bed, which was where she kept her passport and some extra cash. She didn't really have anything to hide. None of the materials she kept in the wall cabinet were sensitive. If anything, Ben or anyone else who might have stumbled upon them would probably just question her strange hoarding habits. Besides, Ben didn't notice much of anything in her apartment, including the fact that she rarely, if ever, ironed. She wondered how long he would leave those shirts piled there before giving up.

She began removing the pushpins from the left side of the cubby and dropping them into the little plastic case that hung on the rear wall. Marcher's phone records, credit card bills, photocopies of receipts, and e-mails with personal identifiers blacked out came down first. Nobody could learn from looking at these papers who the target was. Hickman knew the kind of materials she liked to work with, the kinds of patterns she specialized in discovering. For example, it didn't matter who the phone numbers on the record belonged to. That was Fay's specialty. What mattered to Dani was how often they were dialed, how long the calls lasted, and what time of day they usually occurred. Regardless of status, pressure, or fear, humans were creatures of habit. Figure out the habit and you could predict the next move.

The right side of the cabinet looked like a modern art take on public trash. Wrinkled brochures, snack wrappers, Metro Passes, valet parking stubs, even a champagne cork—the kind of stuff people dumped out of their pockets at the end of the day. In fact, much of what she'd tacked to the wall had been obtained just that way. Hickman didn't list pickpocketing as one of his skills but he was known for it. He'd seen Dani pull results, patterns, and secrets out of the debris targets kept at the bottoms of their handbags and in their raincoat pockets. He knew to skim the detritus from desk drawers and office supply trays. If he couldn't swipe it, he photographed it, blowing the pictures up for Dani to study. To Dani, strangers dragged trails of information behind them like a comet drags a tail. She read them. All she knew for sure about Marcher was that he ate an awful lot of fois gras and had a weakness for Argentinean steakhouses. Nothing earth-shattering on its own and might never have led to anything but it was the kind of detail that Dani noticed. To say the least, the materials were not sensitive.

Dani had no illusions about who had the more dangerous job. She knew what she provided was color and background, the type of information that could make a big difference in an undercover operation. Hickman and Evelyn and the other Faces put themselves into the thick of the job. The Stringers worked in even rougher terrain, skirting the shadier ethical questions for Rasmund and operating under full anonymity. Even Choo-Choo didn't know their names, only their identification codes. Dani, Fay, and the other Paint crews operated safely in the well-protected bosom of Rasmund and that was just the way she preferred it.

Which is why it pained her to have to disassemble her materials board. Dani didn't just enjoy her job; she loved it. She loved this point in a job where ideas and patterns lurked just beyond the grasp of her fingertips. She could feel her mind reaching, stretching, and just barely bumping the soft edges of whatever the random bits of information were trying to tell her. She dreamed about her jobs, imagined she could see the swirls of colored papers rising and bending into arrows and shapes that would become worlds to her. These little bits of debris triggered associations that she couldn't consciously explain but that she and her employers had come to trust. To have to pull the plug at this stage in a job felt like being cheated.

She stuffed all the materials into the blue canvas Rasmund pouch. Like everything else Rasmund, the pouch only looked like a simple book bag. In truth, the bag was waterproof, fireproof, and, unless Choo-Choo was pulling her leg, could stop a small-caliber bullet and a sharp knife. It certainly weighed enough to be lined with Kevlar.

She had to hurry. She still had to get across the bridge and out to the estate, log the materials back in, and slip out of sight before the client's liaison came for the package. Maybe Hickman would treat them all to lunch the way he usually did after a job. He wasn't all oozy charm like many of the Faces. When he was off-job, Hickman's easy laugh and adolescent humor could occasionally eclipse even Fay's resentment. As a matter of fact, the thought occurred to Dani more than once that her two teammates might have more going on than just a professional relationship. It wasn't the kind of thing her friend would talk about. Fay joked about Dani's sex life but her own private life she kept pointedly private. Still, Dani knew she wasn't the only one who got a touch of a thrill peering behind the curtains of strangers' lives. Some might even call it a kink.

Speaking of kinks, she realized she was standing there holding Ben's shirts up to her face hoping to get a whiff of his scent. All she got was laundry detergent and she threw the shirts onto the ironing board, now back in place in front of the hidden cabinet. She threw them with enough force to lock the board in place. She threw them like it was their fault. Closing the accordion doors and hauling the Rasmund pouch up onto her shoulder, she promised herself not to dwell on just how weird she probably was.

X X X

She made better time on the way back but she was still cutting it close. Her phone beeped as she pulled off the interstate but she ignored it, concentrating on not getting smashed between two semis as she merged onto the two-lane highway. It seemed she had timed her arrival perfectly with a convoy of enormous trucks that stretched for miles in either direction. At least the turnoff for the back road to the estate came several miles before the turnoff for the client entrance. Maybe the liaison would be sandwiched in the same convoy, giving her an advantage.

She turned left onto an unmarked county road then took the right fork onto another unmarked road, this one narrow enough to barely be considered two-way. The trees hung low over it, pin oaks and poplars already dropping enough of their leaves to obscure the little bit of shoulder the road provided. Blackberry bushes and brambles crowded along the sides, sometimes scraping the edges of her side mirrors. This service road was for Rasmund employees only. Dani could just imagine what the reaction would be from the company's elite clientele if they had to drive their Beemers and Jags over this rough stretch of road. Well, they could keep their overpriced ego-rides. Dani whistled to herself as the little car hugged the curve. With its front-wheel drive and heavy body, she knew the car could drive up the side of a tree if necessary.

"What the hell?" Dani slammed the brakes unnecessarily hard, since she wasn't even going ten miles per hour. She slammed her fists on the steering wheel. "What is this?"

An unmarked black panel truck was parked facing her, blocking the opening of the rear Rasmund security gate. Dani stared at it for several seconds, her mouth open. This could not be happening. Was someone trying to get her fired? She climbed out of the car, stomping up to the cab of the truck, but it was empty. The engine was warm. Whoever left it here hadn't left it long. Pounding her fists on the hood of the truck, she swore her way through her frustration.

"That's it. I'm fired. I'm fired. Life hates me and I'm fired." She marched back to her car, noting without surprise that there was no way to squeeze it past the truck. Backing up on the narrow road required an optimism she didn't feel and besides which, she was out of time. She grabbed the heavy pouch from the car along with her purse and keys. She could imagine the sight she would make, standing muddy on Mrs. O'Donnell's carpet. "See, there was this truck and Ben's shirts were on the ironing board and there's never anyplace to park on my street and there was this convoy on Route Seven and . . ." She double-timed it up the road.

"Oh and the gate's open," she said out loud to nobody. "That's safe. Not like we have security measures in places, stupid trucker-fucker." She knew the security cameras were filming her and could just imagine Choo-Choo watching her running and talking to herself. She held the pouch up to a camera she knew hung hidden along the fencing, mouthing "Please!" to the lens. Hopefully they hadn't sealed the box yet. Hopefully the client's liaison was having the same trouble she was having getting into Rasmund.

She punched in her code at the garden door, barely waiting for the soft snick of the latch before barreling through. She took the steps to the main floor two at a time, no easy task with her short legs, and tried not to pant as she ran down the hall. The carpet muffled her footsteps and she strained to hear the sounds of Mrs. O'Donnell through any of the oaken doors leading to the front of the house. Materials would be signed off on in the library, and if she could just make it to the rear door she could signal to whoever would be sealing the box. She hoped it was Hickman. He'd be watching for her, stalling for her.

She didn't hear anyone talking. That could be a good sign, a sign that the liaison hadn't made it yet or was still being greeted in the foyer. It could also mean she had missed the drop altogether.

Slowing down, pulling the pouch to her chest, and quieting her breathing, Dani peeked around the rear doorway of the spacious library. At first glance it looked empty and she didn't know whether to swear or sigh. She tiptoed through the door, trying to spy any sign of the plain white materials boxes that would be stacked under the front windows. Instead she saw a patch of blue sticking out over the arm of one of the high leather wingback chairs.

"Hickman," she whispered, knowing that cashmere elbow any-where. She could see his expensive wingtip-clad feet casually kicked out in front of him. "Todd!"

She crept up behind the chair, hoping she could just pass the pouch off to him and sneak out before Mrs. O'Donnell's inevitable entrance with the liaison in tow. If Hickman felt relaxed enough to sprawl in the chair rather than grooming himself for the meeting, she figured she couldn't be as late as she feared. She let out the breath she'd been holding.

"I thought I'd missed this." She kept her eye on the door to the foyer as she stepped around, slinging the pouch off her shoulder. "Some asshole parked his truck right at the—"

The words died in Dani's throat when she came around to face Hickman. Her first thought was that he had ruined his beautiful sweater. Two black-and-red holes marred the soft cashmere just under his collarbone. They matched the small black-and-red hole in the center of his forehead.

CHAPTER TWO

She didn't scream. She didn't feel faint. She didn't even feel fear. All she could do for several loud heartbeats was stand there and stare, her brain scrambling to figure out which out of all the many, many things wrong with the tableau before her was the worst. Different. That was the only word she could think of. Todd Hickman looked different; he looked wrong. He didn't look like he was sleeping or unconscious or made of wax. He looked like Todd, but he looked like a wrong version of him. Finally the correct word rose to the front of her mind. Dead.

Todd Hickman looked dead.

A *pop-pop-pop* sound came from the sunroom just past the library. Dani knew that sound, a sharp, crunching sound like someone stomping on bags of popcorn. She'd researched it and filed it away with the thousands of other pieces of random knowledge she'd acquired over the years. She'd thought that factoid interesting—that silencers don't actually silence a gun, they just muffle it. Silencers muffled gunshots until they sounded like *pop-pop-pop* in close quarters.

Close quarters.

Like the next room.

Then the thoughts came flooding. The breath whooshed out of Dani's open mouth and like an animal caught in the high beams she dropped to a crouch and froze. Glass shattered, a radio crackled, and another round of *pop-pop-pop* sounded, this time accompanied by a brief but unmistakable human scream. The sound of a dull, wet thump on hardwood made her jump and that jump became a scrabble across carpet until her brain got the message to her feet, or maybe it was vice versa, and Dani charged headlong out the rear door of the library and back down the carpeted hallway toward the exit.

Her plan, such as it was, involved hurtling herself through the same garden door she'd come in. Fortunately, fear made her vision sharp and she caught the hint of a shadow moving in the garden room before she cleared the corner. The carpet muffled her skid and it was only her low center of gravity that kept her from face-planting in the middle of the hall. The animal part of her brain that screamed "trapped trapped trapped" ran the show and she didn't think to let go of either the Rasmund pouch or the purse she clutched tight against her chest as she cannonballed up the back stairs.

More pops sounded below. Somewhere a door slammed.

So many sounds rushed through her adrenaline-flooded mind she couldn't think, couldn't make a plan that involved anything more than moving, always moving. Footsteps sounded from the front stairwell but Dani couldn't tell if they were ten feet away or a mile, if they were coming closer or retreating. Her fingers crushed the bags to her chest as she bounced from locked door to locked door, her brain and her body fighting for control over the situation, both losing miserably.

A muffled vibration made her jump straight up in the air. For one horrible second she was certain she'd been shot. No. Her phone. Her phone in her purse was vibrating, which meant it was probably making noise that she couldn't hear over the pounding of blood in her ears but which was probably audible to anyone looking for her.

It didn't take long for her reptilian brain to get on board with the idea that the people making the *pop-pop-pop* sound were probably looking for her and that this would be an ideal time to silence any and all noises that would assist them.

Getting her fingers in on the solution was another thing altogether. Dani dumped the bags on the floor, shoving her fists into her purse to find the beeping phone. Instead she found her keys, or rather they found her, stabbing into the webbing between her index and middle finger hard enough to break the skin. That pain broke through the clamor of panic and as she sucked the blood from between her fingers, Dani felt the odd sensation of time stopping.

She had to move. She had to hide. She had keys.

This meant something. This added up to something. Her brain and her hands translated the jumble of messages and managed to single out the fat brass key from the other contemporary keys on the ring. Moving slowly, so slowly, as if the floor would crumble beneath her should she disturb it, Dani crawled across the carpet runner, dragging her purse and pouch behind her. Her left hand shook as she neared the lock and she used her right to steady it. A click, a horrible moment when the lock resisted, then another click and the door swung open. Still scrambling on the floor, Dani winced at the sound of canvas on carpet as she dragged the bags in behind her. With infinite care, she snicked the door shut.

In the silence of her office, Dani's brain snapped into focus. This was her office. She knew this space. The door was locked. Had anyone seen her come in?

Had she just trapped herself?

Her breath broke ragged through her clenched teeth and she couldn't seem to get her fingers to perform anything but the grossest motor movements, but they would be enough. Even as she crawled across the ugly brown rug, some small secretary in the back of her mind listed her condition.

Adrenaline dump. Loss of coordination. Rapid breathing. Shock imminent. Muscle memory tendency—freeze in place. Distorted understanding of time. Loss of sensory conception. When had she learned this? The Dixon case, studying the video of the office workers flooding out of the Dixon Express Building in Dallas after a shooting rampage. She'd watched the video with Choo-Choo. The client had wanted . . . what the hell was she doing?

Dani crawled over to the denim beanbag she used as her office chair. She was talking to herself, listing details of old cases and factoids and symptoms of shock. "Self-comfort," she whispered aloud. Self-comfort, familiar ground to anchor the conscious mind from the impact of trauma or shock. A natural psychological response. Expected. Normal.

"Not normal." She spoke louder, trying to jolt herself from the spiral of panic. There was nothing normal about this situation. More gunshots sounded from somewhere below her. She could hear them through the vents. The vents. Why wouldn't Rasmund insulate their ventilation system better? It would be so easy to eavesdrop.

"Goddamn it, Dani." She banged her knuckles against the bags squeezed to her chest. "Get your shit together. Get it together *now*."

She forced her breathing to slow down, quieting it to a slow, softer panicked pant.

"What do you know for sure?" She heard a door splintering down the hallway. There were six doors on this side. Three Audio suites on the other. Her room was at the end of the hall. "They're not here. They're not here yet. What do you know?"

She knew Hickman was dead. Shot. She knew someone, possibly several someones, was moving through Rasmund and nobody was screaming. Why not? Why wasn't anyone screaming? She certainly wanted to scream. Someone had screamed. In the foyer, after she'd found Todd. Who would be in the foyer? Evelyn? Mrs. O'Donnell?

Was that Mrs. O'Donnell who'd screamed before hitting the floor? Dani could still hear that wet thump, that sound she'd been unable to acknowledge was a body hitting the floor.

It was just like the Dixon hit. She could see those shocky wide-eyed stares of the people fleeing the building as two armed gunmen blew through walls and doors and windows, killing thirty-seven people and wounding a dozen more before a SWAT team had taken them out. Rasmund had been brought in to analyze the incident.

Who would analyze this one, she wondered. Would they find her body like the bodies she'd seen photographed from a hundred angles? Arms and legs sprawled and flung by the force of automatic weapons fire? Bloody streaks on the carpet where they'd tried to drag themselves away from the killing floor? Thirty-seven people. She could still remember most of their names and why couldn't she stop thinking about it?

"Debra Maxwell. Daniel Tarrant. Christina Bomer." The names stuttered out of her mouth. They weren't the dead. They were survivors. She had listened to their interviews. They had survived in the building. They had survived in the presence of the gunmen. Another door collapsed somewhere down the hallway, this one closer.

"Behind them," Dani whispered. "Behind them." That's what Debra Maxwell had said. The exits had been blocked. They had found a way to circle around the gunmen, getting behind them. They stayed behind the gunmen as the killing march moved through the building.

Someone screamed.

Not someone.

Dani squeezed her eyes shut, tasting blood where she bit into her lip. Fay. That was Fay. That was her partner screaming. Was. Not screaming anymore. Dani felt the fuzzy cloud of shock settling down over her and more than most of her wanted to let it take her away from this dusty floor and crowded room and *pop-pop-pop*–filled house. Out out out.

Fay. How dare they shoot Fay? The ever efficient fact-listing secretary in her mind reminded the panicking thoughts about the energizing power of anger. Rage could break the shockiest fugue states and Dani felt the sensation of being of two minds—one watching, one letting anger flood out fear. She wasn't going to die here.

Once she accepted that as a fact, the act of escaping execution transformed from a terrifying and bewildering scramble for freedom into a list of obstacles and options, pros and cons—the most important to-do list she had ever assembled.

She couldn't stop the gunmen. She was outnumbered and had no weapon and she'd never had any illusions of herself as an action hero. A vibration rumbled once more against her chest, sound muffled by her body and the heavy Rasmund pouch. Her phone. She didn't berate herself for her stupidity in not thinking of her phone until now. She didn't have the luxury of worrying about mistakes and wasted time. She had a job to do.

She slipped her trembling hand into her purse to find her phone. Step one, call 911. Get help on the way. Then she would have to find a safer hiding place.

Building the mental list soothed Dani's nervous system and she felt her muscles relax and her thoughts line up in an orderly fashion. Her hearing came back into focus and she could make out the sounds of movement down the hallway. Radios crackled at low volume and from the sound of it, rooms were being searched. She couldn't tell from where she hid but it sounded as if she had at least two more Paint rooms between her and the searchers. Blessedly, the gunshots had stopped for now.

With a sigh of relief she yanked the phone clear of the inner zipper. She had just long enough to look at the message on the screen informing her that the vibrations she'd been feeling were her warnings that the battery was dying. Even as she swiped her thumb to unlock the device, the lights went black and the phone went dead.

That panic she thought she'd dismissed roared back up at her from the shadows but she refused to let it in. Not a disaster. Just an obstacle. Obstacles and opportunities. That's what she had now. Pros and cons. Problems and solutions. That's what she had. That's what she did. That's what she was good at. Over and over she repeated these words to herself, forcing her fingers to release their talonlike grip on the phone. What are the pros and cons, she made herself ask. Everything had pros and cons.

Pro: the phone would no longer make an unexpected noise and give away her location. Okay, that would do.

Con: she was stuck in a house full of murderers, in line to get executed while her best friend lay dead down the hall. No no no. That was panic. That was not fact.

Her teeth chattered as she argued with herself. Con: the con was that she had to find another phone. Another phone. She had to find another phone to call for help.

Another list built itself in her mind. As she had ignored her mistakes, she ignored the absurdity of how difficult she found it to put together a simple conclusion like that. Her world, her life, had come down to inches, to a string of small movements that she had to perform one after another to get her out of this room, this house, alive.

Another door splintered. She heard the sound of shattering glass and bells. That was Anderson's and Keller's Paint room. Anderson annoyed the shit out of Choo-Choo with his little bell choir performances. No gunshots. Dani let out a slow breath, listening to the sound of drawers being slammed, imagining Keller's meticulously organized file cabinets being tossed. Three doors. She was running out of time.

Forcing herself to fight the paralysis of panic locking her knees down, she pushed off the beanbag and dove into a pile of cushions beneath the window. She and Fay never used their phone. Fay kept it buried and unplugged, claiming it emitted an ultrasonic vibration that interfered with her concentration. Plus she hated being paged. Dani squeezed her eyes shut, blinking back tears, remembering her ridiculous outrage. She would have time to mourn her friend later. She corrected herself. Friends.

Another door collapsed, this time on the other side of the hallway. Two teams were sweeping the building, one side clearing Paint, the other Audio. She pressed her head to the wood, dizzy as the blood rushed in her ears. *Pop-pop-pop.* Surprised grunts, what sounded like shelves or maybe chairs being slammed into walls. Someone was throwing something solid around, something solid like furniture, not fragile. Not bodies.

Another crash and a rash of shouting broke out. An animal scream, a crash, a rumble of footsteps.

"Down! Down! Down!" a rough male voice shouted over the scream and the crashing until *pop-pop-pop* brought the uproar to a halt. Someone had fought back. And lost.

She found the multiline phone stuck to an old paper plate. No lines were lit up. Obviously, Dani thought. Rasmund business was currently on hiatus. She lifted the cradle and heard nothing. Of course. They cut the lines. Trying not to cry aloud, she dropped her head against the useless machine.

And she saw the cord sticking out from beneath a cushion.

It took three tries, each more desperate than the last, to get the plug in place, and by the time she heard the dial tone, she had once again bitten her lip hard enough to draw blood. Pressing nine and then pound, she heard the connection made to an outside line. 911. Keeping an eye on the door, she gripped the phone in a sweaty palm.

"This is nine-one-one. What is your emergency?"

"I need a SWAT team at Rasmund." The words caught in her throat, the urge to scream almost overwhelming her. "Rasmund Historical Center, 11623 County Road 23."

"Ma'am, can you tell me what's happening?"

The man's voice on the line was so calm, so low and soothing.

"Guns. Guns. There are people with guns and they're moving through the workrooms. They're shooting. They've shot . . . they shot Todd. And Fay. They're kicking down the doors."

"Ma'am, I need you to stay calm. Can you stay calm for me?"

"No! Are you kidding me? They're shooting everybody."

"What is your name, ma'am?"

"My name? What?" Dani pulled the phone away from her ear for a moment to listen, hearing nothing. "Dani. Danielle. What the fuck does it matter? Send a SWAT team. Send cops. A lot of cops. They've got guns."

"Ma'am," the low tone of the operator's voice became maddening when it never lost its soft, low cadence. Dani curled up more tightly into a ball, trying to stay calm. "Listen to me very carefully ma'am. Dani? Can you get to a secure location?"

Dani let out an unfunny laugh. "Secure from guns? No. That's why I'm calling."

"Where are you, ma'am? Where exactly in the house are you?"

"I'm in the . . ."

And that's when she heard the click. She knew that click. She'd listened in on enough tapped lines to know that click. That was a relay click.

"Ma'am? Where in the house are you? Are you safe?"

The house. Why had he asked about the house? Dani had said workrooms, historical center. Why had the operator asked about the house?

"I'm in the basement." Dani's fingers felt like ice and she thought she might drop the phone. "I'm in the basement. Everyone else is dead. Everyone. I'm the last one here."

"Stay in the basement, ma'am." The operator's voice dropped to an even softer, lower tone. "We have a team on the way. Where in the basement are you? Can you tell me where you are? I'll alert the entry team to watch for you."

No question about how many people were in the house. No question about where the guns were. The only question the operator wanted to know was where to find her.

"I'm in the basement behind the furnace room. It's secure. Metal door, metal lined." A calmness settled over Dani as she lied, a coldness that some part of her knew was hatred. "It's on the southeast end of the building. The door is hidden behind a fake furnace panel. They won't find it. I'm safe."

"Is there anyone else in the building with you?"

Dani listened again for the team moving through the hallway. There was no sound. Even the radios were silent.

"No. They're all dead. I heard them die. I heard them all die."

"Ma'am, stay where you are. We're coming for you. I want you to stay on the line with me until we come for you. Can you do that?"

"Sure," Dani said, settling down on the floor. "Do you mind if I don't talk though? I'm afraid they're going to hear me."

She heard muffled radio static coming through the phone. "Don't worry, Dani. We're coming for you."

"Thank you," Dani said softly. "I owe you one."

She held the phone away from her face, staring at it as if she would see the operator in it. She wanted to see the man's face. She wanted to know his name because in that moment Dani Britton knew two things. She knew she was going to live and she knew she was going to find this man and make him pay. She didn't currently have a plan for achieving either of those goals but just seeing them so clearly calmed her like nothing else could.

Her focus returned and the jittery clumsiness dissipated. She couldn't think more than two steps ahead but two steps was further than she'd gotten so far. She knew whoever they were, they controlled the building. Had they seen her come in? Maybe not. They'd left the fence open in the back, the truck blocking the rear driveway. It didn't matter now. Now all that mattered was getting out unseen and unheard. Dani pushed the speakerphone button and replaced the handset in the cradle. Before the man on the other end could say anything, Dani pushed the down-volume button to zero, silencing the speaker. She then pushed mute. The operator wouldn't be able to hear Dani; anyone coming into the room wouldn't hear the phone. It would look like any other phone in the building.

Dani scoured the room for a place to hide, tamping down panic and frustration at the lack of cabinets and cubbyholes. She and Fay had insisted on open shelving everywhere. They would joke about all the locked doors in Rasmund and how theirs was a knob-free world. It had been funny and easy, since neither was the filing cabinet type. Now all it meant was the room looked like miles and miles of open ground.

She considered risking a run across the hall, maybe hiding in the wiring cabinets in Audio. Pressing her ear to the outer door, she heard an outburst of radio static. The target had been acquired. That's what it sounded like at least. Dani heard the words "data" and "drives" and someone said "Say again."

The radio made it sound tinnier but Dani recognized the low voice of the man on the phone. "We've found our rabbit. Repeat. We have found our rabbit. Hiding in the southeast basement of the house. Split the team. Team A, retrieve the package and make a final sweep. Give me a head count. Team B, join the boys downstairs to find our rabbit. Hidden panel behind the furnaces. Once head count is confirmed, we are smoke. Understood?"

"Roger that." The radio went silent once more, muffled commands given, and Dani heard heavy footsteps running toward the front stairwell, away from her. She had bought herself a few minutes and hopefully a less vigorous search. That didn't help her much though. The best she could hope for was that the team assigned data retrieval would search the Audio room first before heading to Templeton's office. Templeton kept her cabinets packed, Dani knew. If she was going to hide anywhere, it had to be here.

Fay's fainting couch wouldn't hide her well enough. With so little to search, even a careless seeker would think to look under the only solid piece of furniture in the room and Dani didn't want to bet on this team being careless. She made a quick circuit of the room, dodging under a partition of hanging corkboards now bare of the Swan Technology materials. A big dented cardboard box lay discarded beside the mostly flat denim beanbag chair with a yellow crocheted afghan in which Dani usually sprawled. While technically she could probably fit into the box, as hiding places went, it was stupid enough to border on suicidal.

But it was big enough. She couldn't hide in the box but if she could fit in it that meant anything her size would also fit into it. Dropping to her knees, Dani flipped the beanbag chair over, searching for the sturdy zipper that always seemed to find a way to the top of the chair and dig into her back when she lay on it. She refused to listen to the little voice in her head screaming to her about how epically stupid this plan was, choosing instead to listen to the monotonous droning of her inner engineer who had taken to running ratio calculations in her mind. Displacement and area and depth-times-width-times-length— phrases and equations and diagrams flitted through her skull as her fingers worked open the zipper.

She had to get this right. Her odds were bad enough without being careless. Pinching the bag closed, she dumped the opening into the empty box and as carefully as she could with the adrenaline rushing through her, she poured out the foam pellets that filled the bag. A fog of white dust rose up in a burst and Dani fought back a cough. As the chair emptied, getting flatter and flatter, Dani's faith in her plan flagged. There was no way this was going to work. But as the door to Templeton's office shattered under heavy boots, Dani knew she was out of options.

Hers was the last room left.

The cardboard box was more than halfway full. It looked like any other shipping box, the crushed pellets like any other shipping protection. The most anyone would do to search it was maybe run a hand through them to see if any objects had been left behind. The voice in the hallway said all data had been retrieved. They weren't looking for objects; they were looking for people.

Dani dragged the mostly empty beanbag chair, the afghan, and the box closer to the wall. The "there's no way this will work" chorus grew in volume but fortunately, or unfortunately, so did the sounds of the team next door. She had literally made her bed and now she was going to have to lie in it. She jammed the box into the corner, close enough to distract but not so close anyone would have to move the beanbag to get to it. She threw her purse and the Rasmund pouch into the bag first, not wanting to leave any personal traces behind. It had to look like the room had been vacated.

Cabinet doors in Templeton's office slammed open and shut. The search continued. Stepping into the beanbag, Dani folded herself down into the dusty fog of pellets. She shook out the afghan over the front of the bag, punching at the denim from within to wrinkle the yellow blanket. There was no way this was going to work. Taking a deep breath, Dani pulled the top of the denim bag over her head and laid down on her side, curling up into what she hoped looked like a lumpy comma. Fay had called her that this morning, a comma. She pulled the neck of her T-shirt up over her nose to keep out the dust, squeezed her eyes tight, and forced herself to be still.

She heard the familiar squeak of the door hinges and footsteps sounded close by. Dani wished she'd thought of a way to place the zipper or her head so that she could peer out, maybe through the holes in the afghan, but she knew it was better this way. If they saw her, if they recognized the shape of a human body underneath all that rumpled denim, they probably wouldn't give her any warning. They would probably just shoot her again and again, hopefully killing her quickly enough that she wouldn't have to know how stupid she looked.

She hoped Fay had died quickly, that she hadn't been too frightened. She hoped she hadn't seen it coming, that the screams hadn't been Fay's. It was selfish, she knew. Who else would she hope had died screaming? Nobody. But not as much as she hoped Fay hadn't.

Dani almost sighed but caught herself. The urge to scream and kick and pray to just get it over with was stronger than she might have imagined. Not that she had ever imagined herself hiding inside a beanbag chair. But she'd hidden lots of times before in smaller spaces than this. Like in her dad's rig. Dani thought of the little spot she used to snuggle up in on the floor of her father's truck, behind his seat, beneath the seat cot he used to sleep on. He used to call it her rabbit hole.

Now she was in another rabbit hole. Now she really was a rabbit. Wasn't that what the operator had called her? The rabbit? Curled up like a bunny, frightened and hiding, waiting to be shot without ever seeing her killer's face. She curled her fingers tight against her chest, refusing to give in to the suicidal urge to scream. Water slipped out from beneath her lashes and she didn't know if she was crying or it was from squeezing her eyes so tightly shut but she felt little foam pellets clinging to the wetness. She breathed through her nose and thought she could smell Ben on her T-shirt.

A doorknob clicked and more hinges complained. The door to the hallway had been opened. A radio crackled and a male voice spoke.

"All clear. Team A has the package and we are on our way down. The only one we're missing from our head count is our rabbit."

Dani couldn't move even as she heard him shut the door behind him.

CHAPTER THREE

She sneezed. Loudly. There was no stopping it. She froze after the spasm, feeling wetness on her T-shirt, but no heavy boots kicked down the door. The only sounds she could hear over her ragged breathing were the footsteps growing fainter. They were gone. She was alive.

They were going downstairs to look for her. She wouldn't fool them long.

Kicking her way out of the dusty chair, Dani grabbed her bags and hurried into the hallway. She had become so certain she wouldn't survive her hiding place she hadn't bothered to think even one step further. Now she had minutes at best before the invaders realized there was no hidden room behind any furnace panels. She felt certain their next sweep would be thorough to a fault. She had to see if anyone else had survived.

She threw herself through the door into Choo-Choo's Audio room and her feet slid through something wet.

She wouldn't look down; she couldn't. Her eyes locked on the wide strip of windows above a rack of equipment, straining only to see the yellowing leaves on the trees beyond, telling herself that the splashes of red she spied on the edges were the fiery red of sugar maples or a flickering glimpse of cardinals.

It couldn't be what she knew it had to be—blood. Arterial blood spatter. She knew the phrase even as she refused to say it to herself. She'd studied it before on jobs. (Dixon again—how she wished she'd never worked that Dixon case.)

A squat metal equipment rack lay on its side on the floor by the door. That must have been what she heard crashing. A gap in the racks on the far wall showed where it had come from, where someone had grabbed it to throw it, someone hoping to stop the invaders with guns. Her eyes slid down the wall, past jumbles of cables and wires and bits of chrome. A receiver of some sort stayed plugged into the wall, dangling from an unseen hook, its wires and filaments trailing out of it like intestines. Those wires and filaments snaked across the floor, joining up with a dark ribbon that looked like chocolate sauce but Dani knew it wasn't. She knew what it was and even if she wanted to fool herself into thinking it was anything else, the ribbon spilled under the upturned heel of a canary yellow pump (ladies' size eleven, she knew) and that told her everything she didn't want to know.

Fay's wide eyes stared up at nothing, her beautiful silk blouse torn and blackened by the close-range shooting. Dani was sorry to see that she'd lost two fingernails on her left hand, probably from hauling the rack from the wall. Somehow that seemed to be the worst part of the whole scene. Fay had beautiful hands and had always taken pride in her impeccable manicures. Dani wanted to cover up her hands, to wrap them up in a towel to protect them from further damage. She didn't want anyone to see Fay with missing nails. She didn't want anyone to see any of this. She didn't want to see any of this.

Swallowing hard, Dani fought against the cloud of shock and denial she knew was descending upon her. If Fay was alive, she told herself, she'd smack the crap out of you for just standing here. Get away.

That became her mantra. Get away.

Make someone pay for what they did here. Make sure the world knew about the killers with guns who dared break her friend's beautiful fingernails and soak blood into her favorite pink scarf. Dani heard the words low in her throat. Get away. Get away. The sound vibrated through her throat, centering her. More important, it kept the scream she knew lurked somewhere below it from erupting.

Dropping her chin to her chest, feeling bile rise in her throat as dizziness washed over her, Dani realized she had stepped on the sleeve of a thin windbreaker. The toe of her boot brushed against a tan hand and her early chant morphed into a low moan.

Look at him, she said to herself. It's Choo-Choo and you need to look at him. He was your friend. He was killed. The thought that the killer might have been looking over his shoulder as he watched Dani running up the driveway made her stomach flip in pain and rage. "Choo-Choo," she whispered, crouching down to see below the console, bracing herself to see the damage done to his beautiful face.

She saw black hair. She thought maybe it was blood blackening the tech's Nordic hair but the surprise of the sight startled her into a weird clarity. Choo-Choo would never wear a windbreaker, not even the high-quality navy blue Lauren one she stood on. Again, unbidden, the fact checker in her brain kicked into gear, recognizing and categorizing the clothes before her by style and price and quality and use. Phelps. Phelps wore Lauren when he golfed. This was Phelps lying at her feet. She didn't need to roll him over to see his face. Judging from the blood spatters and exit wound, she doubted there would be much to convince her.

Why was Phelps here? He was supposed to be at the Greenbrier golfing with the client. Choo-Choo had said so, had said he wasn't coming in. Mrs. O'Donnell would have notified Phelps by phone, would have called the job for him while he was out. She probably would have let him enjoy a round of golf at the luxurious resort on the client's dime.

Dani spun from the console, careful not to step into the ribbons and puddles of blood. Climbing onto one of the console chairs, she balanced herself and rose, trying to see the entire room from a higher vantage point. A high rack of receivers rose like a chimney in the middle of the room and behind it she could see one foot sprawled out from beneath a workstation. One white calf peeked out from beneath a rucked-up leg of pale blue twill pants. Eddie. Eddie, who had been transferred to the Miami office. Why had he come back?

Fay, Phelps, and Eddie. Hickman downstairs. Where was Choo-Choo? She didn't have long until the killers realized they'd missed her, that their rabbit wasn't in the hole it had promised to hide in. Grieving would come later. If Choo-Choo lay dead somewhere in this or any other room, she would have to process that at another time. Now she had to get out of the house.

Part of her wanted to hide again, hide someplace brilliant and unfindable, but she knew such a place did not exist. If they were willing to kill a houseful of people, they were probably willing to take the time to dismantle every nook and cranny to be sure the job was done thoroughly. But with the front and back exits of the compound blocked, where could she go?

She had heard radios crackle in the stairwell. She couldn't go down that way. The back stairs would be watched as well. One peek out the high windows made short work of any farfetched ideas of jumping to safety. She stepped carefully from the wheeled chair onto the console, thinking somehow the higher vantage point would give her an idea.

Plus Phelps' blood was running across the floor toward her.

She picked her way over headphones and keyboards, careful not to knock over Choo-Choo's army of Mountain Dew cans. She moved quickly, her small feet finding room on the crowded surface until she got to the second window of the row. Even this close, Dani could barely make out the thin line between the window and the frame. She hoped she'd be able to open it without having to touch any of the blood.

None of the windows in Audio were supposed to open; they'd been painted shut years before. They weren't wired for security so as not to interfere with the many sensitive surveillance devices and none of the lower gables came close enough to offer any real point of entry from the ground. The only thing close to them was an architectural flourish beneath the windows, just a narrow ledge of brick.

But Choo-Choo was a smoker and hated to walk all the way downstairs to light up. He'd given Dani one of his "poor me" sad-eyes and she'd been helpless to resist. It had taken her three hours, a packet of razor blades (plus a roll of gauze and tape to treat a nasty cut when a blade had slipped), four shades of paint, and a can of WD-40, but finally she had gotten the window open. More important, she'd layered and stained the paint around the edges such that nobody would be able to see the change. Choo-Choo had tears in his eyes when the window had slid open silently that first time.

Dani placed her fingertips carefully to avoid the arc of blood spray against the glass and gave a sharp push. The window slid up with expected ease. She took one last look onto the killing floor of Audio and whispered, "I hope they have cigarettes wherever you are, Choo-Choo." Then she slung her purse and Rasmund pouch over her shoulder and hoisted herself up through the frame.

A quick peek down to the estate below assured her that nobody was watching the upper levels and she folded herself enough to get one leg, then another, through the frame. It took most of her upper-body strength to lower herself down to the ledge that had looked a lot bigger in her memory. She slid the window back into place as she heard heavy footsteps pounding down the hallway.

She didn't think it was possible for her body to produce any more adrenaline, but pressed back against the rough brick of the building three stories up, Dani's throat tightened and a new shower of sweat ran down from her hairline. Only the sound of voices coming closer prompted her to take that first inching step away from the window. She thought she might be short enough to not be seen through the glass, but she had neither the nerve nor the room to turn her head to check. All she could do was slide her left foot and then her right foot, over and over again, until she put distance between herself and the bank of windows.

Perspective really is everything, she thought as she looked down the ledge at the nearest gable of a jutting dormer window. It had looked a lot closer when she'd seen it from the ground. But if she could get atop that, at least she wouldn't be exposed as she was now. Dani hoped like she'd never hoped before that she would be strong enough to get up there.

Behind her, Dani heard furniture being overturned and shouting voices. She had no time to worry about what they'd discovered in the basement. If she fell from the ledge all the way to the flagstone path beneath her, a bullet to the skull would be a kindness. All the fact checkers and calm talkers in her brain had grown horribly silent and Dani dug her nails into the rough brick to focus her nerves.

She focused on the gable, measured the distance to it. "Five steps," she rasped, more from the tightness in her throat than from the urge to remain quiet. "One after the other, Dani. Just one after the other."

A bundle of cables were clamped and bolted into the brick beside the gable and she noticed with a whisper of elation that the closer she got to them the sturdier they appeared.

Finally, with something concrete to focus on, the mechanical part of her brain kicked in, calculating just how she was going to get one foot then the other onto those brackets and hoist herself onto the gable's roof. She felt that familiar separation in her mind—one part problem solving, one part trying not to scream.

The chattering of sparrows made her jump, slamming her head against the brick and nearly overbalancing herself right off the ledge. She adjusted, leaning to the side and grabbing the bundle of cables. Seconds before she made contact, the thought that they might be electrified flitted through her mind but at that moment it seemed a small risk to take, all things considered. Her fingers raked between the brick and the dirty wires and she cried out when she couldn't pull the cables free from the brackets. Having something solid, something more reliable than her balance to count on, made her let out a breath she hadn't realized she'd been holding. Before she could think, she spun on the ledge, gripping the bolted bundle with both hands, resting her forehead against a sun-warmed steel bracket.

"Think, Dani. Think."

She had to get onto the gable. The problem was that the cables felt so solid, so dependable, every survival instinct in her body screamed at her to stay there, to cling and wait and stop taking so many ridiculous chances with her safety. She knew that if she let those voices take a vote, she'd wind up clinging to the side of the house all night or until she lost feeling in her hands or dozed off or got dizzy and plunged to her death. But those options seemed so far in the future compared to the very likely event of her not having the strength or coordination to finagle the climb.

She studied the brackets containing the cables. A hand span wide and maybe three inches thick, the brackets were attached to the rough brick with screw bolts as thick as her middle finger. Dani glanced down to the bracket near the ledge, prodding the bolt with the toe of her boot. They weren't long enough to work as reliable toeholds. She risked getting on tiptoe to better see the bracket above her head.

The gap was small, not much more than half a fingertip's width, but it might be enough. It was certainly more than she had just standing there clinging to cables waiting to learn to fly.

Dani carefully lifted the Rasmund pouch strap from her right shoulder. The rough strap scratched her nose as she lifted the bag over her head. Forcing herself to focus and relax, Dani pinned the pouch between her chest and the wall, taking the bulk of the weight off of her exhausted arms. Working only by touch, she pushed and twisted the strap of the pouch into the gap between the brackets and the brick, forcing the thick canvas into the small space. When the strap no longer felt free to move, she risked tilting her head back to see her handiwork.

The canvas strap pressed against the cables, wedged behind the brackets. She tugged gently at first, more to force the fabric down than to test the strength. When the bag didn't budge and the brick didn't crumble and the bracket didn't wiggle, she tugged harder, going so far as to yank the bag away from the facade. Still nothing budged.

This is a miserable escape plan, she thought. She comforted herself with the grim fact that if it didn't work, she wouldn't have long to worry about it.

Like the distance between the windows and the gable, the gap between having a plan and executing it yawned before her. Dani's hands shook hard enough that it looked like she was drumming on the brick when she let go of the cable, alternating hands to restore her grip.

Reaching as high up as she could, she gripped the cables overhead and pressed off her right toes. The bolt cut into her sole and she didn't have much leverage but it was enough to lift herself high enough to wrangle her left knee onto the top of the pouch. The fabric bent beneath her, the straps straining closer together, as she shifted her weight to her left leg, using the pouch like a stirrup.

She scraped her forehead against the brick, every inch of her trembling as she lifted her right foot from the stability of the narrow ledge. If the ledge had felt dangerous, this felt suicidal, and she knew she had to work quickly or her nerves and her muscles would fail her.

With the pouch bending nearly in two beneath her weight, she started to panic when she couldn't get her right foot into the narrow space between the straps. She kicked at the canvas and finally her toe found the gap and she felt herself shift with a nauseating lurch as her right foot pressed down on the bag. She tried not to listen to her high-pitched panting as she pulled herself up to a standing position, her entire body weight relying on a canvas pouch, two metal bolts, and a steel bracket.

It might have been a minute, it felt like a week, but Dani clung to the cables and found her balance on the straining canvas of the Rasmund pouch. The thought of taking even one more step did things to her stomach she could never express. She was going to have to move almost a foot to the right into open space with nothing to grab onto.

"It could be worse," she whispered to herself, fighting back tears. "It could be raining."

At that moment, it wouldn't have surprised her to feel the heavens open over her. Instead, she felt a pattering of fine dust and gravel bouncing over her cheeks and lips. She didn't dare look up and risk getting grit in her eyes, much less seeing the brackets pulling loose from the building. She had to move immediately. Leaning as far to the right as she could, she let the pouch swing out to the left so she lay almost horizontally above the ledge. Her right hand clutched at the rough shingles and she felt a wiggle of hope move through her that she might actually be able to keep her grip.

Digging in with her nails and pulling her body with her abdominal muscles, Dani shifted her balance toward the roof. Her body and her mind flew through weight and balance calculations and Dani knew she had to act. She had to grip the roof as tightly as possible, push off with her feet, and throw as much of her torso as she could onto the sloped surface. If luck was on her side, her feet would find something to kick off from beneath the gable and she'd be able to haul herself onto the surface.

She gripped.

She kicked.

Her fingers held as her body twisted and her legs slammed hard against the underside of the roof. Her stomach cramped as she fought to clamp herself against the sloped roof, and for two or three seconds, Dani hung suspended. Sheer will struggled with gravity.

The balance between supported and unsupported weight tipped out of her favor. She kicked and clawed and even dragged her teeth against the filthy tarred shingle and then wondered what it was going to feel like when her hands gave way and she floated through space before hitting the ground. She wondered if it was going to hurt a lot.

"Ow!" Her left wrist burst into a flame of pain and a shingle folded up and dug into her neck, confusing her. She felt weightless and weighted down at the same time as her body slid along the roof. She was falling. But she was falling up. Her boots and the button fly of her jeans and the buckle of her purse caught on the raised edges of shingles as her body inexplicably moved up and onto the roof.

"Dani!" The voice came from above her and it took a concentrated effort for her to understand how to raise her head, how to focus on the sight before her. A pale hand clamped around her wrist, dragging her from the precipice. She followed the pale hand up a pale arm to a red face framed with pale hair.

"Choo-Choo?"

CHAPTER FOUR

Choo-Choo dragged Dani high enough to get a leg over the peak of the gable. Even once he was certain she wouldn't slide, he kept his grip on her arms, releasing them only when she broke free to throw her own arms around him in a bear hug.

"How did you get out? Who are these people? What's going on?" The questions poured out of her as Choo-Choo squeezed her against his chest.

"I don't know. I don't know. There was screaming from downstairs and Phelps had his gun," Choo-Choo talked over her questions, his breath warm in her hair. "He told us to stay down, to stay quiet. He said to watch for him but the monitors, they didn't . . . someone had cut the recording, cut into the feed." He finally let her go, pulling back only far enough to rest his flushed forehead against her sweaty one. "We could see them, saw them storming the foyer, and Hickman, oh God, Hickman never had a chance. I tried to zoom in, to move the cameras, but they had taken control of the video. I couldn't move it or record it or—"

"They were watching," Dani said. "From outside. In those trucks. They took the phones too. I tried to call nine-one-one and I got an operator. Their operator. That's how I got out. They're looking for me in the basement. I lied and said I was down there."

Choo-Choo risked a glance over the edge. "That must be why they're still here. They're looking for you. They know they're missing someone."

"What about you? How did you get out?"

He pressed the heel of his palm against his eye as if he had the world's worst headache. "I don't know. It was panic. Fay came in and told me to get the feed out to the police, to alert Rasmund, and I kept telling her I couldn't control it. Then I remembered the window and I thought, I don't know, I thought maybe I could see what they had done to block the signal. I wasn't thinking. And then doors started breaking and I just climbed out. I called back for Fay but she told me to run and I did. I just dropped out the window and crouched on the ledge for, like, hours I think. I heard them shooting. I heard Fay—"

Dani squeezed his hand to make him stop talking. She didn't want to hear this, she didn't want to hear any more about Fay than she already knew. "Who are they? Do you know? Did you hear anything? What are they looking for?"

"It all happened so fast. They were in and up, just like that. They took all the Swan materials in the foyer. Two men took them all and the rest just poured up the steps. It was like something from a movie." Choo-Choo pulled a crumpled cigarette box and a lighter from the pocket of his jeans. His hands shook so badly Dani had to help him get the flame of his lighter to the tip.

"Phelps and Eddie." Dani watched him gulp down smoke, wishing she had a habit like that to fall back on for comfort. "Why were they there? When did they get in?"

"Down!" Choo-Choo folded his spine, grabbing Dani and lowering them both closer to the roof. "They're searching the grounds." Two men jogged through the back gardens, poking into hedges and heading for the ring of young poplars near the koi pond.

"We've got to move," she said.

Choo-Choo crab-walked back along the peak of the gable, holding his hand out to keep Dani steady until they climbed up to a flatter expanse of roof that ran the length of the building.

"The pouch. They're going to see the pouch." She pointed where she knew the dark blue Rasmund pouch hung from the bolts. It would stand out clearly against the pale red brick and it wouldn't take a great leap of logic to figure out how it had gotten there.

"I'll get it." Without waiting for her to agree, Choo-Choo climbed back out on the gable, slid on his butt and heels down to the edge of the sloped roof. Dani clamped her hands over her mouth, certain he was going to pitch over the edge, but he stopped himself with a twist of his ankle. A quick flip and he slid forward on his belly, his long arm easily grabbing the pouch and yanking it free from its hook. Slinging the bag over his neck, he spun himself around and ran back up to her, barely grazing his fingertips along the shingles.

"What the hell, Choo-Choo?" She gaped as he ran past her to a shaded spot behind a turret. "Are you part goat?"

"Close," he smiled, holding out his hand to pull her up with him. "Boarding schools since I was seven. You get really good at sneaking out."

"Good to know," Dani said, grabbing him. "I don't suppose any of your schools shot students for sneaking out, huh? Any experience dodging bullets and snipers?"

"Unfortunately, no." His smile faded and he squeezed his eyes shut tight again. Dani leaned against him, reminding herself that unlike her, Choo-Choo had actually seen people getting shot. Not just their bodies and not just on film, but real live shootings before his eyes.

"We're going to get out of this, Choo-Choo." She put as much conviction into the words as she could muster. "We're going to get to the police."

He nodded. "Just as soon as we get off this third-story roof."

"Yep. Just as soon as we do that."

They stood that way silently, listening to voices shouting below, people moving in and out of the building. The metallic sound of truck doors slamming rang out but they heard no signs of the trucks pulling out. Choo-Choo sighed. "What do you suppose the odds are that they'll just give up and go away?"

"They don't really seem the type, do they?"

He grunted his assent. "Well we can't stay here all night. I think it's safe to assume the police aren't coming and process of elimination is going to eventually lead them up to this roof."

"Should we try to find an access panel and get back inside?"

"And do what?" He shook his head. "Sneak past them?"

"There aren't any cameras in the back of the house, right? There's no surveillance of the employees. If we could drop down and do like they did in the Dixon case. Remember? They got behind the shooters and followed them out the front?"

Choo-Choo kept shaking his head. "The Dixon shooters were madmen on a killing spree. They were just cutting a line through the building, killing everyone. They were crazy. These guys? They're pros. For all we know they could be sweeping the building with infrared looking for your heat signature, making sure nobody is alive."

"Yeah but this is a huge building. They've been sweeping it but they can't watch it all at the same time. If we listen and we stay low and quiet we could make our way down at least to a window we could jump from. We could make it down to the tunnel to the airstrip."

"First thing they sealed. Heard them report it."

"Then we go off the west end of the building, closest to the rose gardens. We find a window low enough to lower ourselves onto the hedges—"

"Where the guards are watching the back gate."

She gripped his arm tightly enough to make him wince. "Then what the hell do you want to do, Choo-Choo? You want to stay up here and wait for them to find us?"

"I don't want to get shot!" Tears brimmed over his lower lashes, the pale blue of his eyes disappearing behind the flood. "I don't want to get a bullet in my skull and just land on the ground like a heap of garbage. I don't want—" His voice broke. She loosened her grip and rubbed his arm.

She needed to think. Choo-Choo was understandably terrified. Her father used to tell her that everybody handled fear in their own way. "When it comes to danger," he'd say, "everybody's chicken. But there are two kinds of chickens—chicken hawks and chicken shits. And it doesn't matter how high up you throw chicken shit, it ain't never going to fly." He'd laugh and squeeze her knee and no matter how bad the storm they'd be driving through got, she'd feel her fear melt right out of her. It didn't matter that she was nearly a foot shorter than the man beside her, she had to accept facts.

"Looks like I'm the chicken hawk."

"What?" Choo-Choo looked at her, confused. "You're a what?"

"I'm going to get us off this roof. We can find a way down and do it now while they're still distracted by their search in the basement. My car is parked on the back service road. They don't even know it's there. We just get to the ground, make a beeline for the trees, and then head to the cops."

"They're going to shoot us, Dani."

"Choo-Choo, there is that possibility." She held his gaze with her own, trying to keep her voice steady. "But if we sit here and do nothing, that possibility becomes a guarantee. Probability and odds, it's what I do, remember? Analyze a situation."

"From a beanbag chair." He didn't manage to get quite the level of snark she suspected he was aiming for.

"Hey." She wagged her finger in his face. "When we get out of here and we're sitting in some cush Capitol Hill bar drinking expensive vodka and collecting our citations of bravery from the D.C. police, I'm going to tell you just how important that beanbag chair was."

He huffed out a reluctant laugh. "Virginia. We're in Virginia. We'll get our citations from the Virginia police."

She pulled him to his feet. "After our daring escape, we'll get our citations from the freaking FBI. Let's go."

They headed west, toward the rose gardens, a thick cluster of rosemary shrubs, and the wide flagstone path that led to the umbrella-shaded patio behind the garden room. It also came closest to the road accessed by the rear gate.

The ground rose higher at this end of the house and it seemed to Dani that if they could get to the second floor, they might find a spot slightly less likely to break their legs upon jumping. It was far from ideal but the ticking clock in her head demanded action.

"Do you see a way down?" She turned to Choo-Choo but found him wandering over the highest part of the central roof, crawling along on his hands and knees, trying to spy the front of the estate.

"Isn't that more open?" she asked, climbing up behind him. "Won't we be easier to see?"

"Something's happening." Choo-Choo slid farther over the slope, craning his long neck as the sounds of voices and radios rose from the portico below them. "They're coming out." He held up his hand to shush her, turning his head to listen more carefully. Dani knew the analyst had scary accurate hearing, and so tried to quiet even her own breath. He closed his eyes, tilting his head more, and whispered, "They keep saying that they've got the bird. They've got to get the bird in the cage."

"They called me a rabbit. Who's attacking us? Jack Hanna?"

Choo-Choo shot her a questioning look. "Who?"

"Jack Hanna? You know, he does all that animal stuff on TV?" She shook her head. "Never mind. Trivia."

"Yeah, well unless that trivia contains blueprints for building a hang glider out of whatever you've got in your purse—" He pointed down to a cluster of men moving in a tight knot toward the front truck. Their movement seemed awkward, tiny steps setting them off balance, and Dani watched as they kept their gazes moving in all directions while each keeping one hand on something in the middle of the pack. A person shorter than all the men bounced between their crowding bodies, stumbling and unsteady since a black hood cut off any chance of the person seeing their way.

"Who is that?" Choo-Choo leaned up on his elbows. "I thought they shot everyone."

Dani just shook her head, watching the awkward race to the now-open truck. The men in the back of the huddle, their own faces covered in ski masks, turned with weapons drawn to face away from the truck. The men in the front weren't gentle as they bundled the bound hostage up to the waiting arms of men within the truck. Only when the victim rose above the shoulders of the escort team did Dani understand.

That gray cashmere sweater cost more than Dani made in a month. She'd know it anywhere. "They're taking Mrs. O'Donnell."

Choo-Choo's arms gave way and he landed on his chest with an *oof*. He and Dani could only stare at the rigid posture of their supervisor as she was manhandled by kidnappers. To Dani it was like seeing Superman taken down by forest gnomes. Somehow it didn't seem possible that guns would work on Mrs. O'Donnell. The team of men shouted into radios and gestured to one another and Dani could hear answering shouts coming from the other side of the building.

"Maybe they're pulling out now that they've taken her?" She wanted to hope.

Choo-Choo looked back at her, doubt all over his face. "Or maybe now that they've got what they've come for and think they're missing someone who's hiding in the building, they're just going to blow the building sky high and erase all evidence."

They stared at each other for a long moment, both realizing which scenario was more likely. Dani broke the silence first.

"This would be an ideal time to get off this roof."

"Agreed. Sun porch."

"Sun porch?"

He scrambled over the peak, holding out his hand to pull her over before breaking into an easy jog across the roof to the northwest corner at the back of the house. "I figured the path down last summer when I was sitting outside smoking. The layout of this house isn't much different than where I spent sixth and seventh grade in Switzerland."

"What?" Dani hurried to catch up with him. "You knew how to get down this whole time?"

"Maybe it was Belgium. I don't remember."

"You knew how to get down this whole time and didn't say anything?"

He grabbed her by the waist of her jeans to keep her from tripping over a gutter junction she didn't see. "I knew how to get down, Dani. What I didn't know was how to get down and not get shot by the balaclava-wearing death squad below, okay?"

"And now?" She resisted the urge to look down at the steep drop below her.

"And now I would rather take my chances dodging a bullet than seeing how far I can fly when propelled by several pounds of well-placed C-four." He pulled her to the edge of a narrow gable that dropped off near the corner of the house. He planted himself on his butt, feet flat in front of him, and urged her to do the same. Once she was in position, he slowly sat-crawled toward the edge.

His feet slid off the roof, his body twisted, and he gripped the gutter braces on the edge of the roof. "Real simple, Dani. Just drop down and hold on. It's not far." Before she could talk herself out of it, she swung her legs out into space. She felt Choo-Choo's strong grip around her waist as she let go of the gutter and crumpled onto a lower section of level roof. He took her hand, leading her several feet to the left, positioning her to drop or shimmy or slide down from one architectural feature to another. Before she knew it, Choo-Choo lowered her softly onto the tile roof of the sun porch off of the garden room.

Choo-Choo held his finger to his lips and Dani nodded. She had been paying no attention whatsoever to what was happening on the grounds below them, concentrating fully on not falling to her death. Now, perched on trembling legs on the hot roof, she could hear voices directly beneath them. She realized with some shock that this was the door she had come in through what seemed like days earlier.

A radio crackled close enough beneath her to make her feel physically ill.

"Cleaners are on the ground, sir."

"And our rabbit?"

"Still in the hole, sir. I repeat, we have no sign of our rabbit."

They could hear a sigh through the radio, then the man's low voice came back. "Roger that. Place the cleaners, cover everything. I want everyone inside that house right now placing cleaners. We've got the locks. We're going to seal that house up; she's not getting out. And Duncan, when you set the detonators, I want a full team head count inside the building before we open the locks, am I understood? I don't want anyone unaccounted for."

"Yes sir. Team is ready to clean."

"One more thing, Duncan. Don't be chintzy with the firepower. Let's teach that little bitch a lesson about the dangers of lying."

"Yes sir." Dani could hear the chuckle in Duncan's voice and she flipped her middle finger toward the spot in the roof she imagined him standing under. Heavy footsteps sounded across the flagstone patio beneath them and orders were shouted within the house. When the sounds diminished, Choo-Choo risked a whisper.

"Think they're all inside?" He heard a metallic click. "Oh, okay I guess we can go."

"What?" Dani gripped his arm as he started to rise.

"That was the locks. The electronic locks have been thrown."

"So, what does that mean? They're locked in with their own bombs?"

Choo-Choo shrugged. "I guess so, yeah. I guess they've locked down the doors until they get the explosives set. Making sure somebody"—he wagged his finger at her—"doesn't try to sneak out behind the killers." He slid to the edge of the roof and Dani was certain she would be sick when he tipped his head over the edge and looked around. "All gone."

She followed him to the edge of the roof that hung over a low evergreen hedge. "No time like the present, I guess." She could see the fear in her friend's eyes. It felt like they were just passing a terror ball back and forth, only enough courage in the air for one of them at a time. This was her turn. "We drop. We stay low. Go by the rose garden and past the hedges. The truck is parked in the gate so as long as we beat the driver to it, we can get through. When you run, Choo-Choo, run like hell. Remember, it's really hard to shoot a moving target."

He lowered himself off the edge of the roof, hanging by his hands before dropping softly onto the patio. "How sure of that are you?"

Dani tried not to grunt too loudly as he kept her from falling all the way into the hedges. "Kind of sure?" They crouched behind the hedges, listening for any sign of alarms.

"Terrible answer."

"I'll give you a better one when we're in the car."

"Deal." He grabbed her hand and they took off running.

X X X

Dani Britton had never been good at gauging distances. If someone had asked her yesterday the distance between the sun porch and the rear gate she would have hesitated, probably answering that it was somewhere between fifty feet and fifty yards. After her dash with Choo-Choo, however, Dani would have answered the question with certainty: the distance between the sun porch and the rear gate was approximately one hundred and eighty-six thousand miles. With the low autumn sun in their eyes and death at their backs Dani felt pretty confident they had broken more than one land speed record, every pounding step certain to be cut short with a bullet.

With his long legs, Choo-Choo hit the gate several seconds before she did and she saw his shoulder slam into the truck in his haste to get through the gap. The impact made him stagger several steps and it looked like it hurt. Seeing this did nothing to prevent her from doing the very same thing as she hurried to clear the gap, and as she careened off the black metal she wondered how much her shoulder would ache when she could be bothered to think about things like that. He was in the passenger's seat of her car before she reached the handle.

Although she well knew there was no way to silently start a car, she couldn't help but turn the key gingerly. Choo-Choo rolled his window down to listen for any cries or alarms while Dani dropped the car in reverse.

"Are you going to drive the whole way in reverse?"

She pointed to the branches scraping the windows. "See any place to turn around?"

"Probably a moot point. The explosion will probably kill us anyway."

"Jesus, Choo-Choo, do you ever have a positive thought?" She slapped his head with the hand she'd slung over the back of his seat as she drove backward. "Get my phone out of my purse and plug it into the charger."

"The phones are jammed. They jammed the cell phones."

"All over North America? They jammed every cell phone in the United States or do you think there might be a limit to the jamming signal? We are driving away from Rasmund, remember? Away? Out of range?"

"All right, you don't have to be a bitch about it." He pulled out his phone and held it up for her to see. "No signal. No bars. Nothing. Happy?"

"Try mine."

"Why would yours work if mine doesn't? Your service is crap. I told you th—"

She threw the car into park with a jerk and grabbed Choo-Choo by the collar of his soft flannel shirt. He stiffened and pressed himself against the window. "Listen to me. I swear to God, I love you, but if you don't get your shit together I'm going to drag you back to Rasmund and beg them to shoot you. I know you're scared. I'm scared too, but right now what we need is teamwork and positive thinking. Can you do that for me? Can you just focus on possibilities? I think we're both very aware of the negatives. Let's try to find some positives, okay?"

He nodded his head with small jerky movements, his pale cheeks mottled with tears and embarrassment. Dani resisted the immediate urge to apologize for being hard. There was too much at stake.

Instead she fished her phone from her purse, plugged it into the car charger, and pressed it into Choo-Choo's damp hand.

"Are we okay?" He nodded again and she squeezed his hand. "Okay. Check both of them as we drive. The first one that gets a signal, call nine-one-one."

X X X

Booker pulled the hood off the bound woman. The client was right—she was stunning. She was the kind of woman who would have intimidated him if he were capable of being intimidated. He smiled at her steely frown. "Tell me what you know about this Dani."

The radio interrupted them.

"Let's teach that little bitch a lesson about the dangers of lying." Booker grinned as he slipped the radio back into his jacket pocket. He tapped the driver on the shoulder. "You know where you're taking our guest? Good. I'm putting her hood back on. If she gives you any shit at all, shoot her in the kneecaps. We've got to keep her alive. It doesn't mean she has to enjoy it."

"Uh, sir?" The driver turned to him. He was young and the only member of the team Booker hadn't met before. That's why Booker had told him to stay in the truck. He looked nervous. "What about the rest of the team? Are they all going to fit in the other truck?"

"We'll have plenty of room. You just worry about our precious cargo. And her." Booker patted the sour-looking woman on the knee, grabbed his bag, and hopped from the rear of the truck. They'd have plenty of time to chat later. Right now he had a team to take care of.

He took his time along the flagstone walkway around the estate. Such a beautiful building. Sure it was probably built on the blood, sweat, and misery of slaves and prisoners, but that really didn't diminish its grandeur. He trailed his finger over a marble porch railing. Several pounds of C4, now that would diminish its grandeur. It was a shame really. Whoever owned the property would probably replace it with some hideous pseudo-historical monstrosity.

His radio crackled as he cleared a thick hedge of rosemary bushes. Gorgeous. Booker bent down to inhale the woody scent. He wouldn't have thought the climate temperate enough to grow a Mediterranean plant like this year round.

"Cleaners are in place, sir."

"Excellent, Duncan. Let me know when you have a full team head count."

"Yes sir." Booker took his time getting to the back garden door. He opened his laptop and brought up the program controlling the building's electronic system. He kept the channel open to listen as Duncan's team counted off as they lined up to leave. "All accounted for, sir."

"Well done, Duncan. Starting countdown to detonation."

"What? Sir?" The door barely moved under the pounding of his heavy fist. "We need you to unlock the door, sir. Sir? The timers. You need to open the locks."

Booker watched the countdown on his laptop as he strolled away from the house toward the truck at the rear gate. "But if I open the locks, then people will get out. That's not the mission. It's important we stay on mission." He switched off the radio in the middle of Duncan's tirade. The glass on all the lower floors was bulletproof and unbreakable. They wouldn't have time to engineer another way out before the building blew, Booker knew. He'd worked with Duncan and his crew before. He could give them a day and a half and they still wouldn't be able to come up with a solution. Geniuses they were not. He was glad to be ending the association.

Booker squinted at the door of the truck parked in the rear gate. The dirt road had left a fine grit of red dust over the shiny black finish. Something had smudged that finish off the door at two places. He studied the smudge. Something had rubbed up against the door. Something coming from the direction of Rasmund.

X X X

It took several minutes for Dani's phone to charge enough to turn on. They finally hit the county road and Dani was able to turn the car forward. Choo-Choo banged his knees several times on the dashboard as the old car jerked but kept his eyes glued to the two phones. Dani wanted to pet him, to reassure him, but she was scared herself.

"Got it." He straightened in his seat and showed her his phone. "Mine."

She rolled her eyes. "Just dial."

"I'm putting it on speaker." He dialed and held the phone up between them. Dani wondered if he expected her to speak to the operator, if he had handed over complete control to her. With his other hand he flipped through apps on her phone.

"Nine-one-one. What is your emergency?"

Choo-Choo looked at her with wide eyes and Dani leaned toward the phone. "Is this really nine-one-one?" It was a stupid question, but she couldn't stop herself.

"Excuse me? Ma'am, what is your emergency?" It definitely wasn't the smooth-talking man from the black trucks. This voice had a twang and just enough fatigue in it to suggest prank calls were no novelty.

"There's been a shooting. Men with guns. At Rasmund. Rasmund Historical Society."

The operator's tone was all business. "Are you hurt? Where exactly are you?"

"No, we're running. Everyone's dead. Rasmund Historical." They could hear the clatter of computer keys in the background. Dani mentally kicked herself for missing that detail when her first call was intercepted. Dispatch centers were busy places. The operator was already contacting law enforcement.

"Tell them about the bombs," Choo-Choo said.

"Ma'am, can you tell me your name?"

More keys clattered and Dani hesitated. Sure it sounded like 911 but she was no expert. "Look, they're there right now planning to blow it up. They're putting in bombs. Get the bomb squad." Dani could see Choo-Choo scowling at the phone in his other hand.

There was a pause. "Ma'am. I'd like you to stay on the line with me. Will you do that?"

"Shit." Choo-Choo cut off the call. He thumbed the screen on her phone that he held in his other hand.

Dani took her hand off the wheel long enough to jab his arm. "What?"

"You got a text message."

When he said nothing else, just stared at the phone, Dani gripped the wheel so tightly her knuckles hurt. "I don't suppose you could read it to me, huh? I'm kind of busy driving our getaway car." He held up the phone so she could see the familiar image on the screen. "That's me. That's my Rasmund ID photo. From my badge. What's the message?"

He cleared his throat and read with no intonation. "'Hi Dani. Gee, you don't look like the type to be disgruntled. I guess you never know who's gonna blow. LOL.'"

Dani's mouth went dry. "Disgruntled? What does that mean?"

Choo-Choo just shook his head, struggling for words. "I think maybe . . . they know that you . . . I think they're going to blame you for this."

"Me? Who's going to blame me? Who is that?"

He said nothing and when the phone beeped again, he flinched so badly he nearly dropped the phone. "Another text."

"Oh hooray. What's it say?"

He swallowed hard and Dani envied him the ability to do so. Her mouth had turned to dust. "It says 'Hop away, bunny rabbit. Hop hop hop.' And then a smiley face."

The phone beeped once more. "Fuck, now what? 'LMAO'?"

"Uh-uh." Choo-Choo held the phone up so she could see it. "It just says 'Boom.'"

"Boom?"

"Boom."

When the woods behind them rumbled and the fireball blazed through the sky, the impact shook the old car. Neither Dani nor Choo-Choo jumped.

CHAPTER FIVE

They drove without speaking until they reached the highway. If she turned left, she would wind up at the little Italian café where Hickman used to take them all for lunch after a job. Right took her back to D.C. She glanced at Choo-Choo, who nodded. She turned right.

Her eyes flitted over every car and rescue vehicle that screamed past them. Choo-Choo kept flipping through the phones but she could tell he too kept track of the horizon. Dani's mind felt both empty and frantic and she struggled to put words together.

"Text them back."

"And say what?" Choo-Choo asked.

"Ask them what they want."

"They want us dead."

"Tell them we've got information that they want."

"But we don't."

"We'll bluff." She gripped the wheel hard as she accelerated toward the city. "Take a picture of the Rasmund pouch and send it to that number. Tell them they didn't get everything and we're going to the Feds. Tell them we want to make a deal."

"A deal? Are you out of your mind? What if what they came for was Mrs. O'Donnell? I don't want to make a deal. I want to disappear."

"And let me take the blame for all that back there? And how are we supposed to disappear? With what, Choo-Choo? I have about fourteen dollars in my wallet and five of that I owe to Fay." She realized what she had said but she wouldn't let her mind go there. "We need to get some kind of advantage or at least stop circling the drain like this. We work for Rasmund, goddamn it, not some pissant private eye. We have connections. We have people in high places. Mrs. O'Donnell has people in high places."

He seemed heartened by this. "That's true. You're right."

"I mean, I don't actually know anyone any higher than Mrs. O'Donnell but—"

"Okay," he said to himself and turned both phones off.

"Okay what? What are you doing?"

"We need a burner. A couple of them."

Dani nearly missed their exit and had to talk over the blare of horns behind them. "'Burner'? Why? Like camping stoves?"

Choo-Choo sighed. It seemed his nerves had been restored enough to reclaim his feline attitude of casual disdain. "Phones. Burner phones. We need to keep these off unless absolutely necessary."

"They can track us with them, can't they? Can you turn off the GPS?"

"Yeah, I did but that's not . . ." He tapped the phones together, chewing his lip as he did when he was working on an especially difficult gig. Dani could feel her shoulders relaxing, knowing her friend was getting his act together. Choo-Choo liked to play the spoiled pretty boy but he hadn't gotten the job at Rasmund because of his looks.

"It's not what?"

Choo-Choo pointed his phone at her. "They may not know we're both alive."

"Well they know I'm alive. I called them to let them know." She resisted the urge to punch herself for that. She followed the thought through to the next logical conclusion and her throat tightened in fear. "Are you going to go? Do you want to go? They don't know you're alive. You could just . . . I mean, you don't have to . . ."

"What? No." Choo-Choo managed to look simultaneously heartbroken, horrified, and offended. He grabbed for her hand and pried it off the steering wheel. "I'm not leaving you, Dani. That may be the advantage we've been looking for. They don't know I'm alive."

"You could go to the cops. You could tell them the truth, tell them I didn't do it."

"I wish I could, Dani, but these people, whoever they are, just broke into a secure facility and wiped everyone out. They knew who you were and had your picture and phone number. Something tells me they've got more than one contingency plan." He tossed the phones into the cup holders between the seats. "No, we have to work our advantage right now."

"Our advantage?" Dani said. "Everyone's dead, we just jumped off a roof, and we're running for our lives and can't tell anyone because they've kidnapped our boss and are going to pin it all on me."

"We have several advantages actually." Choo-Choo ticked them off on his elegant fingers. "They don't know I'm alive or that you have anyone to work with. They can't track us if we stay hidden. And despite all their stealth and finesse, they have terrible timing."

"How do you figure that?"

He smiled. "Because they broke in before I had a chance to cut the Stringers."

"That's good, right?"

"It's outstanding. The Stringers are very dangerous people and it's good to have them on our side. I can't imagine they're going to be happy when they hear about this."

"How do we know that they haven't been, you know, gotten to yet?"

Choo-Choo snapped a look at her that made her jump. His tone sounded offended. "The Stringers? Nobody gets to the Stringers."

"Oh, I don't really know them. To tell you the truth, the idea of them kind of scares the hell out of me. What is it they do, anyway? I mean, are they like hit men? Does Rasmund use hit men?" Choo-Choo only shrugged. "How do we reach them?"

A flash of tooth appeared as he began to gnaw on his lip once more. "I'm not exactly sure." He shouted down her sound of disbelief. "I mean, I can reach them. I'm the one that sends the signals. But I don't exactly know how to meet up with them. They only go face-to-face with the Faces, and even then only in an emergency."

"So you wouldn't know one of them if, say, they were pointing a gun at you?"

"Why would they point a gun at me?"

Dani shrugged. "Seems the thing to do today." She made the turn, heading for Key Bridge back into the district. "Forgive me if this is a stupid question, but why did we have Stringers on this job?"

"Standard."

"For investigating a group like Swan? Swan seems so, I don't know, groovy? Peaceful? I mean, they make recycling bins and solar panels."

"They also make body armor and portable military structures. They're paranoid as hell and they hired us because they were afraid someone was going after their new research. If it's high enough risk to hire us, it's high enough risk to need Stringers. Jobs like this sometimes require a little more than Face charm. Just ask Dr. Marcher."

"Marcher?" Dani almost rear-ended a car stopped in front of her. Her eyes were wide as she tried to put together a sentence. "You don't think . . . it wasn't . . . how Marcher died . . . we didn't, I mean, Stringers didn't . . . that's not what . . . right?"

"Do I think the Stringers took out our own client? No." When Dani relaxed, he went on. "But I don't think it's outside of their job description, if you know what I mean. It's not like we keep files on that sort of thing. The Stringers are an entity unto themselves. An entity with guns. It wouldn't suck to have them on our side." Choo-Choo pointed to a shopping plaza off the highway. "Pull off here. I'm going to get us some phones."

Dani watched Choo-Choo jog across the parking lot. He was the only man she had ever met who could make faded jeans and a blue flannel shirt look like fashion. When he disappeared inside the Rite Aid, anxiety shot through her. She was alone. He was only a couple of yards away but now, with the silence of the car and time alone, her panic roared up at her. Everyone was dead. Really dead. Not dead like on a videotape or dead like on a news story.

She turned the rearview mirror to stare at herself. Those eyes. Those were the same shocky eyes she'd seen on surveillance videos and news reports, recorded during witness statements and interviews. She was now one of those people. She was a survivor of violence.

So far.

She spotted Choo-Choo coming out of the drugstore with a bag swinging from his arm but instead of heading for the car, he hurried a few doors down to RadioShack.

"Surely to God," she said to nobody, "you're not bargain hunting."

Dani was considering beeping the horn to hurry him up when he came back out and headed to yet another store down the plaza, but couldn't bring herself to risk the attention. Choo-Choo had a plan and she trusted him. If he thought this was the time for a spree, who was she to stop him? Getting to the car without being shot had been the extent of her strategy. It was all improv from this point on.

They needed money. She had money. She had cash and her passport stashed in the cubby beneath her bed. As her father had taught her, she kept little caches all through her apartment and even one in her car that she had completely forgotten about. Popping the trunk, Dani hurried around to the back of the car. Pulling back the fabric floor mat, she pulled up a little nylon bag tucked inside the spare tire. When they had started dating, Ben had teased her about her tendency to squirrel things away. He had no idea how pervasive that tendency was.

Her dad, a long-haul trucker, had instilled this lesson in her. Cash is king, he would say, and a handful of kings can get you out of an awful lot of trouble. Inside the bag she found a change of clothes, some protein bars, and a tightly wrapped bundle of tens and twenties, six hundred dollars if memory served her. Her dad had also driven home the point that, fair or not, it was more dangerous for a woman than a man alone on the highway. That's why she kept a tire iron in the pocket of her car door and a small air horn under the seat. She could see her dad winking at her. Make a lot of trouble and make a lot of noise, Dani-girl. Make 'em wish they hadn't messed with you.

But they had messed with her and all the tire irons in the world couldn't keep her safe now. Still, she had cash and she had Choo-Choo. She had her car and for the moment she had some level of invisibility from whomever was chasing them. They could get back into the city, find a place to hide, and maybe Choo-Choo could contact the Stringers. Maybe the Stringers could get them out of this, get to the FBI. Anything was better than just sitting there, frightened and waiting to be caught.

As if he'd heard her thoughts, Choo-Choo came loping across the parking lot, the lowering sun catching the blond of his glossy hair and, just for a minute, he looked like an ad for some hip high-end clothing line. She slammed the trunk shut and leaned against it, taking one minute out of the panic to enjoy the sight. Choo-Choo swung the collection of bags from his long fingers and when he got to the car, he leaned against it rather than climbing in. Dani was just about to make a crack about lingerie modeling when Choo-Choo bent in two and vomited between his feet.

"Oh my God, are you okay?" Dani came around to his side of the car but stopped outside the puddle spattered in front of him.

Choo-Choo spit once and then again, holding up his hand to stop her from coming any closer. He didn't have to worry. Dani had always been a sympathetic vomiter and just the idea of it made her mouth sweat in that telltale fashion. Choo-Choo straightened up with a long sigh, brushed his hair back from his sweaty face, and opened his car door.

"We never speak of this." He slid into his seat and slammed the door behind him. Dani climbed in her side, not turning to face her pale friend.

"You're not going to do that again, are you?"

"That should be all of it." He wiped his hands on his knees, his fingers trembling. "I'm sorry you had to see that. It's a fear reaction."

"Understood." She pulled back onto the highway. "There are mints in my purse."

They drove in silence until Key Bridge. "Where should we go?"

"Thank you."

Dani looked over at Choo-Choo who had regained some color. "For what?"

"For not laughing at me for blowing it back there. For not letting me stay on that roof."

"You're kidding, right? I'm not entirely sure I haven't peed myself yet."

"Yeah, but you," he looked her over like he was memorizing her. "You don't panic. You don't cry and you're so smart. I don't know if people realize just how smart you are. If you realize it."

"Please." She had to look away to keep her eye on traffic. "I've panicked so many times today I've run out of sweat."

"I'm really glad you're with me."

She reached out and squeezed his hand. "Me too. We're going to get out of this." He nodded and looked back out the windshield. "We need to find someplace to go, someplace safe where we can stop and think and make a plan."

"Turn up M Street. Head to Dupont Circle."

She made the right into the Saturday afternoon traffic. "You know a place?"

"A little hideaway. It's an inn. They know me there."

"They know you at an inn?"

He arched an eyebrow at her. "Don't ask."

"Shouldn't we stay away from places where people know us?" The familiar streets of her usual drive home from work reignited the fear in her, reminding her just how far from normal her life was at the moment. "I mean, if someone is looking for us, if we can't even use our phones because they're tracking them, do we really want to use a credit card to check into a hotel where they know you?"

"Trust me. They're known for their discretion. And I don't need a credit card."

She barely made the light onto New Hampshire Avenue. "You're going to have to do better than that. You haven't even told me what's in all those bags you've got. If you have a plan, you need to let me in on it because my reservoir of freak-out prevention is running a little dry right now."

"I bought phones. Burner phones. Seven of them." He pointed for her to make a turn. "I went to more one store because, believe it or not, people get a little twitchy when anyone starts buying a bunch of disposable phones. It's kind of a red flag for either drug dealers or terrorists and I didn't need some patriotic clerk slash Gomer Pyle wannabe calling Homeland Security to report suspicious activity."

He caught her side-eye and shook his head. "And don't tell me I don't fit the profile. Blond hair and blue eyes do not an innocent man make. We know Rasmund has already exploded. Police and rescue workers are going to be on-site and every news outlet is going to be covering it. They're going to whip up a public frenzy and encourage people to scour the area for suspicious activity."

Dani had to force herself to loosen her grip on the steering wheel. "Jesus, Choo-Choo, this is really helping me calm down."

"I'm just telling you how it is, Dani. You read data, I listen to broadcasts. I listen to scanners and phone calls and radio transmissions. The first twelve hours after an incident are the most active for phone-in tips from concerned citizens. Especially around the Beltway and especially if it involves explosives. Remember when that gas station caught fire in Clarendon last year?" She nodded. "We monitored the state police line for twenty-four hours. They logged in sixty percent more phone calls in that period than they had the entire month. All from helpful citizens who thought they had information."

"You monitor police lines?"

"Of course," he said. "My point is that that gas station blew up because of a faulty electrical system. No foul play. What do you think is going to happen when rescue workers find the bodies inside the building? It's not going to take long for them to realize what really happened. We need to be as low-key as possible."

She couldn't agree more. "So why are we going to a hotel—excuse me, an inn—where they know you?"

"Because they know me. I sort of have a tab there."

She pulled up to the curb before an artfully landscaped gray brick building that she'd seen on dozens of tourist brochures. "The

Milum Inn? You have a tab at the Milum Inn? I didn't know mere mortals were even allowed to stay here. I thought they hired actors and models to be window dressing to make the rest of us look bad." He shrugged again. "I don't want to know this story, do I?"

He sighed as he opened the door. "Probably not."

She grabbed her bags as the valet hurried to the car. "Probably not."

X X X

The interior of the lobby lived up to the inn's exterior promise— understated, elegant, and with just enough quirk that Choo-Choo fit in like the room had been designed around him. He sauntered— Dani could call that walk nothing but a saunter—to the desk, where the young woman behind the counter smiled and blushed when she recognized him.

"Hello again, sir," she said, and Dani would swear she fought back a giggle.

Choo-Choo leaned forward, looking at her through his lashes. "Please, what is it going to take for you to call me Sinclair?"

The giggle she suppressed wiggled through her body as she forced her eyes and her fingers to focus on the keyboard before her. "Probably my job, sir." After a few keystrokes, she looked back up, biting her lip. "I don't see anything."

Choo-Choo leaned against the counter as if exhausted by her announcement. "I'm early. You know me. What am I going to do on a Saturday afternoon?" He smirked at her. "Watch football?"

The giggle would be held back no longer and the blush on her cheeks looked warm enough to be uncomfortable. Looking around her as if afraid of being caught, the young woman winked back and began typing. After a few minutes, she reached under the counter and withdrew a plastic key card. She slipped it into an envelope and slid it across the counter.

"The usual?"

"Mm-hmm," she said. "But it's being cleaned right now. Can you give me an hour?"

Choo-Choo made a comical sound of outrage. "How dare someone use my room?"

The clerk laughed. "Would you like to speak to the manager?"

"I certainly would," he purred, draping himself on his elbows over the counter. "But only if she agrees to do it in my room over martinis."

She laughed again and pushed back from the keyboard as if to physically break Choo-Choo's hold over her. "You're a very bad man, Sinclair."

"I know. That's why everyone pretends they don't know me." He tapped the card on the counter before slipping it into his pocket. "We'll be in the bar. And you never saw me."

"I never do," she said with a sigh. She looked up as Choo-Choo turned, her eyes widening at the sight of Dani. Apparently, short girls in jeans and corduroy jackets weren't the client's usual company. Dani gave the woman a jaunty wave.

She followed her friend into the cool dark expanse of the bar, climbing onto a wrought-iron stool beside him. The bartender placed two napkins before them.

"Good afternoon, sir."

"Good afternoon." Choo-Choo spun the napkin around, looking at Dani rather than the waiting man. "A kir royale."

"Very good, sir."

Dani watched as the man set about making drinks. "He didn't seem to know you."

"He's the bartender. It's his job not to know anyone. Just their drinks."

"He didn't know yours."

"What?" Choo-Choo looked at her as if she'd just spit. "Of course he does. The kir royale is for you."

"I don't even know what that is. And how can you think about a drink?" She lowered her voice when he arched his eyebrow at her. "We have to make a plan. And isn't your stomach kind of, you know, not ready for alcohol?"

"Don't be ridiculous. A dirty martini is exactly what I need. Alcohol to settle my nerves, something slightly bitter as a digestive, and the olives will help me retain fluid so I don't become dehydrated. As for the kir royale, well," he looked her over, focusing on her swinging feet that didn't touch the chair rail. "That's just an educated guess. You don't strike me as a drinker."

She wrapped her feet around the stool legs and folded her arms on the edge of the bar. "I drink. Sometimes. I like—"

"If you say white zinfandel I'm having you dragged out into the street."

She shook her head. "What if I say beer? Just a simple flogging?"

The bartender slid their drinks before them. Choo-Choo took the stem in his long, elegant fingers. "Let's not find out, shall we? A toast." She raised her bubbling drink to his. "To civilized drinks—an eye in the storm of the worst fucking day on earth."

"I'll drink to that." One of the phones between them on the bar beeped. Dani tried not to bite through the crystal flute. "That's mine, isn't it?"

Choo-Choo nodded, thumbing the screen. They leaned in together to read the text.

HER DEATH WILL BE YOUR FAULT TOO. The words captioned a photo of a scowling Mrs. O'Donnell.

CHAPTER SIX

Choo-Choo signed for their drinks and guided Dani up the narrow staircase to their room. She watched landings pass, she was dimly aware of people around her, but all she could really focus on was the ever-growing urge to scream. How was this her life? How could this be real? Once the door was locked behind them, Choo-Choo opened a beer and pressed the cold bottle into her hands.

"I don't want to drink. I don't think well when I drink."

"How are you thinking now?"

She looked up into his worried face and took a deep drink. She liked the taste better than the sweet champagne drink that had somehow disappeared from her grasp. She took another drink and let out a soft burp.

Choo-Choo settled onto the settee beside her, kicking his long legs out on the coffee table. "Technically it's considered wrong to serve Stella Artois beer from the bottle. Some say it can only be appreciated when poured correctly from the tap into the proper glasses."

She tipped her bottle against his. "I'm glad we're not standing on ceremony."

"Well if you can't let your guard down on a day like this, when can you?"

They sat in silence for several minutes.

"What are we going to do, Choo-Choo?" Dani whispered.

"I don't know." He spoke no louder than she did. "I don't know anything."

"We know that the hit came when we were called in for an unscheduled meeting. It was almost only our team on-site, right?" He nodded. "We were hit when the Swan job was called, so it's not a huge leap of logic to assume this is linked to Swan. I mean, if someone just wanted to grab Mrs. O'Donnell, there had to be a million easier and less noticeable ways of doing it."

"True." He closed his eyes and leaned his head back. Dani glanced at his elegant profile, seeing the way his brow tensed just slightly (never enough to cause a wrinkle, she knew). She'd seen that look a thousand times although usually when she saw it, he was wearing headphones. "But why take Mrs. O'Donnell? If they wanted materials—and we know they did because they made a point of humping every box out of the building—why did they need Mrs. O'Donnell? If they knew they were going to kill everyone and blow up the building, what good is she?"

"A hostage? Ransom?"

"From whom? Why go through the trouble of a hit like that only to leave a link? If you're going to kill twenty people, what's one more?" Choo-Choo's voice grew softer, more detached, and Dani could see him mentally removing himself from the situation. He was supposed to be one of those dead bodies. They both were.

"Insurance?" Dani felt her body relaxing, the beer and the familiar discussion of analysis soothing her adrenaline-abused body. "Maybe they had to be absolutely certain all leaks were sealed. Maybe they, whoever they are, want a completely contained information bubble. They knew they were missing someone from the building and so took Mrs. O'Donnell as insurance the missing person would cooperate."

"Or maybe they need to keep Mrs. O'Donnell alive because she has information they need. Maybe she knows something about Swan that they don't."

Dani dinged her fingernail against the glass bottle. "Then why send me her picture? Why threaten to blame her death on me? What threat am I to anybody? I don't know who these people are. I can't finger anybody. All I could possibly do is tell the police that Mrs. O'Donnell is missing, which would be pretty obvious to anyone looking for her."

"Maybe *you* have something they need."

"Like what? Evelyn's real name? Your secret love getaway? I don't know anything. I don't have anything."

They stared at each other, unspeaking, until they both turned to stare at the pouch.

"Would they know you have this?" Choo-Choo whispered.

"Probably. I sort of held it up to the camera when I came in."

She unzipped the blue canvas pouch. "This is all we have. This is the only Swan material that wasn't in the building when the job got called. If they think they're missing something, it's going to be in here." She pulled out the white papers first, stacking them on the corner of the table and dumping the miscellany out in a heap. Choo-Choo poked around the debris and grabbed a shiny piece of cellophane.

"If it turns out that I get killed because of a Ho Ho wrapper, I'm gonna be pissed."

She couldn't help but giggle. "Duly noted." She bumped her shoulder against his and set about sorting the debris into piles. "These are the materials Hickman collected from Dr. Marcher. They kind of got tossed around in the running-for-my-life thing."

"Mayhem can be so messy. What is that?" Choo-Choo picked through the papers on the corner.

"Those are mostly phone records and receipts, all the personal information redacted. I can't take any client material off-site that has personal information. Plus too much information can skew the big picture. It can trap you into alleys of thought so you don't see things. Like this guy eats a shit ton of fois gras—good stuff, too. Look how much he pays for it."

"And that tells you what? Beside his good taste and penchant for cruelty to animals?"

"Well it could mean a couple of things. But look at the rest of the receipt." She ran her finger down the faded print. "Nothing else on the list is high-end. I mean, even the saltines are generic. Beer in a can, generic dish soap, shampoo, store-brand dry-roasted peanuts? Kind of a weird match for the fois gras, don't you think?"

"Maybe he likes the combination?" Choo-Choo asked doubtfully.

"Maybe. I personally love those peanuts. But if you look at the other receipts, it's obvious this guy is treating himself with the fois gras. He's busting his own budget with this one incredibly expensive indulgence. And he's not doling it out either. He's bought several packages of it." She rifled through some pages and caught her friend looking at her sideways, his chin resting in the palm of his hand. "You think I'm crazy?"

"No, I think I'd love to figure out how your mind works. What is your conclusion?"

"I don't have a conclusion as such, but since Swan was worried someone was stealing and selling information, this guy pings for me. This serial indulgence could say a couple of things. Maybe he's become financially embarrassed and fois gras is the one delicacy he refuses to relinquish. That makes him a prime candidate for being tempted to make money on the side. Or he could be ambitious, try-ing to groom himself to step into a higher financial level and life-style. Who knows? He could have read in some douchey upscale magazine that fois gras is the food to eat among the landed gentry and those in the know."

Choo-Choo shook his head. "But you don't think that either, do you?"

"No. This says self-comfort to me. This is someone rewarding himself, pampering himself, when he feels miserable. Either he's done something wonderful and is rewarding himself or—and I think this is more likely—something is really bothering him, he's struggling with it, and this is his reward to himself to keep up whatever agreement he's made with himself."

"You can tell that from fois gras and saltines?"

"And generic shampoo and the fact that he paid for parking eight blocks from Swan when there is a closer but more expensive lot. Also he bought no less than six greeting cards over the past two months. Six greeting cards. I don't buy six greeting cards a year but this guy bought six of them. If he paid for postage, he used cash, because we don't have a receipt for it. Maybe he bought the cards for coworkers. Birthdays, anniversaries, get well, could be anything."

"We've got a guy who's worried and buys greeting cards." Choo-Choo reached across her and stopped the finger she had twisting in her hair. He had to tug gently until she got her finger free and he smoothed the hair down. "And what does this tell you?"

"It's a pattern. It's not always clear what it means but things are consistent. People tend to behave consistently. It's what we do. Even I do in my own weird way."

He turned back to the pages, pulling up a phone record. "Well hats off to you, Dani Britton. The bad news is that if we need this guy, we're screwed. He died in that car wreck a few days ago. Fell asleep at the wheel."

Dani glanced over the bits of Dr. Marcher's life that she'd strewn across the coffee table. She could never explain it to Choo-Choo but she felt a bond to the stranger whose stuff she'd been pawing through. She'd gotten to know him from an oblique angle, making judgments and predictions based on the most fleeting of evidence.

To learn that now she'd never really know if she'd been right or exactly why he'd been eating all that goose liver pâté made her feel a thick, thumping sadness. Or maybe she was just raw from the day.

"Maybe Ev was right. Maybe Marcher was dealing and whoever he was in bed with killed him. But to go from hitting a lone scientist to taking out a facility like Rasmund? And to kidnap Mrs. O'Donnell? What the hell could they be looking for?" She waved her hand over the materials. "Not this garbage."

Choo-Choo stared at her for a moment before asking quietly, "And just who got you all this garbage?"

"Hickman."

"Hickman." He leaned in closer to her. "And in the five years you've been running analysis for Rasmund, have you ever worked with anyone who was better at zeroing in on the focus of the problem faster than Todd Hickman?"

Dani shook her head.

"Hickman had instincts like none I've ever seen. He could read a room faster than anyone I've ever known. And he knew what you were capable of. He always insisted that you be on his team, did you know that?" Choo-Choo's voice lowered almost to a whisper and Dani leaned into him without thinking. "He used to brag about you, about how you could take things apart and put them back together in ways nobody would ever have imagined. He used to make bets with the other Faces, take pieces of their materials and slip them to you as side jobs and bet that you could find out what they were looking for faster than their Paints could. And he never lost."

Dani didn't realize she was crying until a tear dripped onto her hand. "This guy was Hickman's friend. Why did he keep bringing me materials on him? Even after he died?"

"Because he wanted you to keep looking. You were close, weren't you?" Choo-Choo swiped his thumb over a tear that hung off her chin. "You knew this guy was important. You were starting to get . . . what do you call it?"

"The shape of him."

"The shape of him." Choo-Choo trailed his long fingers over the piles of odds and ends. "You were starting to get the shape of him and Hickman knew that when you told him what you learned, he'd have an answer for Swan. Swan thought there was an information leak in the lab. Hickman obviously thought it centered on Marcher. But he didn't think Marcher was guilty. Didn't you get the feeling he thought Marcher was a victim?

"Swan thought that leak was important enough to pay Rasmund's enormous fees to unearth it," Choo-Choo went on, still in almost a whisper. "And these killers think this leak is worth enough to kill dozens of people. Including Hickman. And Fay." His voice broke on the last word and Dani bit her lip to keep from crying out loud. "Now, don't you think it's worth it for us to figure out what is in here, what Hickman passed to you, that is important enough to kill for?"

"But if it was so important, why did Swan call the job? If it's so freaking important that Fay had to die—"

Choo-Choo grabbed her hands. "Maybe that's why he called the job. Maybe he found out that Marcher's death wasn't an accident. Who knows? Maybe they threatened him too. His family. Maybe he thought the information wasn't more important than human life. But whoever these sons of bitches are who killed our friends," he squeezed her fingers, "they made it that important. Now you and I have to do what you and I do best. Only we have to do it alone."

"Alone together," Dani said, feeling about six years old.

"Alone together." He let go of her hands and smiled. "It's not like we had anything else to do on a Saturday night, right?"

"Oh shit. Ben!"

"Ben?"

"It's Saturday night," she said, slapping the cushion around her. "Where's my phone? It's Saturday night. Ben usually comes over on Saturdays. I have to tell him. It's going to be on the news, the explosion, and if they're putting my picture up there . . ."

Choo-Choo grabbed her phone from the side table but stopped her from taking it. "What are you going to tell him, Dani? If you tell him you're being set up, will he believe you?"

"What?" She hesitated before taking the phone. "Of course he will. Who would believe I could do that? He's my boyfriend."

"What if the police have already contacted him? And told him a different story?"

She thumbed the screen to life and brought up Ben's number but didn't dial. "It's only been a couple of hours, right? I mean, even if the police think I did do it, they wouldn't know about Ben. We're not married or anything. We don't even technically live together. It's not like they could ask anyone." She tried to force the image of her dead friends from the front of her mind. "It's not like they could ask Mrs. O'Donnell."

"What are you going to say to him?"

"That I'm okay? That no matter what he hears on the news, I'm okay." She saw the look of worry on her friend's face. "I'm going to wind up dragging him into this, aren't I? You're thinking I'm going to get him killed too."

Choo-Choo didn't disagree. "I think maybe you should just tell him not to come over."

"He's going to see it on the news."

She dialed his number. It went right to voice mail. "He doesn't have his phone on, as usual."

"Says the girl whose phone is never charged," Choo-Choo said. "And who still takes notes with a ballpoint pen on her wrists. Why don't you leave him a message?"

She shook her head. "Because when he comes over to my place he keeps his phone off. He makes a big show of tossing it onto the counter like it's nothing. He always expects me to do the same. He says that when we're together, we're together, just the two of us."

"That's nice."

Dani smiled at his sympathetic tone. "He's not a total dick. Really, he isn't. And he doesn't deserve to get dragged into this. If he's at my place, I've got to get him a message."

Choo-Choo's eyes widened. "We are not going to your place."

"No," Dani grabbed her phone once more. "But I know who can."

X X X

Booker got Dani's lock open in less than a minute. From the other apartments in the hallway he heard the sounds of televisions and stereos but, as expected, Dani's apartment was silent. He shut the door carefully.

"Knock-knock. Anyone home?"

Nobody answered as he moved down the narrow hallway. He loved empty apartments. Even if he wasn't tracking someone, he loved to riffle through a stranger's life. It felt so intimate without any of the sticky realities of human interaction. The old woman had been disappointingly short on information about this Danielle Kathleen Britton of Flat Road, Oklahoma. Twenty-eight, single, short, quiet. What kind of bio was that? He'd figure little Dani out by himself.

Not too tidy, he thought, as he strolled into her kitchen. He liked that. Extreme tidiness bespoke a cheapness of character. He wouldn't have been delighted to find piles of dog poop or a sink full of stinking dishes, but the trails of toast crumbs glued to the counter by intersecting coffee cup rings charmed him a little. He tried to picture Dani standing in the sunny room before work, hair mussed, coffee steaming as she buttered her toast. He peered into the sink. He grabbed the knife he knew he'd find there and gave the greasy end a kitten lick. Yep, butter. Real butter. He wondered if Dani was a morning person or if she stood there grumpy and thick with sleep. He imagined she would be cute grumpy.

The refrigerator yielded no surprises. Takeout containers, wilted celery, a half-finished bottle of wine and two beers. A glance into the cabinets made him laugh. SpaghettiOs. Lots of them. He couldn't resist. He grabbed a can, pulled off the pop top, and opened a drawer he knew would have spoons. He didn't even need to look; they were right where his fingers landed. He shoveled a spoonful of the salty-sweet pasta into his mouth just like he used to when he was a boy. They tasted better now, better in Dani's apartment, better off of her spoon.

He stood in the middle of the living room. Cheap furniture, the temporary stuff that gets passed to college students and kids leaving home, getting gradually more broken down and more threadbare until it finds its graveyard in floorless trailers and abandoned houses for whores and meth addicts and pedophiles to find their ease. He dropped with an *oof* onto the last cushion. Dani. This is where Dani sits, he thought, taking up more room than she would but fitting all the same. A blue and white—well, almost white—afghan covered part of the back of the couch, as if flung off. He took another mouthful of the canned pasta, dropped the spoon into the can, and surveyed the room. The TV sat on a crooked pressed-wood table in the corner. He felt around with his right hand, under the afghan, toward the seam of the couch. There it was—the remote. He clicked the power button once, twice. Nothing happened. He slid off the plastic panel on the rear of the remote and smiled. No batteries. Dani Britton wasn't much of a TV watcher.

She didn't sit here too much either, he decided. The light wasn't good and there were no real objects of focus on the shelves or the walls he could see. No, he suspected his girl sat here when she had company. Maybe a boyfriend? A girlfriend? God forbid, a roommate? No, the knife in the sink and the neat array of spoons told Booker that Dani lived alone. He couldn't have explained how he knew it. He just did.

He pulled himself up from the couch, careful not to spill SpaghettiOs anywhere, and wandered around the room. He could feel his pants tenting just a bit as the thrill of his invasion reached him on a visceral level. Booker didn't have any illusions about himself. He wasn't a sadist or sexual psychopath or some mentally enfeebled predator. He was a professional. He learned early in life that he had the capacity to take human life and, more important, the capacity to live with that knowledge. He wasn't haunted by his victims any more than he was sexually aroused by the act. He didn't take pleasure in torture, though he didn't flinch from it when necessary. Booker was a professional. He was efficient and reliable and he made a remarkable amount of money from it for the simple fact that he was willing and able to do well what most people couldn't do at all. And which a surprising number of people wanted done. Rich people.

But the money wasn't enough. The money, the weapons, the travel—it had all seemed a lot more glamorous fifteen years ago. But even then, high on his reputation, Booker had come to terms with the fact that the lifestyle lent itself to solitude. And he was okay with that too. Booker was nothing if not a realist. He accepted situations at hand as they were, not as he wanted them to be. So he adjusted what he could adjust and what he couldn't adjust he learned to live with.

This was one of those things. The lifestyle had taken its toll on his sex life, hell, on his sexuality as a whole. He wasn't so inhuman that he could shoot a person between the eyes, wash his hands, and then jump into bed with some hot body. Maybe in the movies hit men did that. Maybe they did in real life too. He didn't know. It wasn't like they had union hall meetings to discuss the perils of the occupation. If a long enough gap popped up between jobs, he could occasionally manage a hookup here or there but they rarely scratched more than the most superficial itch. Booker had come to terms with the choices he had made. The fact was, in his life, moments like this—alone in a target's home, driven by curiosity and the need to discover—had taken the place of first dates and sweaty-palmed kisses.

Would he find what he needed? Did she have some kinky fetish or hideous habits that would shape his opinion of her? He wanted her. He wanted to find Dani. He had to find Dani. That's what he was getting paid for, but Booker knew firsthand the mind and the body found ways to encourage each other that had nothing to do with outside compensation. Sublimation—he knew it by name. Because of the demands of his job and the isolation it required, he sublimated his sexual urges into his professional prowess until picking a lock took on the same allure as unhooking a bra. Sliding his hands into an underwear drawer produced the same shiver of desire as sliding his hands between a woman's legs.

He wasn't a sicko. He wasn't going to yank it out and jack it off right here in the middle of a job, and all sexual tension dissipated at the moment the target was acquired, but Booker was a realist. He took his pleasure when and where it came. He adjusted himself in his trousers, taking just a moment to enjoy but not lose himself in the shimmer of heat that rose when his fingertips pressed against his increasing hardness, and headed into Dani's bedroom.

This was Dani's space. This was where she did her thinking, where she dreamed her dreams. He knew it as soon as he stepped on the soft blue rag rug that covered most of the floor. A queen-size bed with a white iron frame was covered with a yellow duvet, from which mismatched sheets, rumpled and comfy looking, peeked out. Books and magazines spilled out from beneath both nightstands and Booker caught the winking eye of Dani's laptop resting beneath a crooked lamp. He came around the bed to the side where Dani slept, the pillows bunched up in a cozy semicircle like a flannel nest. He argued with himself over the urge to climb into that little sleeping spot and compromised, letting his fingers trace the pressed wrinkles where Dani's head had lain.

He kept his gloves on. Laptops tended to be filthy devices, covered in spit and food and fingerprints from a thousand people. Using just his fingertips, he lifted the screen, tapping the machine to life. No password—that surprised him a little. Like the flimsy lock on the door. The lack of security created an interesting contrast with the nature of her job as a security analyst. Booker felt something warm inside him growing even warmer as he opened the Internet connection.

She'd set Weather.com as her homepage. Booker laughed. Everyone wanted to know the weather. He checked her history: cleared. He grinned as he crouched down to type in every social media outlet he could think of. Each page opened at an empty login screen. A quick scroll through the alphabet showed that no cookies were stored on any login page. No passwords had been stored on the hard drive. A few more clicks and he saw the computer had no documents, no pictures, no music or videos stored anywhere. He clicked a cloud storage icon on the toolbar and wasn't surprised when it contained no stored login information either. Too bad. Booker had been looking forward to seeing more of Dani than just her Rasmund ID.

A knock on the front door made him jump. Wrapping his fingers around the gun in his waistband, Booker slid to the bedroom doorway. He listened and the rapping came again, this time harder. Walking silently down the hall and keeping to the hinge side of the door, Booker pressed his eye to the higher of two peepholes. He had to peer down to see the red tassel of a knit hat. He saw the broad face of a young Asian man as he leaned in to knock again, his body moving to a rhythm only he could hear through the earbuds peeking out underneath the cap.

Tucking his shirt up to keep the gun accessible, Booker cracked open the door and the boy smiled and held out a plastic bag of takeout food.

"What is this?"

"Thirty-three," the boy said too loudly and through a wide smile as he continued to keep the beat of his music.

"What is this?" Booker asked again, peering around the boy for any surprise guests.

"Yes, thirty-three for Miss Dani." The boy spoke with a thick accent and it took Booker a moment to catch the words.

"Who ordered this?"

The boy smiled, nodding again. "Yes, thirty-three for Miss Dani. Saturday night."

Booker narrowed his eyes as the young man pulled out his phone, careful not to jar the headphones, and flipped through the screen. He looked up at Booker, making a little gesture of impatience. "When did she order this?" The kid didn't seem to understand the question and Booker felt a prickle of cold nerves on his neck. He considered shooting the kid to flush out who had called him. Instead he grabbed the shorter man's arm in a tight grip. "Dani ordered this?"

"Yes, yes," the kid jerked away with a huff. "Saturday. Every Saturday, thirty-three for Miss Dani. She no cancel, you pay for food. She no cancel. I no pay for food."

Booker reached behind him, his fingers playing over the gun, reaching instead for his wallet. "Every Saturday, huh? Same thing?"

The kid scowled at him, ready for a fight. "Yes. Saturday. All Saturdays. You pay. No check. Only cash." He watched Booker pull out two twenties.

"Keep the change."

The young man smiled at that, tucking the money into his pocket and sliding his phone in after it. "Okay. Okay. Good night, Miss Dani."

"Good night, Miss Dani," Booker said and watched the kid dance his way down the hall toward the stairs. Sensing nobody lurking in the hallway, he shut the door and put his nose to the bag. Thai food. He smelled curry and ginger. Dani ate this every Saturday. Holding the bag up against him, he could feel the warmth of the food against his lower belly. This was too delicious an opportunity. He peeled off his gloves and decided to eat in Dani's bed.

XXX

Dani stomped her feet against the cold as she and Choo-Choo waited on the corner across from Big Wong's. The bicycle cruised past them before the rider spotted her and spun around.

"Miss Dani!" The red tassel of his hat bobbed as he pulled the headphones from his ears. "There you are! You no home tonight? You no get thirty-three!"

"Knock it off, Joey," Dani said, checking around them to see if anyone watched.

Joey laughed. "Hey c'mon, it's great for tips." His accent had vanished, replaced by a soft southern drawl. "Plus it gives customers the complete Big Wong Thai experience. So what's the deal, Miss Dani? You stepping out on Ben? And you didn't call me first?"

"Not exactly." Dani led Joey toward Choo-Choo, who remained in the shadows. "Was Ben there? Did someone answer?"

"Yeah someone answered, just like you thought. Some tense little dude, like Ben, only tenser." He stuffed his hands in his pockets against the cold. "Tipped okay though."

She had to lean against the brick wall to steady herself. Someone was already in her apartment. They'd found her. They could be planting anything—bugs, evidence, anything. They could be laying a trap for her or for Ben.

"What did he look like?"

Joey shrugged. "He looked like a tense white guy. He looked like every tense white guy in D.C. Short brown hair, pissy little mouth. You know, like Ben. Like every guy that comes in the restaurant." He winked at her. "You can do better. Give me another chance."

"This is important. Please." She didn't have time to play Joey's flirtatious game even though she knew from experience that pad Thai wasn't the most delicious item available at Big Wong's. "Can you tell me anything about him? Was he alone? Did he look like a cop?"

"Definitely not a cop," Joey said. "And I didn't get past the door. He was real jumpy. Kept looking past me, checking the hallway. Are you okay? Are you in trouble?"

"God, Joey, it's such a long story. Anything you can tell me about him. Anything."

He looked from Dani to Choo-Choo. "He's taller than you, shorter than him. Paler than you, darker than him. Short brown hair. Looked like an accountant."

"Shit." Choo-Choo fell back against the wall beside Dani. "That's half the people in D.C. He could be standing right next—"

"Hey," Joey cut him off. "Who do you think you're dealing with, Dani? Chimps? You asked for my help; I came to help. Just because I said I couldn't describe him doesn't mean I can't help." He pulled his phone from his pocket and flipped through the screen. "Will this do?"

There in the alley beside Big Wong's Thai Delivery, Dani got her first look at a photo of the man who was trying to kill her.

CHAPTER SEVEN

Booker wiggled his toes against the flannel sheets. His gray slacks bunched up around his knees and the yellow duvet covered him almost to his chest. He ate carefully, not wanting to spill any food in Dani's bed even though he could make out little splashes of soy sauce on the comforter. He smiled as he pulled out his phone. Dani ate right here, probably just like this.

He snuggled against the pillows while he waited for her to answer. She was a tiny thing, wasn't she? He hated breaking her cozy little ring but he wanted to be comfortable when he talked with her again. He wanted to hear how her voice had changed from the panicked breathy hiss he'd heard coming from Rasmund. She'd sounded pissed then. He could only imagine how she sounded now. She picked up on the third ring.

"Hi Dani."

"What do you want?"

Traffic sounds. She was outside, poor thing. "Don't tell me you're just running around the streets on a night like this? It's supposed to get cold tonight."

He heard a harsh puff of air, like a laugh but hard. "Thanks for your concern. I guess I know where there's a nice big fire I could warm my hands by, although I guess by now the police have got that area pretty well roped off."

"Yeah probably." He took another bite of noodles. "What are we going to do here?"

"That sounds like it's up to you. Maybe we could start by exchanging names."

Booker wiped sauce from his chin. "I already know your name, Dani."

"Well, what do I call you?"

"Hmm, how about Sir?" He waited, hearing the sounds of car doors slamming and people walking by.

"Sir? What's the matter? 'My Lord and Master' is too formal?"

He laughed, relieved. There was still a chance, albeit a small one, that Dani had gone to the authorities. If so, the call would not only be monitored, it would probably be steered by a trained negotiator who would instruct Dani to engage him and please him, draw him into a lengthy conversation. He had been lulled almost to sleep by too many conversations like that in his career. No, that edge in her voice wasn't coached. It sounded like a raspier version of the frightened voice he'd heard earlier in the day.

"Call me Tom. I like Tom. It's a good name. Solid."

"It's fantastic. I can't wait to shout it to the police."

"I had a feeling you'd be funny, Dani."

He heard her sigh and the sound made him frown. "I don't feel funny, Tom. I'm scared and I'm tired and I don't want to run from the police. I don't know why you killed my friends. I don't know what you want. Tell me what you want."

He bit down on the plastic fork. He heard so much honesty in her voice, so much raw pain. She wasn't playing him. She was alone and frightened and running for her life and she still wasn't engaging in subterfuge. She wasn't pretending to have an advantage. He liked that. Growing up, he'd known all too well what it was like to be the smallest person against impossible dangers. It took guts to be honest. "What I want really isn't important right now, Dani. Unfortunately for both of us, what matters now is what the client wants, and the client wants you and any information you have under your control."

"That sounds a lot more unfortunate for me than it does for you."

"True," he sighed. "But it doesn't mean I like it."

"Well then, Tom, what do you say you blow off work today? So to speak, of course."

He laughed, swinging his feet out from under the covers and dropping them to the rug. "I wish I could. Believe me, I'm about ready to retire. As a matter of fact, I was—"

"Hey Tom?" Dani said. "Can I call you right back?"

Before he could answer the line went dead.

X X X

Dani shut her phone off. "You're keeping time on these, right?"

"Yep," Choo-Choo said, dropping Dani's phone into her purse. "We keep each call under ninety seconds just to be safe. It's almost impossible to trace cell phone calls, but that's by people using legal means. Until we know who this guy is and who he's working for, we keep the calls short." He handed her a burner phone. "His number is programmed in each of these."

"'Killer'?" Dani read on the screen. "A little bit on-the-nose, don't you think?"

"You want me to reprogram them to read 'Tom'? Maybe load his picture?"

She shook her head and hit dial. The man picked up on the first ring. "Hello?"

"Hi, it's me." She hurried along beside Choo-Choo down the sidewalk. "Sorry, my phone was dying."

"Lucky for you that you happened to have a spare."

"Yeah, I'm lucky that way."

"You're afraid I'm tracing your location through your phone."

"Wouldn't you be?"

She heard him hum. "Probably. And I probably shouldn't tell you this but I'm not tracing you. You were smart enough to turn off your GPS in your phone. I guess we could go through the trouble of accessing your account and reactivating it, unless of course you've already contacted your service provider and prevented that. Huh, did you Dani? You really are clever."

"You're no slacker yourself, Tom. Taking over Rasmund like that."

"It's easier than you might imagine if you have the right intel. Hey, wait a minute." He spoke in a singsong. "How do I know *you're* not tracing this call?"

The sound of the smile in his voice made Dani grip the phone hard. She tried and failed to keep her voice low. "Because I'm standing in the middle of a fucking sidewalk!" She wanted to continue to scream at him to get out of her apartment, to let her go home, but she knew that nugget of information was one of the few advantages she had at the moment. It didn't keep a rough sob from escaping before she clamped her lips together. Beside her, Choo-Choo held her elbow, keeping her out of the flow of traffic on the sidewalk.

"Dani, please." His voice was soft through the phone. "I know you're upset. This has been hard for you, I know that. I wish it didn't have to be this way."

"Then make it stop. Make it go away." The horrible tenderness in his voice unsettled her. "I don't have anything you want."

He cut her off. "Don't say that. Don't ever say that." She could hear his voice get harder and louder. "You have to have something. Listen to me, if the client believes you don't have anything, my only job is to kill you. If you have something, anything, then you can leverage yourself with that information. You can make a deal."

Choo-Choo leaned away from where he'd been pressing in to listen. Dani knew she looked as confused as he did. "Are you . . . trying to help me?"

The sigh was loud enough to hear without putting the phone back to her ear. "This job, Dani . . . I don't know. Hey, do you need to switch phones? What are you doing, like ninety-second, two-minute sprints?"

Choo-Choo's eyes widened and he drew a circle around his left temple, mouthing the word "crazy" as he did it. Dani nodded. "No, I'm okay." She waved off a panicked Choo-Choo and kept walking. "I trust you." She could hear his happy sigh.

"I'm glad. If it makes you feel any better, those guys who went in shooting today? They're all dead too."

Dani closed her eyes and felt the world swirl around her. This man, this killer, was obviously insane, but she wasn't lying when she answered him. "That does make me feel better."

She heard him fumbling. "Hey Dani, can I call you back? I have to take this call. It's the client. Maybe I can find out what they're looking for exactly. Would that help?"

"Yeah, it would. Hey Tom, you wouldn't lie to me, would you?"

"No, Dani. I wouldn't."

"If I can't find this thing or they won't make a deal, are you going to kill me?"

She heard him breathe a long sigh. "I've really got to take this call."

"Okay. Thanks, Tom."

XXX

She stared at the dark phone in her hand. The evening had grown cold enough that she couldn't really feel her fingertips, although the shrinking part of her rational mind told her that might partly be from shock. Choo-Choo stood in front of her, his lips moving, but it took more than a few moments before she could make out his rant.

". . . your mind? He wouldn't *lie* to you? What do you think? You think this is some kind of blind date?" He grabbed her arms and bent down to stare into her eyes. "Dani, tell me you don't really trust this guy."

"I don't." She didn't. But she did. "I do. I mean, I trust what he tells me. I can't explain."

"I can." Choo-Choo released her arms and cradled both of her hands in his. "You're afraid and you've been through a horrible trauma. You don't want this to be happening and he knows that. He's a professional killer, Dani. He knows how people think. He's in your apartment right now—your apartment, where you should be eating Thai food, sitting in your pajamas watching crappy movies on your crappy couch with your crappy boyfriend, getting ready to have some crappy sex. But you're not. You're not because that man on the phone killed everyone we work with. He blew up our building and kidnapped our boss and now he's in your apartment trying to figure out how to find you so he can kill you too. Do you hear what I'm saying, Dani? He is going to kill you."

Choo-Choo was right. She knew he was, but something in her brain refused to catch on to the truth. As she had learned to do a long time ago, Dani let herself be of two minds. The sensation comforted her. It felt like her brain operated by committee and she only had to observe. She wrapped her arm in Choo-Choo's and led him down the sidewalk. "We're going to go to my apartment and wait," she said. "We're going to wait outside for him to leave and we're going to follow him."

"He knows what you look like."

"He doesn't know what you look like." She could feel the wonderful reassurance of thoughts taking shape and lining up in orderly ranks. "He doesn't know you're alive. Nobody does. You can follow him and see where he goes, who this client is."

"What makes you think he's going to see the client?"

"He took the call. He's not going to stay in my apartment forever. He's got to go look for me. I bet he's going to try to find out more information about me. Maybe he's going to ask Mrs. O'Donnell. We're going to wait out here with a cab and when he comes out, you follow him."

"What are you going to do after we're gone?"

"I'm going to go up to my apartment and get some things. Some clothes, some money. A warmer coat, since I'm freezing to death. You tell me if he's headed back my way."

"Maybe he won't even come back here."

She shook her head. "He will. I know it."

"Dani," Choo-Choo started to say more and then stopped. He gripped her arm more tightly and let her set the pace toward her apartment.

XXX

Booker let the client rage while he slipped his socks on, followed by his shoes. He didn't bother to keep the mouthpiece in place as he bent to tie the laces on his black wingtips, knowing it would be more than a few minutes before he got a chance to speak. He made little noises of agreement as he tucked the pillows back into their narrow curve. He got a few "okays" and "uh-huhs" in as he trailed his fingers over the clothes hanging in Dani's closet. A lot of black, he noticed. It probably set off her black hair nicely. He tried to stifle a delighted laugh at the size of the boots and shoes scattered on the floor. He had concealed weapons on his body that were longer than her little soles.

"We've got surveillance footage of her car as well as some additional background." The client's tirade seemed to be fading. "There's no conclusive evidence that she's got our ticket."

"She's got it," Booker said, sliding the closet shut. "She's got it and she's trying to figure out the best way to use it. She may not know what it is, but she knows that you want it."

He heard a clatter. The client had thrown something glass against something hard. Booker said nothing to calm the situation. "We're meeting in fifteen minutes," the client said. "The Black Door on M Street."

"That's kind of public, isn't it?"

"Hiding in plain sight. That seems to be the trend right now."

X X X

Choo-Choo flagged a cab and bundled Dani inside it. A hundred-dollar bill convinced the old woman driving it to shut off the availability light, crank up the heat, and keep her eyes forward. She took the opportunity to read *People* magazine while Dani and Choo-Choo crouched low in the backseat watching the door to Dani's apartment.

"How long are we going to wait?" Choo-Choo asked. "Are we sure he's going somewhere tonight?"

"He'd be a piss-poor . . . hunter if he didn't go looking for me." She caught herself before she said hit man. The woman in the front seat might be ignoring them, but that didn't mean she wasn't listening. "He won't stay out all night. He'll come back here."

Choo-Choo pulled at the placket of his blue flannel shirt. "Let's hope he's not going anywhere with a dress code. I'm dressed like a skank. This couldn't happen on a day I wore something presentable? Do you have any clothes on you?" At her questioning look, he reached for the nylon bag she had carried since pulling it from the trunk of her car. Despite his assurance they would return to the Milum Inn, Dani had insisted on carrying all her bags with her. They were starting to get heavy but their solidity grounded her.

Choo-Choo stuck his hand into the bag she'd kept in her trunk and pulled out a faded black T-shirt. "This'll do."

"What? That's my size." The words died on her lips as her friend peeled off his flannel shirt and lifted the hem of his stained Cap'n Crunch T-shirt over his head. All that pale skin she'd dreamed of over the years working with him rolled into view, every inch of it as pale and smooth and lovely as she had ever imagined it. He caught her staring at him just as he started to pull the smaller black tee over his head and winked at her.

"What do you think?" he asked.

"It's small. It's . . . it's really tight in the . . . It's tight." Her fingers fluttered in the general area of his chest and biceps that stood out in detail against the stretched fabric.

"Give me your jacket."

"My what? Choo-Choo, it's not going to fit." Even as she protested, her arms moved without her conscious permission, taking off the loose corduroy jacket. "You're going to look ridiculous in it. The sleeves won't even reach your elbow."

"I know." He slid into the jacket, the unstructured shape of it giving him just enough room for his shoulders. He unbuttoned the wristbands and rolled them back with a big flared cuff, pushing them almost up to his elbow. The coat barely met at his chest and he didn't bother trying to button it. "It could be worse," he said, gently pulling the long knit scarf from around Dani's throat and wrapping it loosely around his own. "I should probably swap jeans with you. But even I draw the line at skinny jeans."

The thought of Choo-Choo stripping off his pants in the narrow confines of the cab made Dani's mouth go dry and her face burn. He rummaged through her messenger bag, found her ChapStick, and smeared it over his fingertips. With a little puff of resignation, he ran his greasy fingertips through his blond hair, pushing it against its natural fall, the lip balm breaking the locks into a messy, tousled mop of hair. He reached down into the darkness of the floor well and did something to the cuffs of his jeans that Dani couldn't see, then leaned back in the seat.

It took her several seconds to see but when she saw it, she couldn't look away. "How did you do that? You look like—"

"A hipster. I know." Choo-Choo didn't sound thrilled.

"How did you do that? I wear that jacket all the time and people tell me I look homeless."

He smiled at her. "You don't look homeless, Dani. A little down on your luck maybe." She continued to stare. "Look, if he's meeting this client, he could be going anywhere. Hopefully it's not some black-tie place. Fortunately those are rare in the city anymore. He's probably going to a bar or club or someplace high-end, with lots of shadows and discreet seating. If there's one thing I have plenty of experience with, it's shadows and discreet seating. And I'm not proud to admit that this isn't the first tight black T-shirt I've used to open doors. Nor is it the first time I've stripped in a taxi."

Dani forced herself to look back at the apartment building. "When we're done with this, when we're drinking that really expensive vodka that the FBI is going to buy for us, we're going to have so much to talk about."

"That we will, Dani B. But for now, there's our boy." Choo-Choo leaned over the seat with another one-hundred-dollar bill, resting his chin close to the driver's ear. "Marilyn, at the risk of being a cliché, do you see that man coming out of that building?"

"Let me guess," the driver put down her magazine. "You want me to follow his cab."

"Sorry to be so dull."

She considered him in the rearview mirror as Dani gathered her bags to slip out. "Honey, I get the feeling there is nothing dull about you."

Dani closed the door on Choo-Choo's soft laugh, staying low in the shadows behind the cab until she saw the man hail another cab. She tapped on the window and Choo-Choo pressed his hand against the glass as the cab pulled into traffic.

She wished she had seen more of Tom when he'd come down the steps to the sidewalk but she couldn't risk being spotted. As far as she could tell, he didn't know she knew where he was, that he had gotten into her apartment, that she knew what he looked like. It wasn't much of an advantage but she'd take anything she had. Now she didn't know if she had minutes or hours, but she needed to get into her apartment and get some things.

Dani wondered if she would have felt the invasion if she hadn't known about it. As soon as she opened the door, she could feel the difference in the air. She had no idea what Tom had touched, where he'd been in her space, what he had gone through, but Dani would swear she could feel the change. It wasn't all paranoia either. Dani had always been able to tell as soon as she opened her door if Ben had stopped by in her absence. But Tom wasn't Ben and she doubted very seriously if the killer would have stopped by just to bring her some shrimp lo mein.

She moved to the kitchen. He'd been in her silverware drawer. The roll rail for that drawer had broken months ago and if you didn't lift the drawer just so it closed crookedly. Dani knew how to close it without even thinking. The half-inch gap in the top right corner screamed at her like a siren, telling her to run and never come back.

She couldn't tell if he'd disturbed anything in the front room. She hardly ever sat out here when Ben wasn't around, hating that lumpy couch she'd never gotten around to replacing. A flush of embarrassment rose on her cheeks as she looked at her living space with the eyes of an intruder. What impression had she made? The furniture looked cheap and lonely. Dani made good money at

Rasmund and the rent wasn't inexpensive. She'd taken the apartment because she liked the neighborhood. There just never seemed a convenient time to shop for better furniture or wall art. Did she look poor? Trashy?

"What the hell, Dani?" She spoke loudly enough to shake herself from her thoughts. What did she care if the man who was hired to kill her didn't approve of her décor?

She was starting to sound as weird as, well, as weird as Tom sounded. He did sound weird, like he was attached to her in some way she couldn't understand. Maybe that was a psychology of killers that she wasn't familiar with. Maybe they needed to personalize their victims. Maybe he was trying to trick her into thinking they had a connection.

It didn't feel like a trick. It didn't sound like one. Dani didn't have Choo-Choo's ear for the human voice but she prided herself on having an introvert's natural manipulation sensor. Dani had always had a good sense of when she was being played and while it seemed bizarre to admit it, this didn't seem to be one of those times. He hadn't lied to her about being obligated to kill her either. Rather than lose herself in the ever-darkening possibilities these thoughts were leading to, Dani decided to file them away under the pros list in her ongoing pros/cons tally.

Then she stepped into her bedroom. She knew immediately where Tom had been. Dani only made her bed before and after Ben came over. Otherwise her flannel sheets stayed in the shape of the nest she made in them. Dani considered her bed and the act of climbing into the warm little pocket she'd left there to be one of life's most sublime pleasures. She'd set up everything in the area just so, from just enough room on her nightstand for a bottle of beer or a glass of water to the fold of the yellow duvet. She knew that when she climbed in, laptop in tow, her feet would dip naturally into the shallow indents she'd created in her mattress and the down comforter would puff up around her knees high enough to make her feel cozy but not so high as to block the fan vent on her laptop. Her pillows would be just where she needed them.

She wondered if she would ever be able to get into her bed again.

He was good. She had to give him that. The pillows were almost exactly as she'd left them and the comforter hadn't been misshaped to any extreme, but Dani knew. She could feel it and the feeling of violation bordered on revulsion. She had to snap out of this, she knew. She had to get her things, get the hell out of here, and do something to keep that promise she'd made to herself in Rasmund when Tom had lied to her on the phone. She was going to kill him. She didn't know how but right now, staring at the perversion of her safest of safe places, she knew she would kill him.

She dropped to the floor beside her nightstand, trying not to look at her sheets. The thought that he might have done something revolting like jacking off in her bed made the blood pound in her ears.

Later, she reminded herself. Later she could figure out how to kill him. Now she had to stay alive. Now she needed to gather whatever supplies she could.

She lifted the edge of the rag rug and slid her hand along the floor. There was the knot in the pine floor. Two boards over and she pounded the side of her fist against the plank, popping it out of place. She worked by feel, moving her fingers along the narrow space until she found the plastic baggie stuffed with two thousand dollars and her passport. Choo-Choo seemed to have plenty of hundred-dollar bills in his wallet and she could only imagine why he carried that kind of cash, but neither of them could use their bank cards until this was over. Dani had little doubt that her accounts had been flagged and she would be tracked immediately. So far it seemed nobody knew about Choo-Choo making it out of

Rasmund but they had to assume safeguards had been put in place. From this point on, they were a cash-only operation.

Dani could work with that. This was just one stash she had in her place. She moved back to the laundry room, the same room where her work cubby lay hidden behind the prayer scarf and ironing board. She didn't bother with that; she grabbed the plastic step stool and climbed on top of it in front of the washer/dryer combo. She had to lean to reach the Styrofoam pad she'd taped to the wall, the pad she'd told Ben she'd put there to keep the machine from rattling so loudly against the wall. It was true that the pad had that quality. What it also had was a hollow center. It was a piece of packing material from a printer she'd gotten years before and she'd saved it for just this reason. Sliding her hand between the dryer and the wall, Dani's fingers found another plastic baggie tucked into the foam opening. She pulled it out without dislodging the pad and saw the red rubber band wrapped around the bills. Five hundred dollars.

There was one more stash of money. Dani didn't know if or what they'd need the cash for but there was no way she was leaving this security behind for that crazy man. It was stupid, she knew. She had to get clothes and other supplies and she probably wasn't even going to survive the night but she had learned early that cash is king; cash is freedom and Dani wasn't giving her freedom to anyone.

She flipped on the light in the kitchen. It had to have been more than twenty years earlier, before her mother had "taken a turn," before Dani had spent her summers with her father in the cab of his big rig, that she used to go along with her mother on her job as housekeeper. She still remembered the badly concealed frowns of displeasure on the faces of the women her mother cleaned for, the looks of annoyance that their cleaning "girl" had brought a child along with her. Her mother always promised Dani would behave and Dani never let her down. She'd follow behind her mother like a ghost, peering into people's laundry rooms and closets, into their medicine chests and food pantries. Dani would curl up like a mouse and watch her mother tackle soap scum and wine stains and stains on bedsheets that would make her mother blush.

Most of the time, especially as her mother's illness took hold, she would work quietly, lost in her own thoughts, looking up only occasionally to be sure Dani was minding her. Every once in a while, however, her mother would smile while she worked, winking at Dani and sharing little secrets with her about the people whose houses she was cleaning.

"Lookie here, Dani," she said one day as they stood in a huge, shadowed library full of heavy wooden shelves and more books than Dani thought even the public library had. Dani crept over to where her mother stood on a stepladder, feather duster raised. "There's nothing easier to find than that which someone thinks they're hiding clever. Tell me what you see."

She lifted Dani up to see the broad wooden shelf. Several leather-bound books in a series took up one end of the shelf. A statue of a dancing lady looked so pretty Dani had to stop herself from reaching out for it. There was a ceramic jar like the one they kept flour in at home, only this had all kinds of bright colors and looked like it was carved with real gold. Two girls with big noses frowned from a black-and-white photograph in a silver frame, an ugly little dog panting between them, and behind the frame sat a plain wooden box.

"See that box, Dani?" Dani nodded. "I'll bet you dollars to doughnuts there's something wicked in that box." Dani didn't know what sort of wicked thing could be in a box that small, but if her mom said it was in there, she didn't doubt it. "That's a real good hiding place for it too. You can't see the box unless you're up high and even then it just looks like another knickknack. But what did they do wrong, Dani? Can you see?"

Dani studied the shelf and all the items on it. She glanced at the shelf next to it and the ones below them. They all looked pretty much the same to her. Her mother held her index finger in front of her face, making it inchworm as she whispered, "Here's a clue." She ran her fingertip along the edge of the shelf, leaving a clear line in the dust. That's when Dani saw it.

"There's no dust on the box. And there's no dust where they pulled it out."

Her mother had given her a big squeeze and a kiss, praising her for being so smart. Dani hadn't wanted to let go but her mother finally put her down and got back to dusting but not before tapping her on the head with the feather duster.

"You remember that, Danielle. If you really got to hide something, it's always better to be careful than clever. You hear me?"

And she had. She had never forgotten it. She opened the door to the white microwave that sat amid the crumbs of the toast she'd eaten at a breakfast that felt as if it had happened a decade earlier. Bracing her right hand on the inside roof of the microwave, she tilted the machine back just enough to get her left hand to the envelope taped to the bottom. Working carefully, she peeled off the duct tape, released the last stash of cash she'd hidden in her apartment, and lowered the microwave back into place. She blew softly on the crumbs on the counter, scattering them in a random pattern that left no trace of her handprint, and closed the microwave door.

She still had a few more things to grab but she wasn't going to rush it. When it came to hiding, Dani knew it was better to be careful than clever.

CHAPTER EIGHT

Booker hung back by the bar at the Georgetown night spot. The Black Door had enough polish to keep the drunkest of the college students out of its oaken interior but still retained enough hipness to draw an attractive crowd. Most men in the bar were dressed in a more polished version of his own wool pants, white shirt, and modest tie. Booker knew he looked like any other harried young executive in the metro area. Or maybe he didn't look quite so young anymore. Age in his profession was calculated more along dog years. At forty, he was prime for retirement. He leaned against the bar and scanned the room.

The client would be in one of the paneled booths toward the back of the room. He saw several pairs of expensive-looking shoes peeking out from beneath tables along the dark row. They could wait. Booker wanted to try to identify any other players in this game. The client was in a free fall of panic, adjusting and readjusting to whims and mishaps with more flailing and more killing. It didn't really matter to Booker. He got paid by the head and he got paid in advance. If it looked like the job was going to disintegrate into a law-enforcement-drawing melee, he would just absent himself from the shenanigans and disappear. What could they do? Report him?

A group of red-faced men were getting aggressive and handsy over double martinis and Booker wasn't sure if they were getting ready to fight or have a gang bang. Or both.

Farther down the bar, two stunningly beautiful women who seemed incapable of smiling made a point of keeping their backs to the yelling men and thus to Booker. Their thin backs and smooth skin shone under the twinkling bar lights.

Waiters and waitresses in androgynous black shirts and pants slipped through the growing crowd, dropping off drinks and trendy little plates of elaborate tapas.

Booker watched the faces.

The front door opened and closed, more people coming than going, and the volume of the room rose. A well-built man in an Armani suit moved closer to Booker with a look of expectation. Booker took a moment before dropping his eyes and shutting off the come-on with a blink. The two beauties at the end of the bar finally found something to smile about as an equally beautiful man draped himself over their bony shoulders. This room is drunk enough, Booker decided. It was time to get on with the meeting. He shouldered his way through the crowd, lingering just long enough to decide that the martini men were definitely heading in the direction of a gang bang.

X X X

Choo-Choo asked the driver to pass the Black Door and head to the next block before stopping. He watched Tom watch the sidewalk without seeming to do so before slipping into the bar. Choo-Choo had monitored enough surveillance footage to spot a pro. Suddenly this seemed like a terrible idea.

He walked past the bar, pretending to be on the phone, before making a show of noticing the door. He could feel his heart pounding in his chest and would not have been at all surprised to open the aptly named black door and find a roomful of people with guns all pointed at him. He felt obvious and awkward until he checked himself. This was a bar. He was Sinclair "Choo-Choo" Charbaneaux. He had been getting in and out of better bars than this all over the world since he was fourteen. With a mental adjustment, he pulled open the door and sauntered in.

He almost stopped when he saw Tom standing in the shadows at the far end of the bar watching the room with experienced eyes. Again, Choo-Choo had seen enough surveillance footage in his lifetime to know the signs. He also knew what sort of behavior triggered suspicion. Furtive wasn't going to cut it. Choo-Choo had to make an entrance.

He saw two women frowning at the bar. He didn't blame them. They were way overdressed for the Black Door and the closest alpha males were a clot of florid-faced ex-jock heart attacks waiting to happen. His entire life Choo-Choo had relied on his charm to smooth over life's difficult bumps. He prayed it was now up to the challenge, corduroy jacket be damned.

Pasting an expectant smirk on his face, he strolled up to the two stiff-backed women and draped his arms over their shoulders. The look they threw back at him became only slightly less withering once they took in the details of his face. Choo-Choo tossed his hair and leaned in close between them.

"Tell me, I beg you, tell me that you two lovely ladies drink champagne. Because I've just gotten the most sensational news." He leaned closer to the one on the left and purred in her ear, "I mean, sensational." He saw the smiles in their eyes before they reached their well-trained faces. "It would just be tragic to have to celebrate all by myself."

He didn't wait for them to respond. Instead he caught the bartender's eye and ordered a bottle of Cristal. The bartender brightened at that and asked how many glasses he would like. Choo-Choo raised an eyebrow and one finger. The woman on his left, whose ear he had tickled, broke first, raising one perfectly manicured finger. Her friend on the right didn't hold out long before she too raised a finger. At his knowing wink, the two beauties threw their heads back in a laugh synchronized to perfection. He leaned in to whisper his appreciation to the woman on the right, all the while keeping his target in peripheral view in the bar mirror. When the man walked past him without so much as a glance, Choo-Choo let out the last of his tension and reached for the champagne.

X X X

The client sat in the booth along with his assistant, a pinched-face young man who Booker decided had paid way too much for his trendy haircut even if he'd gotten it for free. The young man had made a point from the first meeting of keeping his name out of the proceedings, insisting, even though nobody had asked him, that he be referred to only as R. The client had introduced him as "an internal security consultant" but as far as Booker could see, his only job seemed to be handing pieces of paper back and forth and occasionally getting the car door for the client. It was apparent that R fancied himself a player in this drama, probably imagining he had finally reached the point in his career where he was running with the wolves. Booker looked forward to the moment when R learned that guys like him were usually the last mess to be cleaned up at the end of a job like this.

Booker didn't care about names or titles. He knew the client's name but he never used it. He liked to know his target's names, for clarity and certainty. What Booker cared most about were numbers—the long strings of numbers that accompanied bank transfers. He couldn't tell you the first names of his last three clients but he could still recite every transfer number and dollar amount, even with the international conversion. After all, he had a retirement to consider.

At the client's nod, R slid a manila envelope across the table. He imbued this simple task with such cloak-and-dagger pomposity that Booker felt like pulling out his gun and finishing him right there. Instead he did something he knew would bother the man even more. He ignored him.

"We've found her car." The client seemed likewise inclined to overlook R. "It's in a valet parking lot off Dupont Circle. Several hotels and restaurants use the lot. The manager of the lot says he thinks hers was checked in from the Milum Inn, but we haven't been able to confirm if she is indeed checked in there."

Booker slid out the photo of the car—a four-door maroon Honda that had seen plenty of rough use. "She lives in the neighborhood. What makes you think she would check into a hotel? Maybe she had friends she's staying with."

"That's not what our information suggests. Our sources tell us that Miss Britton is a loner, spends most of her time at work or working at home, and, aside from the occasional fleeting sexual relationship, her primary bonds are with her coworkers."

"Who are all dead."

"It seems that way, yes."

Booker looked up at the uncertainty in the client's voice. "It seems that way?"

R spoke up. "Your concern at this juncture should focus entirely on retrieving the missing data which was not at the si—"

Booker held up his hand to cut the man off. He kept his hand up—keeping R silent and open-mouthed—longer than was absolutely necessary, long enough to be awkward. Finally he asked in a soft tone, "Do you know why they're called 'search and destroy' missions? Because that is the order in which the mission is carried out. First you search, then you destroy. Whoever is calling the shots on this job seems to be getting that backward."

R jabbed his finger across the table. "The chain of command in this job is not yours to question. Just know that you are at the bottom of it. Do you understand me?"

Booker had been told as far back as grade school that there was something wrong with his eyes. The general consensus seemed to be that his gaze lacked a certain vitality or humanity. Or as his second foster mother had told the social workers, "That boy's dead behind the eyes." It didn't bother him then and he'd come to appreciate the quality in his line of work, though never so much as when he got to level his cold stare at some underling overstepping his bounds.

Personally he always thought he had nice eyes, gentle and blue, but judging from R's sudden paleness as Booker stared at him, he guessed the man across from him would disagree.

It saved him time in pointless discussions. Booker turned back to the client, who didn't do a much better job of hiding his nervousness. "Why don't you tell me what it is you think she has? If I can take care of her in a private setting, I can get the materials and return them to you with little hassle."

"We're not entirely sure Miss Britton has the ticket."

"What is the ticket?"

"That's not for you to know." R had regained some of his starch, or maybe he was just reacting with an adolescent urge to hit back. Booker didn't acknowledge the outburst with as much as a blink, waiting instead for the client to answer the question.

"It is research material," the client said with slow caution.

"Could you be a little more specific?"

"No, I cannot." When Booker sighed, he hurried to continue. "I mean I cannot. We are not entirely sure what form the research is in. We thought we did. Our earlier intel suggested that. We know several components of critical research are not where they should be and we have good reason to believe files have been altered and/or removed from the facility."

Booker brought his fingertips together and raised them to his lips like a schoolboy at prayer. He breathed in the smell of Thai food that lingered on his fingertips. "Let me get this straight. You hired Rasmund because you were told there was a leak in your enterprise. Then you brought me in to stop that leak. Now you have brought me back again to stop an even bigger leak within the company you hired in the first place. And now that all those leaks but one are sealed, you still don't know what's leaking?"

The client paled as Booker spoke, his eyes looking everywhere as if expecting a police raid at any moment, as if the innocuous phrasing would somehow damn them all. His boy assistant, R, made the point moot.

"If you had done what we paid you to do with Marcher, none of this would have happened."

Booker leaned forward on his elbows. "Would you like to say that a little louder? The FBI didn't quite pick all that up." He looked back to the client. "I did exactly what you paid me to do on the first job. It's not my concern that you dropped the ball. But I have to ask you what your plan is if this doesn't work. Are you just going to keep hiring me? Or are you going to get proactive and just blow up the eastern seaboard? Because you know you have to have a finish line, don't you?"

"We know perfectly well—" His boss's hand silenced R mid-sentence. Booker didn't even bother to enjoy the flushed look of frustration on R's face. Was it just him or were clients getting more stupid every job? It seemed like more and more of these jobs involved more and more hand-holding and problem solving, like the clients expected him to teach them how to be dangerous men and women.

Maybe he was already too old for the job because the absurdity of it all had become glaringly obvious. Bullets and dead bodies didn't fix everything. Bullets and dead bodies often created bigger problems that needed more money and more bullets and more dead bodies. And even then, those increasingly large body piles usually did little to solve the original problem. They just created a whole new set of problems that made the original problem pale in comparison. Booker wished he'd ordered a drink at the bar.

"What do you suggest we do?" the client asked.

He had to fight the urge to put his head down on the table.

X X X

Choo-Choo watched what he could from his bad angle. Maura on his left had made herself very comfortable against his hip and he'd be lying if he said he wasn't enjoying the attention her fingers were giving the soft skin on his back below his waistband. He continued with his tale of good fortune, some ridiculous confection of inheritance and invitations to royal functions on private islands. He knew the trigger words to keep women like this engaged. When Maura's middle finger took an adventurous turn south, Choo-Choo realized he was going to have to make a clean break soon or someone would create a scene and, based on her apparent familiarity with the terrain, he worried that someone might be him.

"Damn it," he whispered in Maura's ear, not trying very hard to hide a sigh of pleasure. "My phone. Hold that thought."

Choo-Choo pulled his phone from his back pocket, tensing as he saw Tom look out from the booth and scan the room. He typed, "STILL HERE. CAN'T SEE WHO HE'S MEETING. DON'T KNOW IF I CAN FOLLOW WHEN HE GOES."

His phone beeped back in seconds. "OK LEMME KNOW WHEN HE LEAVES. ALMOST DONE. MEET AT MILUM BAR?"

In his distraction Maura and the other one—Lily? Lilah?—seemed to have worked out a plan. He nearly tossed his phone into

116

his champagne as now two hands worked discreetly and in tandem on one narrow band of his anatomy. He knew from experience there were far worse ways to spend an evening. He also knew this evening would probably not be one of those nights.

"You're going to hate me."

"We could never hate you, Sinclair." Lily/Lilah nipped at his lower lip.

He brushed his lips across her temple, watching as someone climbed from the booth in the back. Not Tom. This man was younger, with an unfortunate haircut and eyes so squinty with emotion Choo-Choo wondered if he'd been crying. Choo-Choo whispered silly words of admiration into the woman's hair as he watched Tom watch the young man leave. Another set of shoes appeared at the edge of the booth but before he could see a face, the group of martini drinkers beside them finally broke their stalemate of rage. One shoved another, shouts and grunts pounded out from the group, and an ineffective tussle flared up and died out as soon as it started. It took only minutes but by the time the bartender threw out bar towels for the mess, Maura's hand was gone from his ass and Tom was gone from the booth.

X X X

Dani slipped the box back into place at the top of her closet, careful to return it exactly as she had left it. It irritated her to have to use such caution in her own home but the less Tom knew about her whereabouts, the better.

She'd tried to imagine her predicament from his perspective. He thought she was alone and terrified and hunted. He thought she would return to the only safe place she knew. He was mostly right, of course. She was terrified and hunted and she had returned to her home, but she wasn't alone and she wasn't flying totally blind. She knew what this Tom man looked like. She could see him coming.

He'd gone through her closets. She knew this because just this morning when she'd slammed the door shut, she'd heard the ugly knit shawl slide from its hanger. Her aunt had knit her that shawl. (Poncho? Wrap? She didn't even know what to call it.) Aunt Penny had been one of the few relatives who had been truly kind to her and Dani didn't have the heart to throw it away. She kept it on a plastic hanger at the edge of her closet where it continually slid to the ground. Before Dani had opened the closet on this trip, she'd seen a clump of fringe peeking out under the door. She'd picked that shawl up enough times to know it always puddled against the door, never slipped under it. Someone had opened the closet door and the shawl had spilled forward. Not just someone—Tom.

She took care not to rustle the clothes. She pulled a heavy black shirt out and slipped the hanger onto the shelf overhead. She had to assume Tom was a man of details and she didn't want to give him any sign that she'd been here. Her phone beeped again.

"HE'S GONE. GET OUT."

All caps. That couldn't be good.

Dani shoved the shirt into the bag on top of the binoculars and all-purpose tool she'd gotten from the box. She'd grabbed a few other items as well, not certain any of them would be useful but she figured nobody ever regretted having duct tape. With a quick check to make sure she hadn't disturbed anything, Dani let herself out of the apartment, opting to slip down the stairs rather than take a chance in the elevator.

The temperature had dropped at least ten degrees, the dampness of the low-lying city raw against her skin. People huddled together as they passed her, the neighborhood still busy for a cold Saturday night. Dani wrapped Choo-Choo's blue flannel shirt around her more tightly. She'd added a few layers in her apartment as well as grabbing a set of gloves, a knit cap, and another scarf. Her now overstuffed bags banged against her hip and the smell of Thai food had awakened her hunger. She hoped the inn had room service.

Choo-Choo texted again that he had finally found a cab and would meet her at the bar. The need to see him throbbed in her. Dark, cold, alone, scared—those words banged around her head as she hurried down the dark sidewalk, watching every passing face for signs of danger or recognition. The cold combined with nervous exhaustion to make her face feel numb, her eyelids heavy and dry.

She almost missed him.

On the last block, she spied the elegant awning of the inn and knowing she'd be back with her only ally, she could feel the energy surge through her legs, wanting to hurry her those last few yards. She stopped watching the faces around her, she stopped thinking about anything other than putting her bags down and warming up every inch of body. Night, cold, dark, and fear had turned her into a burrowing animal seeking only a warm nest to hide in.

If he hadn't stopped at the streetlight to glance up at the facade of the inn, she would have walked right past him. She really didn't even know how she recognized him. True, he stood out from the rest of the people on the sidewalk since he stood in just his shirtsleeves, seemingly unaffected by the damp night. But the photo Joey had taken of him had been at an angle, showing three quarters of a tense face. Under the streetlight, though, hands stuffed easily into his pockets, white shirtsleeves rolled back to reveal muscular forearms, his shoulders looked relaxed, and his profile was almost a smile. Her first reaction was recognition, a sudden irresistible "Hey!" the human brain shouted at familiarity. That he had chosen that moment to be looking anywhere but in her direction, Dani knew, was the only reason she managed to not give herself away.

He knew where she was. He'd found her hiding place.

He turned back to the sidewalk when she was less than half a block away. She'd gotten a grip on the freeze/jerk/halt motion that had kicked through her muscles, had a half-second argument with herself about running away, and managed to resume what she hoped was a normal gait. Feeling exposed and obvious, she racked her brain trying to remember what her eyes normally did when she walked, how she normally held her hands and her shoulders when she wasn't strolling past the man who had murdered her coworkers and was now targeting her.

Would he pull a gun? Would he shoot her right there on the sidewalk? Or would he drag her into an alley and slit her throat? His arms looked strong, the white fabric taut against a long line of muscles in his shoulder. He could strangle her. He looked like a strangler. Where were her hands? He was looking at her. Should she look away? Would she look away if she didn't know who he was?

The struggle to appear normal made each step feel like a hulking lurch and she felt as if her eyes would fly out of her head if she didn't blink. If he'd found her here, he could find her anywhere.

She bit down hard on the inside of her cheek as she moved to within a dozen feet of him. When she cleared the outer ring of light from the streetlight, she looked up just in time to see that flicker, that minute widening of his expression that told her he recognized her. As she had when hiding blind in the beanbag in her office earlier that day, Dani used every ounce of self-control to resist screaming and flailing, anything to end the suspense.

He held eye contact with her, his expression warm and expectant. If it had been any other situation, Dani would almost think he was flirting with her. Or getting ready to approach her to pitch his lord and savior. D.C. afforded plenty of practice dodging pitches of every stripe and Dani clung to her small advantage. He didn't know she knew what he looked like. He had missed her moment of recognition. He thought he was observing her unseen.

When they were close enough that they either had to speak or avert their eyes in the urban fashion, Dani wondered if she could do either. He made the decision for her.

"Hi." He tipped his head back with a nod and smile. Dani felt her neck creak in tension when she nodded back. "Cold night."

"Yeah," she managed to breathe out. She slowed her pace but kept walking to the inn's steps. She couldn't stop the words. "Where's your coat?"

He looked down at his arms as if just realizing his arms were bare. "I don't get cold."

"Really?" She wanted to continue with a spit-screamed rant along the lines of "Because you're a slice of hell off of Satan's ass, you crazy son of a bitch!" But she managed to keep it to "I do. I'm cold."

He nodded at that and flashed her a big smile. He had beautiful eyes, one part of her brain mentioned, while another part wondered if they'd be the last thing she'd ever see. She forced herself to turn her back on him to head inside. When he spoke again, she half expected to see a bullet tear through the front of her shirt.

"Excuse me." He took a step toward her as she looked over her shoulder. "Do you know if there are any good Thai restaurants around here? Somewhere I could walk to?"

That did it. That settled the stone that had been rolling jagged and rough over her nerves. Just as she had known when she'd realized she hadn't reached 911, that certainty of "enemy" settled over her. She'd seen the Thai container open in the kitchen. She'd smelled it all over her apartment. Cold, hungry, and scared, she'd smelled Thai food, her Thai food, number thirty-three that he had helped himself to. He knew who she was, he knew what he planned to do to her, and what he had done to her friends, and he had the nerve to ask her about Thai food.

"There are a bunch of different places. Head up Mass Ave toward Dupont Circle. From there go north." She nodded her head in the direction from which she'd come. Maybe it was suicide but she wanted to see how far he would take this.

He took it farther. "Yeah, there are a lot of restaurants up there. Any you recommend?"

"Oh yeah." She peeled her lips back in what she hoped looked like a smile. He was testing her, smug fucker. "Big Wong's. They have the best crispy noodles."

He grinned at her and Dani decided that given the chance, she would shoot him in the face. "Big Wong's? Thanks for the tip. You better get inside. It's cold. Have a good night."

"You too. Enjoy your dinner."

Given a chance, she was definitely going to shoot him in the face.

CHAPTER NINE

It was definitely time to retire.

Booker kept his hands in his pockets as he hurried down the sidewalk, trying to keep his grin under control. He probably looked like a crazy person but he couldn't help it. This had to be a sign that he should retire.

It was nothing new to find the target more interesting than the client. That was the case more often than not simply because the target required more attention than the client. As long as the client could type in the bank transfer or hand over the cash, that was as interesting as they got. Targets had to be studied and understood, even boring targets.

But Dani Britton?

She was something altogether different. In her situation, not knowing him from the man in the moon, to stop and smile and talk about restaurants? Unbelievable. Booker had killed nice people before. He harbored no illusions that he only exterminated people that needed killing. There were more than a few occasions when he actually thought the deaths were a shame. It didn't keep him from killing them but he did take a moment to acknowledge the loss to humanity as a whole. And to be honest, he wasn't that big a fan of truly "nice" people, if such a thing really existed. In his experience, nice often worked as a blanket phrase for people too cowardly to stand up for what they wanted or too boring to know any better.

But Dani Britton?

She'd snuck out of Rasmund right under Duncan's nose. Right under his nose. She'd had the presence of mind to lie to him on the phone about that hidden room. That was clever. And resourceful. And brave.

Why couldn't clients ever be that interesting? He answered himself: because clever, resourceful people didn't usually need their messes cleaned up with his particular skill set. Ergo his increasing frustration with his career.

Booker indulged himself with a moment's fantasy of turning the job upside down, of blowing off the client and finding a way to whisk Dani away from it all. He let himself imagine her tiny feet under the covers with his, snuggling up and enjoying some real Thai food, maybe even in Thailand. It was ridiculous, of course. He was going to kill her because that's what he got paid to do. Plus, if he really peeled back the layers and looked at the truth of the matter, the fact that she had eluded him thus far irritated his ego. It might be temporarily fluffing his libido but in the long run that irritation would win out.

Still, the job had enough dead hours and dark spots; he couldn't think of a thing wrong with taking time to enjoy a fleeting sweetness.

He knew where Dani was—God, she looked adorable bundled up in that big blue shirt—and he would bet his life she had no plans to go out again this evening. He'd seen her bed. Dani Britton was a woman who enjoyed her comfort. Everything about her was low to the ground and he could just picture her cuddling up in a fluffy hotel bed, telling herself that tomorrow was another day. She'd praise herself on surviving thus far and promise herself that tomorrow she'd find a way to survive. Booker almost wished he could drop off her pajamas to her so she'd sleep well.

He had work to do, however. He had to head back to his hotel, where his gear waited for him. He had to look back on his notes on Marcher to see if he could find any trace of the materials the client thought missing.

What a mess this job was. How many times had he asked the client to be sure the job on Marcher was ready for him? How many times had he offered to break into the lab or his house, to be on-site with communication, and retrieve whatever it was they needed before he took the final step? Booker didn't mind being thorough. He charged a lot of money for his expertise and took pride in being a problem solver.

At the first meeting to set up the Marcher job, that little rat-face R had mentioned something about his widow. It took Booker all of seven minutes to discover that the scientist wasn't married, had never been married. Did anyone respond when he'd passed that information back to the client? They sure did. They let that kid send Booker the abrupt message "Do your job." So he did. And now it seemed like he had to do it again. And backtrack. Booker hated backtracking.

He was just irritable tonight. The thrill of being face-to-face with Dani had diminished, dropping him down into a deep funk. He made a decision. He would go back to his hotel, get his things, and return to Dani's apartment. He'd reheat the remaining takeout, climb into Dani's bed, and do his work there. The thought of that cozy little nest made him smile, taking the edge off the darkest part of his mood.

X X X

Dani lurched through the lobby of the inn, her feet remembering the way to the bar since her brain could do nothing but focus all its energy on keeping her mouth from letting out a primal howl of rage and fear. She wanted to lie down on the carpet, maybe crawl under one of those antique couches, and never ever come out again. She felt like she had looked into the face of the devil himself.

He had found her. Maybe it was suicide to confirm her location for him like that, but what could she do? He knew about her apartment. He knew about the hotel. Maybe he knew about Choo-Choo too. Maybe he was dragging this out for some sadistic reason she could never understand. Maybe. But the whole situation had come down to shades of awful—it felt less awful to be inside than to be outside. It felt less awful to be by Choo-Choo's side than to be alone.

She managed to get herself onto a bar stool, her bags piled high enough on her lap to almost block her face, and get a beer. She needed something to eat. She could probably use a cup of coffee to take the chill off but the word "beer" was out of her mouth before she could stop it. The idea of putting together sentences fit for polite company was beyond her ability at this moment. Instead, she buried her chin on the heap in her lap, her feet swinging free below the stool. She could sleep like this, she thought. She would sleep like this if she wasn't certain she would wake up screaming at any moment.

When Choo-Choo tapped on her shoulder, she started. It turned out she could sleep in the chair without screaming, at least for a few minutes. He climbed onto the seat beside her and motioned for the check. A quick scribble and he once again led her to their room. Either he thought anything he had to tell her was too confidential to risk saying at the bar or, more likely, he could see the circles of fatigue and strain below her eyes and acted with compassion. In either case, Choo-Choo didn't say a word until he had gotten her back on the settee, boots off, feet up.

He dropped a bag on the table and started pulling out groceries. "I seem to recall you telling me one day as we sat in the sun behind Rasmund that your father used to make you bologna sandwiches on white bread with yellow mustard and nacho cheese Doritos. Am I remembering this correctly?" He lined the ingredients up, not checking to see her answer. "And I'm ninety percent certain you said he would let you wash it all down with root beer. Or was it Dr Pepper? Damn it, I got root beer but now I'm doubting myself."

"It was either. I like them both." Her voice cracked seeing the humble buffet her friend laid out for her. "Man, I must have bored you to death with those details. How many times did I tell you this? That you'd remember all this?"

"Hmmm." Choo-Choo studied the ceiling, appearing deep in thought. "I think it was exactly . . . once."

"And you remembered?"

"Of course I remembered." He squirted mustard out on a slice of bread. "A: Listening is what I do. B: You're my friend. And C: It's not like you used to bury us in personal information. I think I know four details about you. Three of them are what you put on your sandwich."

"There just hasn't been that much to say. I'm kind of boring." She stopped him before he put the second slice of bread on top of the lunch meat. "The Doritos go on the sandwich. Between the bologna and the bread."

"Really?"

"Don't look so grossed out. It's delicious." She laughed and reached forward to smash the chips between the meat and the soft white bread. It sounded just the way she remembered. The sour tangy smell rushed up at her, dragging up the feel of memories without the memories themselves. The too-sweet vanilla smell of the root beer bubbles would have brought tears to her eyes if she'd had any left. Instead, trembling took the place of crying or laughing or raging, her nerves too jagged to settle on just one emotion. She didn't know if she'd be able to swallow the crunchy mustardy mess of a meal but she would certainly give it a try.

Choo-Choo watched her eat. He watched her eyes and the grind of her jaws; he watched her fingers tremble as they reached for the root beer. "He looks like a pro."

"I know."

"I mean in person. The way he scanned the bar, the way his eyes took in the crowd. He's definitely a pro."

"I know. I saw him too. Out in front." She fumbled through a disjointed account of the interlude. "He smiled at me, like a real smile. And he asked me about a good restaurant."

"Jesus, Dani, you didn't think to lead with that?" He sat up straight. "I'd have gotten you a sandwich to go, you know?"

"He's not coming here. Not tonight."

Choo-Choo looked like he might drag her out of the room by force. "And you know this how, exactly? Like you know you can trust him to tell you the truth?"

She nodded. When he took a breath to start in on her again, she shook her head. "He found us here. Nobody knows we're here but he found us here. He was in my apartment. He was in Rasmund. He's probably in my fucking car right now. But he says he's going to find out what the people behind this want and I believe him. You know why? Because I don't have any other choice. Apparently I can be gotten to anywhere. I don't know shit about shit and I have nowhere else to go. You know what I do have?"

Choo-Choo shook his head.

"I've got a delicious bologna and Dorito sandwich and I'm going to eat it."

He sighed. "How are you even holding it together?"

She talked around a mouthful of sandwich. "You."

"I'm a very bad person to rely on." He sounded as tired as she felt.

"I don't believe that."

"You don't know me."

She shoved the last corner of the sandwich into her mouth. "I guess I don't really, do I? If you'd asked me yesterday I would have said I did. I would have said we were good friends but I'm sitting here thinking about Fay. I'm thinking she was the best friend I had and I don't even know where her parents live. If they're even still alive. How is that possible? We worked together, close together, for five years and I don't know anything about her family. I don't know who to call to tell about what happened to her." Some small part of her wondered why she didn't cry at those words.

Choo-Choo spun a chip on the table, watching it with red-rimmed eyes. "I guess you don't take a job like ours if you're a real people person."

"How did you get the job? Why do you work there?" She watched the chip with him, not having the energy to look away. "I mean, you always kind of struck me as a trust fund baby. Fay and I used to wonder why you even worked at all."

"See? You know me better than you think you do. I am a trust fund baby. Typical story. Been told a thousand times. My parents were in the diplomatic corps; I was raised by nannies and drunks until I was old enough to ship off to boarding school. I rebelled. Spectacularly, if I do say so myself." He laughed at that and flopped back in the seat beside Dani. "Anyway, Grandfather didn't find my stunts amusing and after I got kicked out of college—again—he pulled some strings and got me an interview with Rasmund."

"As an audio analyst?" Dani asked. "Was that your field? Spying?"

"No, my field was—what the hell was it? Oh yeah, Renaissance art. Yawn. But my specialty was phone tapping, which sat very badly with the university president and his undergrad girlfriend." He grinned at her. "Which was a shame because truly creative and effective dirty talk is rarer than you might imagine. The calls were quite a hit when I slipped them into the university's radio playlist."

Dani laughed out loud, sinking deeper into the small couch. Choo-Choo put a warm hand on her leg. "I know my parents thought this job would be like a punishment for me, a lesson learned. So did I until I got here. And then when I started working I realized that for the first time in my life I was good at something that actually mattered. I was part of something." He squeezed her knee. "Don't get me wrong. I didn't abandon any of my less respectable skills. Ergo our little hideaway here, courtesy of a far more respectable senator's wife."

"Ah," Dani said. "Who is far more respectable—the senator or his wife?"

Choo-Choo thought for a moment. "I guess that depends on what you respect." He watched her laugh and then nudged her. "And what about you, Danielle Britton? You're from where? Omaha?"

"Oklahoma. Norman, Oklahoma, originally. Flat Road, Oklahoma, by default."

"Flat Road, Oklahoma? Is that as glamorous as it sounds?"

"Pretty much, yeah. We weren't in what you would call the heart of the jet set." She saw him arch an eyebrow in anticipation and she shrugged. "Not much of a story. My dad was a long-haul trucker. My mom was crazy. The crazy finally won and I had to spend my school years being shuffled around to relatives who didn't want me, going to schools that didn't know I was there, and waiting for summer breaks. Then Daddy would swing by and get me and we'd spend the whole summer on long hauls. We went all over the States and into Canada. We even went to Mexico once."

Choo-Choo smiled. "That sounds kind of jet-setting to me. Or maybe truck-setting. It sounds like you liked it."

"I did. I loved summers in that truck. We'd go everywhere and everybody knew my dad. He'd let me listen in on everything, sneak me into poker games, hide me in bars. We'd pick up hitchhikers from all over the place and they'd just tell him anything. We'd even talk about Mom. Nobody ever talked about Mom. God, I used to love summer. I used to love being in that truck."

"Is he still driving?"

Dani shook her head. "High winds in Missouri took his truck off the road. There was a question about faulty brakes and I wound up with enough money to go to Oklahoma State. Got enough money to get my PhD if I'd wanted it."

Choo-Choo rubbed her leg and let the silence stretch on before asking, "So how'd you wind up at Rasmund?"

Dani laughed. "You wouldn't believe me if I told you."

"After today, I'd believe just about anything."

"Okay, are you ready for this?" She let her Oklahoma accent fill her words. "My plan was to become a proud member of the Federal Bureau of Investigation."

He howled out a laugh. "You? A Fibbie? Special Agent Dani Britton, FBI. What were you going to do? Be the special agent in charge of height crimes?"

She jabbed him in the ribs, still laughing. "I didn't say it was a good plan, but it was my plan, conceived as most bad plans are, in a haze of post-sex naked drunkenness."

"I get some of my best ideas that way."

"That's because you probably look a lot better naked than I do." She pressed her face into her hands. "I can't believe I'm telling you this story. Okay, I was a bartender at this shit-hole bar in Flat Road. For fun—and occasionally a little profit—I used to do this trick

Daddy showed me. I'd convince people that I was psychic and I'd tell them things about themselves that I couldn't possibly know."

"Cold reading?"

"Exactly. I didn't know that's what it was called then but you know how it works, you start hinting around about an old girlfriend and watch their body language, keep pouring the booze. Before you know it you're telling them about the time their ninth-grade girlfriend licked their no-no hole or something." By this point, she and Choo-Choo were huddled together on the settee, shaking with exhausted giggles. "One of my favorites was that, if I knew they were in town for a few days, I'd get them polluted, really trashed, and get them talking about their first dog. Well, you get some rigger soaked through and get him talking about his first dog and you wind up with an hour-long, tear-soaked, snot-flinging version of *Old Yeller* every time."

Choo-Choo had to choke the words out past the laugh. "That's terrible! Why would you do that to someone?"

"Well that wasn't the fun part. The fun part was the next night when they'd come back in and have no recollection of the story at all and I'd say, 'Oh my lord,'" she laid the accent on thick, drawing out the words. "I'd say, 'I had a dream about you and you was with the most beautiful dog I ever seen.' Buddy, they ate that shit up with a spoon. They'd do anything for me. Buy me dinner, put gas in my car. They'd have married me if I'd wanted."

He stared at her, his eyes wet from laughing. "So how does this translate to the FBI?"

"The Feds raided this drug line coming up from Mexico and were camped out in some shit motel on the highway. Why, I can't imagine, but we had a bar full of them one night. I was young and bored and prone to falling for men in bad suits—"

"Something that hasn't changed."

"Something that hasn't changed at all. Thank you for pointing that out. I pulled the old 'message from grandma' game on one tense-looking fellow in hard black shoes and we wound up back in my apartment violating several of Oklahoma's decency laws. He figured out how I'd been playing him and told me I should apply as analyst to the bureau. He said they'd appreciate my unique skills."

Choo-Choo pursed his lips. "I'm assuming he meant your ability to read body language, not commit acts of indecency."

"One can only assume. Anyway, I applied, took a bunch of tests, and failed. And my FBI dreams were over just like that. But the woman who gave me the results told me she'd write a recommendation for me to Rasmund and it seems that whatever I lacked for Uncle Sam was just what Rasmund wanted and five years later, here I am."

"Here we are."

"Here we are." She pared back the accent that had flooded her words. "Here we are, sitting in a hotel while some psychopath is eating my food and sleeping in my bed, planning how he's going to kill me." Choo-Choo said nothing. "You know what's funny? It's still better than Oklahoma."

X X X

Back in his room, Booker checked the clip on his backup SIG Sauer and tossed it into his briefcase. He'd never been much of a gun man. All this crap his clients expected when he showed up, silver cases of precision weapons nestled in custom-cut foam, he could only imagine how he disappointed them. Guns were tools. He remembered the words of Big Eddy Eddy, a sadistic meth dealer with a surprising sense of humor who had become one of Booker's earliest mentors. "Guns don't kill people," he'd said. "Bullets going really really fast kill people."

Booker had laughed when he'd said it even though he didn't get it. He couldn't have been seven years old and had learned quickly to laugh when Big Eddy Eddy told a joke. All these years later, however, Booker got it. Hobbyists and enthusiasts and weekend militants could rhapsodize on and argue the merits and shortfalls of Walthers and Glocks and Berettas but the truth was the only gun worth carrying was the gun you were willing to lose.

Duncan's team had insisted on silencers on their high-tech weapons—big hulking canisters that made the guns look like cannons. The weapons were clunky and huge and Booker could still hear the shots from outside. He hadn't said anything to them and they returned the favor by not openly mocking the .22 he carried in his waistband. One of them had muttered something about it being "a woman's gun," but Booker had ignored that. He didn't measure his dick by his gun. He didn't worry about things like silencers and hollow-point titanium this and that. When it came time to end another human being's life, what mattered were speed, precision, and proximity. If the only thing protecting you from apprehension was the silencer on your gun, you wouldn't last long in this business. That's why Booker preferred low-tech weapons—blades and wires, shivs and lead pipes. He didn't like counting on machines and technology. He didn't mind getting his hands dirty.

But even he needed a laptop. The digital age demanded it. Booker slid the computer into the briefcase. He wasn't fastidious about destroying evidence chains. If the Marcher job had gone wrong enough for the police to suspect him, a man with eleven names and five citizenships, whatever research he carried on his computer would be small potatoes. The only way the police would suspect Booker was to see him over the body with a bloody knife or bruised hands. He knew that day was coming—nobody's luck held out forever. Booker figured if he ever went down on a job, he'd keep enough evidence on hand to take the client down too. Fair was fair.

He grabbed the gray woolen overcoat he'd packed. He didn't need it. Booker hadn't felt the ambient temperature since he was a boy, but he knew he'd stand out on the D.C. streets without one. Dani had noticed. She'd been cold.

He smiled at the memory of her rosy cheeks and messy hair peeking out from all those bags and shirts she'd been buried in. Grabbing his briefcase and letting himself out of the room, he wondered what she had in all those bags. Did she have the client's intel? Had she stopped somewhere to shop while fleeing for her life? It would be clever of her. Some people panicked when hunted, running in circles and wasting time. Not Dani. She'd gone straight to ground, checking into a hotel in her own neighborhood. At first he'd thought that careless, until the client's research had shown no activity on any of her credit cards. Any credit cards that were known, at least. Despite the background that showed Dani to be a loner, she wasn't without resources. He'd have to do a little digging at her place.

The lobby was nearly empty, two maintenance men buffing the marble floor while three businessmen huddled together in club chairs beneath a shaded lamp. New York may be the city that never sleeps, Booker thought, but in D.C. the games never ended. He paused before a flat-screen TV tucked into an alcove near the fireplace to catch the headlines of the evening news.

On his list of tasks for the evening was making the anonymous tip regarding Dani's involvement in the Rasmund explosion. Despite what he had messaged Dani, he'd held off on misleading the authorities. Everything about this job had been off from the start and Booker had decided to play a tight game. There was no rush to put Dani on the hot seat. He knew where she was. Once the law got involved, it probably wouldn't take them long to find her either. They'd start canvassing her neighborhood and the inn wasn't far outside her known whereabouts. And as cute as Booker thought Dani looked bundled up in her flannel, he doubted she blended in with the stately inn's usual crowd. Why had she gone there? The tingle of being temporarily outwitted shivered up his spine. He loved it and hated it at the same time.

The news anchors laughed about the sports headlines as Booker sidled up closer to the screen. Local news came next. He was surprised to see the lead story focused on a bank scandal, followed by a charity event put on by local teenagers. Maybe he'd missed the Rasmund story; maybe it had run before the sports report, although this late in the year it seemed every American news report started with football. Shrugging his overcoat on, Booker bent to pick up his briefcase and froze. The news show cut to commercial but not before running a banner with the upcoming stories, among them a gas explosion in Falls Church.

Gas explosion?

He scanned the lobby to see if anyone had noticed him. Another white fortysomething man with a tie and briefcase didn't exactly stand out, but Booker liked to make a point of remaining in motion. Just standing still made him feel vulnerable but he stood there, hands down by his side, attaché forgotten. Stillness settled over his muscles, his expression neutral, as his brain kicked into an unfamiliar gear. He felt nervous. He didn't know why he felt it but Booker had learned early in life to trust that reaction.

The commercials finished and the news anchors returned with aerial footage of smoke billowing out over the late fall foliage of Virginia. A close-up shot of fire trucks and state trooper cars circling the scene framed a young reporter huddled in a fleece jacket trying to shout over the chaos behind her. Without realizing it, Booker leaned forward toward the screen, listening with his entire body.

When he stood almost on the balls of his feet, he felt a sensation he had not felt in over a decade. He felt a rivulet of sweat trickling down his back.

X X X

"Want to go over the materials again?"

"Sure." Choo-Choo packed the sandwich ingredients back into the bag. "It's not like I'm going to sleep tonight. Or ever again."

Dani hauled the heavy pouch onto her lap, pulling out the papers first, then the odds and ends. Choo-Choo took the pages, sorting them by type while she lined up the rest. She made a point of placing the cupcake wrapper in front of him and he shook his head. Beside that went the drug company's stress ball keychain, a champagne cork still in its wire cage, two valet parking stubs from two different lots, an empty box of cough drops, an expired Metro Pass, an origami swan, and a wrapper from a grape Tootsie Pop.

"Hey look," Dani pointed to the wrapper. "It's got an Indian on it. That's good luck."

Choo-Choo looked at the purple waxy paper and saw the silhouette of the boy in a headdress shooting an arrow. "Didn't really seem to pay off for Marcher, did it?" He continued sorting the white papers into categories: receipts, statements, and scattered notes. Below the three piles closest to the edge of the table, he removed the folded pictures that Hickman had taken from various angles throughout Marcher's work area. He had to move the TV remote to make room for the last two shots.

"Is the news still on?" Dani asked.

"It's probably almost over. We can try."

She hesitated before nodding. "I kind of hope we missed it."

They hadn't. Choo-Choo muted the set as a group of kids held up signs and posters on a busy sidewalk that looked like the Capitol Hill area. Dani turned back to the materials that looked even less meaningful now than they had when Hickman had brought them to her. Her brain couldn't kick into an analytical frame and she rested her chin in her palms. Choo-Choo elbowed her hard enough to make her teeth clack when he lunged once again for the remote.

He unmuted the screen, catching the reporter in midsentence. ". . . a natural gas explosion. Fortunately, the historic research facility is closed on Saturdays and the building was empty at the time. Authorities say that preliminary reports show there are no signs of foul play and there have been no injuries reported." The reporter looked almost sorry to relay that last bit of information. Her face looked grave as she peered into the camera. "Had this explosion occurred just twenty-four hours earlier, Steve, authorities say the news would be a good deal grimmer. I'm Natalie Harding reporting. Back to you, Steve."

The shot cut back to the two anchors straightening out papers and nodding in agreement before the weatherman cut in with promises of a chilly day for the Redskins game. Dani had to press down on Choo-Choo's thumb, where it rested forgotten on the remote, to turn off the set.

"I don't understand," she said in a whisper.

"There had to be at least a dozen bodies in there." He whispered too.

"How did they . . ." She couldn't begin to phrase the question. When a phone beeped to announce a text message, she and Choo-Choo turned to the floor where her corduroy jacket sat in a heap, his phone chirping within. It took her more than a few seconds to put together the actions needed. When she reached down for the jacket, she only held it up, begging Choo-Choo with her eyes to reach in and pull the phone out.

He moved in the same slow motion she did, as if any faster and the last shreds of reality and understanding would disappear. His thumb slid across the screen and Dani leaned in to see.

"'See the news?'" the message said. They read aloud the next line together. "'Four, four, one, eight, six.'"

"Is that from Tom?" Dani asked. "What are those numbers?"

Choo-Choo stared at the phone. "That's a Stringer code."

CHAPTER TEN

"Did you . . . I thought . . ." Dani couldn't put words in order. She didn't know what she was asking or what she wanted to hear. Rasmund had exploded. Fay had been killed along with the Faces team. Mrs. O'Donnell had been kidnapped. Dani didn't hold local law enforcement in low regard. She knew they were more than capable of understanding a crime scene much more subtle than Rasmund. Anyone would recognize the presence of bodies in the ashes.

"What should I say?" Choo-Choo looked as sideswiped as she felt.

"How about 'Help!' That seems kind of fitting." When he still didn't move, she squeezed his arm. "The Stringers, they're hit men, right? I mean basically that's what they are. Isn't that what you said? We know the people that attacked Rasmund had hit men. Don't you think it would be nice to have a hit man of our own? Someone on our side? Maybe he knows something."

If it was possible for Choo-Choo's fair skin to become any paler, it happened at that moment. "That's exactly what I'm worried about. Maybe he does know something."

"What?"

"What if we're looking at this all wrong, Dani? What if Rasmund didn't get hit but we did?" He stared into her eyes, waiting for her to catch on.

"But we did get hit. Rasmund got hit."

"No, *we* got hit. You and me and Fay and the Faces. Who worked on the Swan job? You and Fay, me, Hickman and Evelyn, Phelps and Eddie. Everyone got hit but us because we escaped. Mrs. O'Donnell walked out."

"Tied up with a hood on her head."

"Because that's so hard to fake?" He scowled at her. "That might have been for your benefit, did you ever think of that? The people who hit us knew someone was missing. They saw you come in and then they couldn't find you. Maybe they knew you were watching. Maybe they were trying to draw you out. Dani, they got into Rasmund. They got the codes for the locks, the cameras, the phones, everything. That is not an easy place to get into. And to get into it without setting off any alarms? You know who gets in and out of Rasmund without being seen? Stringers."

She shook her head. "No, whoever it was must have come in with the Swan liaison. They collected all the materials. This has got to be part of the Swan job."

"We don't know that."

"The job was called!"

"Says who?" Choo-Choo asked. "Says Mrs. O'Donnell. She's the one who called the job. There was absolutely no chatter about that beforehand. There was nothing in the audio I heard to suggest that the job was off track. And what was in the materials? Did you see anything? I had shit on audio. There was zero evidence of anything wrong at Swan."

"But why would she . . . ? Who is . . . ? Tom said that the people who hired him think I have something. All I have are the Swan materials that Hickman gave me. What else could it be?"

"I don't know." He slumped back against the couch. "Whoever is working this, they have the power to affect the police investigation. That's harder than you might think. It's one thing to alter a police report. It's another thing to convince a battalion of state troopers and firefighters to not see dead bodies in the wreckage of a blown-up building."

"Could they have gotten the bodies out?"

He shook his head, uncertain. "Maybe? My sense of time was pretty warped when we ran but it doesn't seem like there was a lot of time between us hitting that road and the building blowing up. Am I being paranoid?"

Dani laid her head back, her shoulder pressing into his. "I think we'd be crazy not to be."

X X X

Booker cut through another busy intersection before he even realized he had left the hotel. His face burned hot, an unusual sensation for him. He knew his face got red when he exerted himself—he was still a functioning organism, but it had been years, decades even, since he had been aware of the occurrence. He didn't hear the traffic around him. He heard nothing but a pounding in his ears and the steady huff of his breath.

No sign of foul play.

Booker had put nothing in motion to hide the bodies. The plan had been to create confusion. The discovery of corpses was supposed to kick off a gruesome discovery of murder and mayhem. The bullet holes in the skulls of the Rasmund employees would take a few hours but that evidence was supposed to open a trail of suspicion and misdirection. The unexplained presence of the dead team of mercenaries would only add to the cloud of fear and foreboding.

Who the hell was playing him?

Booker knew nobody had gotten out of that building alive except O'Donnell and Dani. Duncan and his crew had died screaming and cursing him. The real question was why would anyone tamper with this plan? Or more to the point, how did it affect him? Booker didn't give a rat's ass if the master plan kicked off the emergence of a new Third Reich so long as he got away free and untouched. What bothered him, on the ever growing list of things that bothered him about this job as a whole, was that nobody had given even an inkling of this wrinkle. The client, his assistant, the site of the big hit, nothing in Marcher's background—nowhere had Booker found even a hint, a trace, or a suggestion that a bigger game was afoot. And Booker had an excellent eye for treachery.

Was someone setting him up? A less experienced professional might feel some relief that the Rasmund hit came up on public record as being a fatality-free accident. Less experienced professionals didn't last long without questioning windfalls and happy surprises. The level of incineration needed to vaporize the number of bodies in Rasmund to a point beyond detection would have left a crater in the Virginia countryside that would still be smoking.

Somebody was covering Booker's tracks. Why?

Of all the many lessons Booker had learned through his forty-plus years on the planet, one of the most important was that nobody did good deeds for nothing. Nobody would cover the tracks of the job Booker got paid so handsomely to do unless he could use it for a payday of his own. Was someone going to try to shake down the client? If so, Booker planned on being on the next flight out of town. Were they going to try to shake him down? He felt the warm hilt of the silver knife he had tucked in the small of his back as it touched his skin. That wouldn't end well for one of them.

Who could pull off a maneuver like this? The questions pounded on Booker as he pounded down the sidewalk, walking without looking, toward the Metro. The bodies were still on-site, of that he had no doubt. Booker had watched the building explode. Nothing had gotten out of the blast area; he himself had barely cleared the perimeter when the rescue workers came on-site.

They had been legitimate rescue teams, right? The tingling thrill he'd felt when he thought Dani had outsmarted him morphed into a hot wave of nausea that roiled like broken glass under his skin. "No," he told himself, speaking aloud despite the strange looks he got from the few people on the sidewalk at this hour. No. Those were local fire and rescue. They had to be. That meant someone in charge of releasing information to the media had chosen or been forced to cover up the deaths. Who had that kind of clout? Who had that sort of reach into local law enforcement? Booker felt his mouth go dry. Higher levels of law enforcement.

Had he been hired to hit the government?

X X X

"I still say we contact them." Dani grabbed her purse from under the pile of bags and started pulling out burner phones. "We have got zero information about what's going on. It's not like we're giving your presence away. You sent them the emergency message. Will they know it's from you? Do they know you're alive?"

"I don't know if they know it's me. I've got to assume they do. Hell, I don't know." Choo-Choo bounced the phone on the tips of his fingers. "If we send the message, if we start a dialogue with them, we're going to have to bluff."

"If they're contacting us—or you—they must want to know something. This is hardly the time for a social chat. Why are they contacting you? To warn you? To fish for information? Let's see what they know."

"What do you recommend?"

Dani took the phone. "You said you all only use tone codes. Well this is a verbal message so clearly the rules have changed." She read her message as she typed it into the phone. "'Saw it. Surprised?'" She looked up at him. "Let's make it sound like we know what's going on. Like we're on the inside of the loop."

The phone beeped in less than a minute. "'Not as surprised as you'll be.'"

Choo-Choo let out a sigh. "That doesn't sound very friendly." Another beep sounded and he read aloud, "'Let's talk.' God Dani, what if they want to finish the job?"

"Well they're going to have to get in line, aren't they? I think Tom already called dibs on that particular activity."

"Tell me you're not being plucky. I hate plucky."

"The alternative is wailing hysterics. Your choice." She trailed her thumb across the phone. "He wants to talk. Let's talk. 'Where, when, and why?'" She showed her message to Choo-Choo before she sent it. He nodded and she pushed the button. The phone remained silent for several long moments.

Choo-Choo spoke around the thumbnail he gnawed. "Did we stump them? Which question do you suppose they're stuck on?" The phone beeped. "I guess they figured it out." "'Dupont Circle Metro, westbound. Fifteen minutes,'" Dani read. "Screw that. We're not just marching to our death. What should I tell him?"

He took the phone and started typing. "'Need more info. How do I know you're secure?'"

The phone beeped in seconds and he held the message up for her to see. "'Because I'm alive.'" Another beep and he read aloud, "'Trying to keep you that way too.'"

"That would be nice to believe. Do we believe him, Choo-Choo?"

He replied to the text. "'How many of us are alive?'" Then to Dani, "Let's see what he knows, if he knows about you or Mrs. O'Donnell."

"'Complicated.'"

"No shit," he muttered at the message and kept typing. "'Not good enough. How many?'"

"'Four. One taken, one in the wind. Only found you.'" Another message came in right behind it. "'Please, Choo2—need help. Dani is target. Must find.'"

He and Dani leaned against each other, their breathing the only sound in the room. Dani kept her voice at a whisper. "We don't have any choice. We're stuck here. We have nothing else to go on. If he doesn't know I'm with you, I could maybe trail him or something. Get the jump on him."

"With what? Your purse? I don't suppose you have a gun in there."

"What else can we do? Maybe this guy really is trying to help us. We know Tom's not. You meet him in public, stay with the crowd. I'll hang back. We'll keep our extra phones on so we can talk. If it looks like he's pulling a weapon or something, I'll cause a scene. You can run."

"That is a terrible plan."

She gave him a weak smile. "So was the roof and we pulled that off."

He didn't look convinced but sent his confirmation to the Stringer. "You know there's a huge gap in your logic, don't you? If this really is a Stringer, a Rasmund Stringer, they're going to know you by sight too. The odds are excellent that this guy has a whole file on you. He's looking for you."

"Let's worry about one hit man at a time, shall we?" She started packing up the Swan materials. "I feel like all I do is pack and unpack this stuff."

"Why are you even bothering? You're not taking it all with you, are you?"

"Yes, I am. I'm taking it everywhere." She rolled the champagne cork around in her palm, her pinkie catching the wire where someone had once bent it into a perfect heart. After all the pouch's adventures, the shape was little more than a mangled loop. "This may be the only thing that's keeping us alive. If there really is something in the material that they want, it's probably in here. If things go really wrong, maybe we can bargain with it."

He grabbed her wrist as she dropped the cork onto the Tootsie Pop wrapper. "What if it has nothing to do with the pouch? What if they're just erasing anyone and everyone who was exposed to the information? What if there isn't a single thing in that bag that's worth them not pulling the trigger?"

She pulled her wrist free of his grip. "You were the one that said they're trying to draw me out because of what I've got. Tom says they want something that I've got. The only thing I've got is this pouch. If it doesn't have what they want, then we'll make them think it does."

X X X

Booker dialed the emergency number. He didn't care that it was nearly midnight. He didn't care that it was freezing outside. The client answered on the second ring. Booker didn't let him finish his hello.

"What the hell is going on here? What was that place?"

The client sputtered, mumbling something about the time, but Booker cut him off.

"Who's covering this up? Are you playing me? Stop talking and let me make two things abundantly clear to you. One, the money is nonrefundable and already out of the country and is nowhere near enough to make me take the fall for you. And two, if I even think you are setting me up, there is no place on this planet I can't reach you. It may take a day, it may take a year, but know like you've never known anything in your entire miserable life, that when you die, it will be at my hand. Are you getting this?"

"Would you stop?" The client's voice sounded gravelly and tired. "Nobody is setting anybody up. I have assurances from people in a position to know. Nobody is setting anybody up. We're looking into the matter right now." Another voice spoke in the background and the client answered in muffled tones before coming back on the line. "We need time."

"You don't have time," Booker said. "Someone tampered with the site, someone with the authority to put a gag order on the scene. Why would someone do that? Why is Rasmund so important that the law is going to protect that scene?"

"No names!"

Booker rolled his eyes, stepping into an alley to pace. "You're kidding me, right? You're worried about your phones being tapped? Now? We just orchestrated a hit that left behind two dozen corpses. There should be outrage and bedlam, demands for justice."

"We're trying to orchestrate an alternative plan right now. We're powwowing."

"Powwowing, Jesus Christ, would you listen to yourself? Would you get your head out of your own corporate ass and look at this situation? What is Rasmund? All my research showed it to be an elite investigation firm. You hired them. Do you know something different? If you do and you didn't tell me, I swear to God I'll start by cutting out your granddaughter's eyes."

"I don't know any more than I told you. I swear."

Booker pressed his forehead to the filthy brick wall. He closed his eyes, wrestling his frustration under control. "All right, let's assume this is a complete surprise to you too."

"It is. I swear."

"Could they have connections high up in the government, maybe the FBI or Homeland Security, someone who could clamp down on a crime scene like this? Someone who could, I don't know, convince the rescue workers to keep the facts of the scene under wraps for national security reasons?"

The client breathed hard. "That could be a possibility. I'll have my team look into it."

Booker dropped his head backward, looking up to the sky in disbelief. "You didn't think to maybe look into that before you started this job?"

"You listen to me, you condescending son of a bitch. You are a very small part of this operation. You were hired to do a job. What you need to know is—"

"Shut up." Booker heard the man choke on his words, shocked at being spoken to like that. "Just shut your mouth and let me think. Where are you on finding out what leaked? Do you even have a clue what Dani is supposedly carrying? Does it even matter now? Don't answer that. Don't speak again. Here's what you're going to do. You're going to find out everything you can about Rasmund—who's hired them before this, what kind of connections they've got. And I mean find out real information. Don't go by their press release. You shake that tree until you get someone on the top who actually knows something. You've got the old woman. You wanted her alive, now use her. Put a gun in her mouth and don't take it out until she starts talking. Are you getting this?"

There was a long silence, then a sigh. "Yes. Yes, I can talk to her."

Booker shook his head at the evident relief in the man's tone. Once again he was having to hold a client's hand when everything fell apart, having to baby talk them through the mess they created by ordering the trigger pulled too soon. It happened so often Booker should charge extra for consultation fees. He really had to get out of this business. "While you're working on that, figure out exactly what is missing from Marcher's files and what you are going to do if it's not returned to you."

"It has to be returned."

"You're not in a position to insist on that. Do you understand me? If it turns out that you are linked to a terrorist attack on a government facility, whatever secret ingredient is missing from your little cake batter is going to pale in comparison to the hurricane of shit that will rain down on you. You. Not me. You."

The man growled through the phone. "Don't think for a second I can't or won't take you down with me. I know who you are and how to find you."

"Do you?" Booker lowered his voice. "Because it seems to me that you can't find your dick with both hands. Don't threaten me. I'm the only thing keeping your plan alive right now. You lose me—and you can lose me very easily—all it will take is one call to the NSA to have you dragged out in chains. Now shut your mouth and do what I tell you. Find out all you can."

"What about the girl?"

"Don't worry about the girl. I know where she is."

"Why don't you go get her?"

"Because I know where she is. What I don't know is who else might be looking for her. What I don't know is how far this shit pile you've blown up has spread." He shook his head, taking a deep breath. "Don't worry about why I'm doing what I'm doing. You do your part. I'll take care of my end. Understood?"

He hung up without waiting for an answer. Pressing his forehead once again into the brick, he puffed out white clouds of breath as he got his temper under control. It wasn't his problem. At the end of it all, whatever giant the client had poked wasn't his problem. Booker had spent a lifetime evading grabbier hands than this. To be sure, tangling with the United States government was not something he ever wanted to do, but Booker had plenty of escape plans to fall back on. He could go to ground indefinitely if necessary and he wouldn't think twice about burning the whole job down around his ears to do so. Fair was fair.

X X X

They argued about the best way to approach the station. The Dupont Circle Metro stop was accessed on either end by wide, steep escalators. Anyone coming down would be visible and exposed. Choo-Choo wanted Dani to stay up top until he had gotten to the platform and made contact. The thought of both of them being spotted on the long escalator ride unnerved him. Dani had another idea. She decided to board the train one stop earlier, the smaller-scaled Farragut North. She told him she would text him as her train from Farragut North pulled into the Dupont Circle platform. He would have time to make it down the escalators while she could hide among the crowds of weekend tourists and nighttime partiers.

Just like at the shopping center when he'd gone off to buy phones, Dani felt a smothery panic at watching Choo-Choo walk away. She could see him trying to keep her in his peripheral vision as he bent his head to light a cigarette and she headed into the Farragut North station. They didn't wave or in any way acknowledge each other. They hadn't even walked side-by-side a block or two after leaving the hotel. There was no way to know who was watching them or how much they knew. Dani was Choo-Choo's only ace against the Stringer; Choo-Choo was it for Dani against Tom. They were silent partners in the truest sense of the word.

She fished around in a zippered pocket of her purse for her Metro Pass. That was another argument she'd won, to carry the bags. She'd given in on leaving her nylon bag and clothes at the inn but wouldn't budge on carrying her purse and the Rasmund pouch. The purse she slung over her shoulder the way messenger bags were meant to be carried. The pouch she'd slipped on between many layers of clothes. She'd given Choo-Choo back his blue flannel and wore her heavy black outer shirt over the pouch. Choo-Choo had made a crack about the added girth but Dani found it hard to worry about her silhouette when there were people with guns looking for her. She'd have worn a barrel if she thought it would keep her safe.

Stepping into the shortest line through the turnstiles, Dani smoothed out a bent edge on the Metro Pass. She kept the card full, renewing it every month because public transportation made life within the Beltway much easier to handle. She knew she was insane for keeping her car; Ben teased her that she spent as much in parking tickets as she did on gas but Dani never could see her way to abandoning her vehicle. Five years she'd lived in the area but she'd never shaken that rural affection for an automobile. She paid her fines and parked on alternate sides of the street and knuckled through the knots of District traffic because she'd never shaken that internalized belief that wheels, like cash, meant freedom. The irony that she now relied on public transportation and an electronic fare card wasn't lost on her.

To be honest, the Metro had always made her nervous. The crowds could be intimidating, especially in the summer when packs of sweaty tourists strong-armed their way on and off the stops around the Mall and the Capitol. Being short on a subway had little to recommend it, especially in the sweltering D.C. summers. In that sense, the cold weather and heavy bundling made her ride easier, insulating her with personal space. What got to her, as it always did, was the futuristic feel of the subway. These weren't the grimy trains of Boston or New York. The D.C. Metro looked and sounded like something from a sci-fi movie. Soft chimes and whooshing carriage doors and the shadowy lighting put her in mind of some alternate universe or planned world that Dani couldn't help feeling she didn't know the rules to.

Now, with her previous world in shambles, the surreal ambience of the Metro seemed fitting. Hell, she wouldn't have been a bit surprised to find out Tom carried a ray gun or that the Stringers were cyborg assassins. It's not like the situation could become any more surreal. She texted Choo-Choo as the train hissed into the Farragut North station and she ducked amid a group of Japanese tourists clutching bags of souvenirs. They'd probably returned from a night tour of the monuments. They were so bundled up they looked like they were planning to sleep outside.

Two girls screamed and laughed at a gang of teenage boys dancing toward the far end of the car, shouting and showing off despite the glares from the other passengers. Dani scanned the faces she could see from her low vantage point. What would it take to stand out on the D.C. Metro? It wasn't like the hit man, whoever he was, would be slinging an AK-47 over his shoulder. And really, would that even stand out? Nearly midnight on Saturday night at Dupont Circle, just about anything was possible.

She stood close to the door, hoping to stake out a secure position to watch Choo-Choo's arrival but when the train stopped, she found herself caught up amid the woolen sleeves and puffy coats of the tourist group. There were more people in the group than she'd originally thought and Dani let herself be bumped and herded from the car across the platform to the lighted map where a petite woman in a red parka held a green and yellow striped umbrella far over her head. She spoke in a high tone that managed to ring out over the dings and dongs and whooshes of the train. The tourists huddled in close together, guidebooks held at the ready, listening to whatever the woman was telling them. As happens in cities accustomed to tour groups, the traffic from the train split around them, letting them create an oasis of stillness amid the bedlam of the Metro.

Dani stood shoulder to shoulder with most of the women in the group. She didn't know how long they planned on standing here or what on earth could be so interesting about a subway stop but she was grateful for the moment of camouflage. She stayed near the rear of the group, nodding and smiling back at the confused look from the tour guide. A train pulled in across the platform, coming in from the other direction, and the noise in the cavernous room rose again. Dani tensed her shoulders against the pressure of the speakers and the lights and the sense of being buried in an enormous ceramic pipe miles below ground. She hated the Metro.

Choo-Choo. There he was. She could see his white-blond hair shining under the artificial light. Even amid the stylish urban fashions preening and posing on display, Choo-Choo stood out. His longish hair, sharp cheekbones, and ridiculously perfect nose couldn't be dimmed by the loose blue flannel shirt. Dani's black knit scarf that he had refused to return to her looked artful. Dani used to wonder how long it took Choo-Choo to achieve that casual look of elegant perfection. Now she knew what she had long suspected—you had to be born with it.

She watched him scan the crowd. He didn't know where she was and the plan was to keep it that way as long as possible. When the Stringer approached him, he wouldn't be able to give her location away with a gesture, however unconscious it might be. Dani urged him to hurry, urged the mysterious stranger to make his move. The tourists were making moves to continue their trek out of the station and Dani let herself be bumped along toward the back of the herd. If the tourists moved too far, too fast, Dani would find herself exposed.

Choo-Choo headed toward his right, toward the platform where Dani stood. He kept his face neutral, just another bored transit patron, but she could see his eyes moving over the crowd. Choo-Choo, she decided, had a spectacular poker face. Until he didn't. It only took a second but his eyes widened, his mouth popping open in surprise. She thought he had seen her and worried he would give her presence away. The tourists surged forward and Dani had no choice but to follow behind them. Choo-Choo stared past her, his face still wide open in surprise. Whatever he was staring at was coming closer to her and for half a second she debated turning around to look.

She didn't need to. A strong hand gripped her elbow, lifting her up onto the balls of her feet. Her breath froze in her throat and all she could do was stare wide-eyed at Choo-Choo, who still moved her way. A breath blew warm across her ear and the hand holding her tightened its grip to the point of pain.

"Well aren't you two a cute couple? I wouldn't have thought you were his type."

At the very feminine pitch of the voice, Dani finally found the nerve to twist her head around to see her captor. She couldn't reconcile the rough gray wool jacket and heavy boots with the glossy red hair pulled back in a ponytail and the faint traces of lipstick. Even the press of what could only be a gun against her ribs didn't shatter the veil of disbelief.

It was the cloud of Chanel No. 5 that gave her away.

Dani turned further, letting her arm hang in the woman's clutches. "Evelyn?"

CHAPTER ELEVEN

"Surprised?" The redhead jerked her closer as Choo-Choo approached. "I have to admit, I'm a little surprised myself. I knew you were in the wind. I kind of assumed you were dead." When Choo-Choo stood before her, his eyes wide and his mouth still hanging open, she pulled Dani to stand in front of her, using her to shield her gun from sight. "Let's all play nice now, understand?"

Dani watched Choo-Choo's mouth move, struggling to find words. "I . . . I don't . . . I don't understand anything apparently. Why are you pointing a gun at her? Why are you even here? How did you get out? You? The message?"

"Let's not do this here." She started to drag Dani, who came to her senses enough to resist. There wasn't any dirt to dig into so Dani did the next best thing: she bent her knees, nearly dropping into a full crouch. Evelyn stood six inches taller and short of actually jerking the shorter woman by the arm, couldn't get her to budge. "You're kidding, right? You know this is a gun I'm holding."

"Yeah, I know it." Dani wrested her arm free and moved to stand by the still-gawking Choo-Choo. "If you're going to shoot me, just shoot me already. Otherwise start talking."

Evelyn regarded Dani with a sharply arched brow. The look lost some of its imperiousness without the normal trappings of her Faces wardrobe. The rough clothes and bare face made her look tough, even dangerous, and Dani wondered if she hadn't pushed her luck. Choo-Choo offered no help at all, stuck gaping as he was. "We can't talk here."

"Well we're sure as hell not going into some dark alley with you. You texted Choo-Choo and said you needed to talk. So talk."

"Well aren't you a power bottom?" The gun she had hidden in the long cuff of her coat until now she slipped into her side pocket. "Judging from the reaction of our pretty boy here, I'm going to guess you're calling the shots."

"We're working together."

Dani pulled Choo-Choo back as a trio of laughing women hurried past them. "Kind of hard to talk here," Evelyn said again. "Plus I could use a drink. How about you?""

Choo-Choo recovered from his shock enough to link his arm in Dani's. "Drinking on the job, Ev?" He made his tone light but Dani could hear the tension. "Doesn't that impede your unique skill set? After all, Stringers are held to a rather high professional standard."

"Don't worry about me," Ev said, standing calmly as a drunken group of college students charged past them toward the escalators. She didn't raise her voice but Dani could hear her all too well. "I can kill you from here if necessary. Let's not make it necessary."

"Charming," Choo-Choo said and then looked at Dani. "It looks like Ev could use some style lessons from your boy."

"Hit men," Dani said with a snort. "Not all created equal."

"You two are really adorable." Ev stepped close enough to kiss Choo-Choo. "Here are your options. I kill you right now and wash my hands of this entire mess. I walk away and let the man looking for you find you—and he will find you. Or you come with me, tell me everything you know, and just maybe we all walk out of this alive. Five seconds. Your choice."

X X X

Booker checked his pockets for cash. He didn't want to take a cab tonight. The way this operation was disintegrating, the less of a trail he left the better. Cab drivers had an irritating habit of remembering their fares by sight and he didn't need his movements tracked any more than necessary. Besides he loved the Metro. He loved its cavernous feel, the bright echoing hallways so clean and wide. More than once he'd had to resist the urge to belt out a song as he descended the many magnificent escalators. The whole system was such a bizarre contrast to the low-slung, buttoned-down federalist architecture above ground. It felt like the designers had sat in front of one too many statues of men on horses and Ionic columns and that once they got belowground, they'd run amok.

He wanted to call Dani. He wanted to hear her voice, to hear in her words what she knew about this cover-up. She'd been so calm so far, so clever. Was that just her way or did she know that he'd just hit a hornet's nest? She had to know. She worked at Rasmund. Then why was she running? If Rasmund had the connections they seemed to have, why would she flee them the way she did? Why not call in to her superiors and have them protect her?

Booker studied the lighted Metro map, seeing the orange line he was looking for but not letting it register. Was she running? Or was she out there as bait? The unpleasant sensation of heat on his skin flushed over him. He was doubting himself. Booker never doubted himself. Doubts led to hesitations and hesitations made a person vulnerable. He reminded himself that he had gotten this far, had developed the reputation he had, by trusting his instincts and his instincts had told him that Dani was truly on the run. And if she was on the run, whatever power or influence Rasmund had, they couldn't reach her. Or maybe they didn't offer their unique brand of shelter to their grunts. The thought of some shadowy figure throwing Dani to the wolves like a bone irritated Booker. Yes, he'd been hired to kill her but he wasn't her employer. She didn't trust him. Maybe she didn't trust them either.

Booker wanted to hear it for himself. From Dani.

XXX

Ev led them into a little Ethiopian restaurant Dani knew by smell more than by name. She knew they served killer *doro wat* but it looked like the business of the night was drinking. As one of the few restaurants on the block open at this hour, business was good. Around the low woven tables, older men huddled together over glasses of sweet wine and tea while college students and young professionals toasted each other with bottles of Coke or beer.

"I like this place," Dani said, nodding to the old woman perched behind the cash register. "Their *berbere* sauce can make your eyes water."

"I know," Ev said, settling onto a low-slung chair. "I mean I know you like it. I have no idea what kind of sauce you're talking about. It smells heinous in here."

"Are you kidding?" Dani eyed a nearly empty platter at the table beside them. "This food is delicious. As a matter of fact, we should each order a meal. Do you know how it works here?"

Ev watched Choo-Choo consider the low armless seat before sliding down into a graceful recline. She scowled at his artfulness. "Dinner? Let me guess. They bring us food. We eat it and the last one to die of food poisoning wins?"

Choo-Choo snorted. "I bet you're fun at Christmas."

"Maybe with you, Ev, the chance of dying is high," Dani said, "but in Ethiopia the custom is that everyone eats off of the same plate. All the meals are served on one huge platter. The idea is that if you eat off the same plate with someone, you'll never betray each other."

"A little late for that, isn't it? Maybe we should have had them cater a luncheon for us."

Choo-Choo leaned in. "You think we betrayed you? How the hell do you figure that?"

"Well someone betrayed me." Ev settled her elbows on top of her knees and let her head sink down.

"And you think Choo-Choo and I did this? Orchestrated this?"

She shook her head, her red ponytail slipping over her shoulder and curling under her chin. "I don't. But I need to blame someone and you're the closest two." When she looked back up, her eyes shone with held-back tears.

"You look tired."

"Fuck you, Dani. You look like you always do—like a hobbit." She sighed and dropped her head back down. "Don't pay any attention to me."

"That's kind of hard under the circumstances."

Choo-Choo pulled his very crumpled box of cigarettes from his shirt pocket and dropped it on the table with a sigh. "And just when you think it can't get any worse, I'm out of cigarettes. Since this night shows no sign of ever ending, I'm going to buy another pack from the machine out there. Assuming it works." He rose and stretched his back. "And if it does, I'm going out to smoke. Don't talk about anything interesting while I'm gone and don't kill each other."

Ev smirked at him. "What if the machine doesn't work?"

"I'll kill all of you and then myself. It seems only right."

Ev leaned back to let his long legs step over the seat she crouched on and she watched him glide through the low tables. When he moved to the register to get change, she shook her head and turned back to Dani. "Unbelievable. Of all the people to make it out of Rasmund, it's you two. Snow White and Dumpy, the eighth dwarf."

Dani took off her purse and lay back against the cushions. Unlike her two long-legged companions, she found the low chairs and tables of the Ethiopian joint to be perfectly comfortable. She considered pulling out the Rasmund pouch from under her heavy shirts but decided she couldn't bear to go through all that disrobing. "Is this what we're going to do all night, Ev? Listen to you talk tough to us? Because I have a few other more pressing issues at hand."

"How much do you know?"

Dani laughed an unamused laugh. "Between me and Choo-Choo? We barely know our own names. I know that I underestimated you."

"Likewise."

"Hey, all we did was get away. You got away with a gun and a Stringer code." Dani saw the guarded expression on Ev's face. "First things first. Which are you? A Stringer or a Face?"

"I don't like to limit myself."

"Cute, but which is it? And what about Hickman? Was he like you?"

"You mean glamorous and deadly?" Ev didn't quite manage to pull off the quip and Dani's humorless reception didn't help. She sighed. "No, Hickman was straight Face. Literally. He was the faciest Face I ever knew. The man was born to it. He could talk the underpants off a nun and have her thanking him for the opportunity."

"I never got the impression that you two were close," Dani said.

"We weren't. Who is at Rasmund? Don't tell me you and the Slavic Stud are in love?"

It took the rest of Dani's tattered and overworked control to keep from kicking the table into the redhead. "Why don't you cut the shit with the cute names, okay Twyla? What? Shocked by that? Didn't think we all knew your real name, Twyla Dawn Cruickshank?"

A mottled flush rose up from the collar of Ev's jacket, leaving a blotchy path along her neck and cheeks. Maybe Ev was dangerous, Dani thought, but if she thought Dani and Choo-Choo were just going to whimper and grovel, she had an unpleasant surprise coming. Before Ev could spit out whatever it was she had planned, Choo-Choo glided in among them on a cloud of night air and cigarette smoke.

"Swapping secrets, girls?" He crossed his legs at the knee. "What next? Braiding hair?"

"What's next," Dani said, "is that we're going to order some drinks so we don't draw any more attention to ourselves and then we're going to settle back and let Ev regale us with what she knows. How about it, Ev?"

Once again Ev got cut off, this time by the arrival of the waiter. Ev and Dani ordered beer, Choo-Choo asked for house honeyed wine.

"You like *tej*?" Dani asked.

"I loathe it." He waved to the dark room around them. "But I'm a slave to conformity."

Dani started to laugh then caught Ev's glare. "Don't let us keep you, Ev. You were just getting ready to tell us everything you know."

"If you're waiting for some big exposition and reveal, you're going to be disappointed. I don't know much more than you, I'd guess. Someone sold us out. Someone got inside and hit us. They took Maureen and they're not going to stop until—"

"Maureen?" Dani and Choo-Choo spoke as one and Ev's blush deepened.

"Mrs. O'Donnell. They got Mrs. O'Donnell and they're holding her. They called me and let me talk to her, so I know she's alive."

"She called you?" Dani didn't think it was possible to be surprised after all that had happened but that did it. "Wait, how did you get out? Why weren't you inside?"

This time Ev looked relieved when the appearance of the waiter interrupted her. She ignored the offered glass and drank right from the bottle. Dani did likewise, trying not to get distracted by Choo-Choo's dainty sips of the pale wine. "Maureen was afraid something was up. She knew the Swan job was screwy. She's been real irritated the past few weeks, real snappy. I knew something was on her mind."

Choo-Choo shot Dani an expressive side-eye and Dani phrased her question carefully. "Did you and . . . Maureen . . . work together a lot? Outside of the usual job?"

When Ev nodded, Choo-Choo snorted a soft laugh. "I've had jobs like that before."

"It wasn't like that, you fucking man-whore." Ev looked like she might smash her bottle against his skull and Dani leaned in.

"Relax, Ev. Take it down a notch, okay? We don't need any more attention."

Ev huffed back in her chair, wiping her nose with the back of the hand that held the beer. Some splashed from the bottle onto her sleeve and she ignored it. She sniffled, her lips set in a stubborn pout. Dani risked a glance at Choo-Choo and saw the same confusion on his face that she felt. It was difficult to reconcile the surly, almost adolescent-acting woman before them with the cold, polished Face they had known before. Or thought they'd known.

"I started out as a Stringer." Ev's voice was soft, with nasal traces of an accent that suggested an upbringing in Southern mountains. "Nah, I started as a mess, a runaway with a record and a habit. I got picked up once for B&E and next thing I know I've got U.S. Marshals asking about me, wanting to put me in witness protection if I'd testify about what I'd seen at this house. Well, I hadn't seen anything and I kept telling them that and then they started getting pissed, like I was playing them. Hell, I would've told them anything if I'd only known what they wanted. They started threatening me with jail time—like that was something I was afraid of, you know?—but they were serious. They wanted something bad and they wanted me to give it to them and when they thought I wouldn't, I seriously thought they were going to make me disappear.

"Then Maureen showed up." Ev took a deep breath, just uttering the name making her accent disappear, her usual throaty tone back in place. "She said she would give me a choice. Of course my track record to that point had proven that my choices always ended badly for me, but she told me to trust her. Funny, because that usually ended badly for me, too, but there was just something about her, something so strong and calm. She told me she worked for a company who could put my skills to a more positive use. How did she put it?" Ev smiled at the memory, mimicking Mrs. O'Donnell's low tone to perfection. "'I work for people who will appreciate your lack of squeamishness.' That's what she told me and that's how I came to work for Rasmund."

Dani found it hard to swallow her beer. "As a hit man? Hit woman?"

Ev shot her a dark look over her beer. "That's the smallest part of what I do. Don't get so hung up on titles, Dani. I could get into places others couldn't. Especially back then. Nobody looked twice at a kid like me. It was Maureen who taught me to appreciate style, to lift myself up from the dirt I'd been wallowing in. She cared about me. We care about each other."

"Well that's good. That's really good." Dani shut down Choo-Choo's questioning look with a small flick of her fingers. She watched Ev pick at the label on her bottle, saw the jagged nails and dirt underneath them. The flush on her cheeks had broken down into hot little islands of burn and her eyes were redder than Dani remembered them being before. Stress. Ev was showing signs of cracking under the pressure of missing Mrs. O'Donnell. Since childhood, Dani had had her share of experience talking to women who were cracking. While she had no doubt the woman was plenty dangerous when angry, Dani could only imagine how volatile she could be when panicked. Dani kept her voice warm and soothing.

"It's really good that Mrs. O'Donnell—Maureen—knows you're out here looking for her. That's going to go a long way toward keeping her courage up. Did she give you any indication what might be behind all of this? Who hit us or why? Or what they want?"

"She always said that Rasmund had a lot of enemies, that a lot of people wanted to keep us from doing the work we do." Ev seemed pacified by Dani's encouragement. "She said that we had important work to do, work that other people wouldn't do, and that real heroes never worked for the glory, they worked for the just cause."

Choo-Choo made a *hmm* sound, nodding as he shifted in his chair. When he'd turned enough that Ev couldn't see his face, his eyes flew wide open in a look that Dani understood perfectly. What the hell was Ev talking about?

"Wow, yeah, that's powerful stuff, Ev."

"Yeah it is. Maureen really knows how to put things. She's really got her head on straight." She rolled her beer bottle between her palms. "It's like I finally have a direction, you know? Like, a mentor I can really trust and, like, what I do matters, you know? I've never had that before."

"Yeah, that's really important, isn't it?" Dani made a point of mirroring her, a trick she'd learned from her father, watching him defuse bar fights and card games gone wrong. She'd watched her father talk jacked-up truckers and freaked-out hitchers into putting down guns and knives and tire irons. He'd talked her mother down from hurting herself. Dani didn't have a tenth of her father's natural charm but she didn't have the luxury of worrying about it. When Ev leaned forward on her elbows, Dani shifted subtly until she too sat that way. Beer bottles hung from their fingertips and Dani meted out the eye contact carefully as she'd seen her father do. Too much meant aggression; too little seemed shifty. Dani had to convince Ev they were in agreement.

"You know, I'm not a Face or a Stringer. I'm just a Paint. I never really could get the hang of what you all do. I don't think I could ever pull off the polish you all do." When Ev didn't come back with a biting remark about her miserable fashion choices, Dani felt she might be getting somewhere. "I never got the chance to work as closely with Mrs. O'Donnell as you did."

"Well, you needed to have clearance."

"I did, well, I mean, I could have had it." Dani readjusted her strategy. "The truth is I always doubted myself. Maureen," she made a point of using the first name, "used to invite me to other jobs, used to encourage me to try new things, but I guess I just chickened out."

"That's too bad," Ev said with what sounded like real sympathy. "The work has been good, really challenging. And I mean, look at what happened. You don't provoke an attack like this from an enemy unless you're really doing good work."

Dani heard Choo-Choo's teeth clink against his glass as he drank. She struggled to find the proper words. "That's so true, isn't it? So it looks like you're the lead on this, Ev. Maureen is obviously counting on you to come across, to keep her team intact." The muscles in Ev's jaw clenched and her eyes got wet once again. Dani risked leaning forward and touching her knee. "You're not in this alone, Ev. We're a team, remember? We're Maureen's team. Damn it, we're Rasmund and nobody pushes us around. We have to work together to make this right. We can't let them get away with this."

"No we can't."

"So did Maureen ever tell you what this might be about? What the enemy wants?"

Ev looked offended. "Of course she did. What are you—stupid? What else could it be about?" Dani was about to kick herself for pressing too hard, that she'd made Ev go back on the defensive, but then the redhead leaned in closer, whispering in a voice for just the three of them. "It's the tunnel at Rasmund. It's the transport of the prisoners. They want to shut that down."

X X X

Booker's phone rang before he could dial Dani. The client was speaking before he got the phone to his ear.

". . . a file. We're assuming it's a digital file but it's possible it's microfiche or a photo. There isn't any way to know for sure but we do know it is a file."

"Hang on." Booker helped an elderly woman lug a loaded wire cart onto the train, slipping his phone into his pocket until he'd gotten her settled on the Metro seat. Once she patted his arm in thanks, he fished the phone out once more. "I'm assuming you've learned something?"

"Yes, goddamn it, aren't you listening to me? You don't put me on hold!" The client sounded as if he'd been screaming for hours. "You threaten my family and now you want to put me on hold? You told me to get you the information. Do you want it or not?"

"Of course I want it. If it's useful, that is. What did you learn?"

The sigh that came through the line told Booker more about the client's anxiety than any words ever could. "The situation is changing. I've learned some information that may call for an adjustment of our game plan."

"Our game plan." Booker knew from experience that when clients like this started talking about changing the game plan, that usually meant they were being pressured by someone higher up, someone with the authority to pull the job, someone who usually suggested tying up the affair by trying to either stiff Booker or kill him. In the fifteen years he'd been doing this job, many had tried to do both and none had succeeded. More than one client had died trying.

"First things first," the client said, clearing his throat and trying to sound calm. "We believe we know what the girl is carrying. Marcher copied a file, an extremely important file that is most likely digital. Of course we can't rule out a photographic record or an alternative information storage system, but all signs indicate digital."

"An important file," Booker said. "So important that you're just now learning of its existence? Or is this related to that widow you had me looking for? A widow file?"

"That is irrelevant to the job at hand."

"Ah, I see." He did see. This file Dani supposedly carried was not what the client had originally believed it to be. The client's superior, whoever was really pulling the strings of this operation, probably sensed the mission was falling apart, and was shedding some light on the true purpose of the job. And judging from the badly controlled tension and anger in the client's voice, the news didn't look good for the client. Booker resisted the urge to laugh. Welcome to the food chain, he thought.

The client continued. "We have reason to believe we will ascertain the target's location shortly, if not completely secure her presence."

"Uh-huh, the target? You mean the girl. Taking care of her is still my job."

"Of course. Of course." He hurried to reassure Booker. "As a matter of fact, we are making arrangements at this time that should facilitate your task. If we can secure the girl, that should expedite your duties. I should have an answer for you shortly."

"Thanks for the update and the opportunity. I'll be expecting your call." Booker ended the call. Now he knew. They were planning to kill him.

X X X

"When you say prisoners in the Rasmund tunnel," Dani kept her tone casually curious despite the chalky taste of panic she kept swallowing down, "what prisoners exactly? I mean, specifically."

"What do you mean?" Ev sounded genuinely confused by the question. Fortunately Choo-Choo recovered his wits and picked up the thread as if they were discussing yachting or an especially engaging polo match.

"Well of course the tunnel is a target. Why else blow the building?" He patted Dani's knee and winked at Ev. "You have to excuse our girl here. She spends all her time in her beanbag chair up in her Paint room. I bet she's never even seen the tunnel, just does the paperwork for it. I think what she's getting at is who would want to target it? Do we know if this was targeted for one prisoner in particular?"

Ev banged her beer bottle against her leg, lost in thought, then said, "I've been trying to figure out the same thing. It's not like we're advertising our services, you know? By the time they get to Rasmund, these prisoners are pretty much off the map. Of course, guys like these live under the map, don't they? They've got their own resources and information networks even we haven't dreamed of. That's why we interrogate them. But I still can't see how anyone could have tracked them. Even the Brits don't know where we operate and we've got some of their cargo too. It's part of that, what do you call it, receptacle . . . receivable . . ."

"Reciprocal?" Dani offered and Ev nodded.

"Of course," Choo-Choo said with a wave of his hand, "the reciprocal prisoner interrogation arrangement that we have with the

Brits. And that we perform at Rasmund. Where we work." He tilted his head toward Dani. "While prisoners are interrogated."

Ev snorted. "I was a little leery of working with the Brits, but they're a lot tougher than you think when you get to know them. They're not afraid to do what needs to be done. Speaking of things needing to be done, I've got to take a piss. Get me another beer?"

"Sure thing," Dani said, unable to take her eyes off of Ev as if she might suddenly sprout another set of arms.

"Yeah," Choo-Choo said as he flagged down the waiter. "I think I'll switch to beer too. We might as well all be on the same page, right?"

Ev slapped him on the back. "You mean we might as well all be pissing like racehorses, right?" Choo-Choo laughed along with her as she stepped away from the table. He kept laughing and kept his eye on her until she disappeared down the hallway toward the restrooms. Then he crowded close to Dani, his voice a low hiss.

"What the hell is she talking about?"

Dani shook her head, her eyes as wide as his. "I have no idea. Do you think she really knows what's going on? Do you think she really knows anything?"

Choo-Choo leaned on his elbows. "I don't know. At first when she started talking about her relationship with Mrs. O'Donnell, excuse me, Maureen—nothing weird about that—I thought she was just being Kooky Cathy McCutsHerself. But the more she talked, the more I think she really does know something. Or she thinks she does."

"But prisoners? Prisoners interrogated at Rasmund?" Dani fought the urge to scream. "In the tunnels? What kind of prisoners does a private investigation firm move through an underground tunnel?"

"A mighty full-service one, I'd wager. With quite an international scope."

"Oh my God, Choo-Choo, what is happening here? Are we being targeted by some kind of terrorist organization? Or are we part of one?"

He held up his hand to stop her. "Here she comes. Let's just play this by ear. Keep her talking, find out what she knows. If she's really in contact with the people who took Mrs. O'Donnell, maybe we can find a way to end this, strike some kind of bargain. If nothing else, maybe we can at least get enough information to go to the police with."

"It sounds like we should be going to the Feds. It's pretty freaking clear that we are grossly underinformed about the situation." She smiled as Ev returned. "So, any brainstorms?"

"Not a thing. Where's the beer?"

"Coming," Choo-Choo said, sounding remarkably relaxed. "So we were throwing around some ideas while you gone. The international flavor of the situation lengthens the list of possible suspects, doesn't it?"

"Tell me about it." Ev sat back as the waiter arrived with three more bottles. She waited until he was out of earshot to speak again. "We've got the usual monitors in place for the big players, the usual thugs, but you know how it is. For every big baddie there are a hundred smaller wannabe copycats."

Dani struggled to match Ev's casual tone. "Sure, there's no end to it, is there? But is it possible that someone even bigger targeted us? I mean, this was a really clean hit."

"Not that clean. You two got away."

Choo-Choo tipped his bottle toward Ev. "Good point, but whoever it was had the clout to erase the evidence or at least keep it off the news. Is there a possibility the goal wasn't to get a prisoner out but to stop the interrogations altogether?"

"Who would want to do that?" Ev asked.

"Gosh, I don't know. Maybe the long arm of someone's law? Just spitballing here. Maybe Mossad? MI6? Hell, the CIA?"

Dani started to remind him that the CIA didn't operate domestically but Ev cut her off with a harsh laugh.

"Right, Choo-Choo. Like we're going to hit ourselves."

CHAPTER TWELVE

It took more than a minute for Dani to realize that ringing she heard wasn't just in her head. She checked her phone and gasped out a little laugh. "Oh look, it's Tom."

"Of course it is." Choo-Choo's eyes were wide and Dani knew he was as close to cracking as she was. "You should probably get that."

"Yeah, excuse me." She didn't know how her legs worked but she managed to get up from the table and head toward the door. She didn't know why she felt she had to take the call outside. She wasn't entirely sure how to even answer a call so she just let her mouth decide what it wanted to say.

"Santa? Is that you?"

"Dani?" Tom's laugh sounded warm. "You're having a long day, aren't you?"

"Yeah, I am and it just keeps getting weirder." She shook her head. "What can I do for you, Tom?"

"It's more what I can do for you." He waited through her semi-crazed giggle. "I'm serious. I know a little bit more about what the client is looking for."

"The client." Dani felt an expansiveness afflicting her thoughts, as if she had nothing but time and no desire for anything other than small talk with the man on the phone. She knew shock did that to people. By this point, Dani knew more about shock than she ever thought it possible to know. "Do you mind if I ask you a question, Tom? Will you tell me the truth?"

"Sure, if I can."

"Who do you work for?"

"Me?" He sounded like he was smiling. "I'm an independent contractor."

"Yeah, I get that. You know what I'm asking."

"I do," he said. "And you know I can't answer that. Professional ethics."

"Ethics." Dani tipped her head back and stared at the dark, heavy sky. A fine mist was starting to fall.

"Besides, don't you think I should be asking you that question?"

She straightened up. "What do you mean?" She hadn't even decided if she believed Ev's story. Did Tom know something she didn't? Besides, well, everything.

"I'm no expert, Dani, but I'd say that sounds like genuine surprise in your voice."

"Well this is certainly the day for surprises."

He said nothing for a moment and Dani felt a strange comfort in hearing him breathing. Chalk another one up for shock, she thought.

"I'm really sorry you're having such a bad day."

"I know what you can do to make it better."

"Oh, Dani." She heard the sounds of traffic behind him. At least he wasn't in her apartment. "This job is a mess. I should have walked away."

"I agree."

"No, I mean it."

"So do I."

His laugh was low and it sounded to Dani just like the kind of laugh a man made during pillow talk or phone sex. What felt even stranger to her was that the sound didn't seem out of place. "This is a weird city, don't you think?" he asked. "How do you like living here?"

Okay, she thought, chit-chat. "I don't think much about it, I guess. It's a place. I work here. It has its upsides and downsides."

"But you don't work here. You work in Virginia. You're probably one of the few people who work in the suburbs and commute into the city to go home. Why? You moved up here for the job, right? Why pay twice the rent for half the space and no parking?"

"National Geographic." She spoke before she thought, unable to filter herself. "When I first came up here I got lost driving around and I saw the National Geographic Center and I thought it was coolest thing I'd ever seen, that it was a real place, not just the magazine with the yellow border. I don't know why but I just thought it would be cool to live near the National Geographic Center. I guess that makes me a hick."

"Hardly."

Dani leaned against the brick front of the restaurant, bowing her head out of the mist. She didn't think it was possible to be this tired. Tom's voice felt warm in her ears. She couldn't say she wanted to keep talking to him, but she wanted it more than she wanted to go inside and face crazy Ev and her insane declarations. What she wanted was for this all to be a dream.

"Hey, do you need to watch the time?" He sounded genuinely concerned. "Are you going back to keeping these calls under ninety seconds?"

"Have you decided to start tracing my calls?"

"Nah," he said with a laugh. "I'm kind of a low-tech guy. So, uh, who's your favorite president?"

"What?" Dani squeezed her eyes shut, not wanting to dwell on what low-tech aspects Tom might be referring to. "I don't think I have a favorite president."

"You must. They're everywhere here in D.C." A horn honked over Tom's shouted threat to someone. "Sorry. Taxi. But the presidents, yeah, they're everywhere. But just the biggies, you know? Lincoln, Washington, Jefferson. You don't see anybody lining up to see a memorial to Taft, for example. And he brought the cherry trees to Washington."

"Well, actually his wife did. She was the one who originally supported the idea."

There was that laugh again. "Brainiac. God, I wish we'd had the chance to meet under different circumstances. I wish you were the client. How come my clients are never like you?"

"Because I don't pay to have people killed?"

"That's all I am to you?"

Dani sighed. "Give me a reason to think of you as something else."

"You're surrounded by killers, Dani. You're in Washington, D.C. Do you know how much work I get from this city?"

"You take the job. That makes you the killer."

"Hmm. Look at it this way, Dani. You can have a linen napkin and a steak knife or a pair of rubber boots and sledgehammer— really doesn't make much difference to the cow."

"Now I'm a cow? Gee Tom, you really know how to sweet-talk a girl."

"Come on, you know what I'm saying."

The horrible part was she did know. She understood his point and it made perfect sense. She also knew she had to be insane to be standing here in the middle of the night listening to semi-flirtatious small talk from the man who had been hired to kill her. Her other option was to go back into the restaurant and face the possibility that she had spent the last five years working for the Central Intelligence Agency.

"You said you have more information about what they think I have."

He sounded relieved. "They think you have a file. Maybe a computer file or photograph that has information they're looking for. It could be microfiche."

"Microfiche? Really? Do people still use that?"

"You'd be surprised where people hide things, Dani. It's got something to do with a widow. A widow file, something marked for widows."

Dani had gone over everything in that pouch. She couldn't think of anything that hinted at widows, but then she hadn't been looking for anything like that. "They don't even know what they're looking for? Or are they just not telling you?"

"Little bit of both, I think. From what I can gather, this guy stole some important information—maybe a formula, who knows? He was a scientist. The client mentioned looking for his widow when they targeted him but the guy was never married."

There was little street noise around her but Dani pressed her finger into her ear to hear him more clearly. "Are you talking about Dr. Marcher? You killed Dr. Marcher?"

He hesitated. "Yes. Did you know him?"

"Does it matter?"

"I guess not. It's the job, Dani. I tampered with his brakes."

She swayed through the rush of heat, struggling to keep her voice level. "That's how my dad died."

His silence stretched even longer. "I'm sorry, Dani." She heard him breathing and it sounded less comforting now. "Look, I'm sorry about a lot of things. I'm sorry I took this job. I'm sorry I ignored my instincts. But none of that matters right now. You have to save yourself. You know that, right? I can't save you. The police can't save you. You have to find the tools to save yourself."

"What do you suppose the odds of that are?"

"What are the odds if you curl up and hide? Come on, Dani, you know you're smarter than that. I know you're smarter than that."

She banged her head against the brick. "You already said you're going to kill me."

"Prove me wrong. Do it, Dani. Prove me wrong." He hissed the words. "And even if you can't, even if you can't get away, do what you can to bring down the bastards who killed you."

"That would be you, Tom."

"Steak knife or sledgehammer, Dani. How much a difference does it make to you at this moment? Whatever it is that you've got, you find it and you get it into the public eye. Take it to the *Washington Post*. Put it online. Whatever it is, they've killed over a dozen people to keep it under control. You may die but that doesn't mean you can't do some killing yourself."

"Why are you telling me how to bring down the people who pay you?"

"Because I hate these bastards. I hate the way they do business. I'm sick of assholes like them pulling strings and making deals, thinking they can buy their way out of any problem with a few stacks of money they probably stole in the first place. I hate the position they've put me in and I hate that they have the audacity to think they can hit me."

"You? They're going to kill you too?"

His chuckle had none of the dirty allure of earlier. "They're going to try and they're going to fail. Bring them down, Dani. You're smart enough."

X X X

His phone beeped. "Hang on, Dani." He didn't recognize the local number. "Let me take this. Find what they're looking for. Will you do that?"

"Yeah, Tom. But hey, don't take it personally if my sledgehammer takes you out too."

He laughed and promised he wouldn't. He answered the incoming call still smiling.

"Listen to me very carefully. I only have a minute." The client whispered, his voice reedy and tremulous. "This is all going very wrong very fast and I need your help."

Booker rolled his eyes. So predictable. "I'm listening."

"These people, these people I'm working for, my God. I hired them and now I'm working for them." Booker couldn't tell if the client was panicked or drunk or both. "It's all been a setup. Every bit of it. Nobody was stealing tech from Swan, nobody was spying on us. The file they're looking for, it's one of theirs. It's a Rasmund file. Marcher wasn't stealing our tech; he was helping move information *out of* Rasmund."

"Calm down," Booker said, and he could hear the old man wheezing through the phone.

"They're going to kill me. They're not going to stop. They're going to kill me and you or send us to prison. Once they get that file—"

"What is the file?"

The client let out a wet cough. "I thought it was a design file. They told me it was the file of patents we're waiting to submit. It's not. It's not our file at all. They set me up to think Marcher was stealing designs but he was working with *their* man, a Rasmund employee, to steal *their* classified information. It's a list of names."

"Whose names?"

"I don't know. They don't talk around me now. They're running the show. I've had to pick up what I could."

Booker started walking nowhere in particular. He just needed to move. "Why did Marcher have this file? What did it have to do with Marcher? Anything?"

"Yes, Marcher. He was the key, what tipped them off. His brother was on the list."

"What is the list?"

"They're calling it the Widow File. I think it's men who have disappeared. Who have been made to disappear. Permanently."

"How did Marcher get this file?"

"The man from Rasmund. Hickham or Hickman or something. He and Marcher knew each other before this job. They're saying that he used Marcher to smuggle the file out of Rasmund. Once they realized what he had taken, they needed to reach Marcher, to find out if he had moved the file or shown it to anyone. That's why they needed me to hire them, to get them access to Marcher. When they get that file, they're going to kill me."

Booker bit back a sound of disgust. Wasn't that just typical? The client had been more than willing to take Marcher's life, had spent the money with no more anguish than he'd have felt tearing open an envelope. But the instant his own life was at risk? Suddenly the moral thunder of injustice pounded across the universe.

"Do you have any idea what the plan is?"

"I haven't heard much. They're getting very quiet around me. They're waiting for a signal from their agent that the girl has the file."

"She's not just going to turn it over to them."

"They have someone on the inside, someone she trusts. They know she's scared and alone. They keep saying her profile says she'll come to them."

X X X

When Dani walked back into the restaurant, she made a decision. If she survived this, she would never play poker with Choo-Choo. He sat with his long legs crossed, his blond hair catching the low light of the restaurant, laughing with ease at something Ev was telling him. Ev spoke with animation, her hands flying, her cheeks flushed, the words pouring from her. Dani almost hesitated to interrupt them until Choo-Choo looked up and his eyes widened just a fraction, just enough to send an unmistakable cry for help.

"How's Tom?"

"Busy," Dani said, settling back into her seat.

Ev laughed and Dani could see the redhead was getting drunk. The number of beer bottles on the table had doubled. "I never would have taken you for the slutty type, Dani. I thought you were serious with that guy Ben, but Choo-Choo's been telling me all about your hot new mystery man."

Dani glanced at Choo-Choo, who gave an innocent shrug. He hadn't told Ev about Tom. "I like to keep my private life private."

"No such thing," Ev said. "Privacy, there ain't no such creature. I got to pee. Again. Never should have broken the seal, eh Choo-Choo?"

He laughed with her, his smile dropping the instant she turned her back. "Okay, two things. One, Ev is a bad drunk and a lightweight. Two, she is bat-shit crazy. The only good part about having her with us is that if someone starts shooting, we can use her as a human shield. Tell me you had a better time with Tom than I had going down that rabbit hole."

Dani almost admitted she'd had a nice talk with Tom but realized how strange that would sound. "He says I've got a file, a widow file is what he called it. He doesn't know what it is or what it looks like but he says that I might be able to use it to stop whoever's behind this. He says it could be a picture, a microfiche—"

"Microfiche? Do people still use that?"

"Like I know?" Dani kept watching the hallway to be sure Ev wasn't returning. "Should we wait until she's gone to look for it?"

181

"Good luck with that. She's already promised me solemnly, and I do mean solemnly, that she is not going to leave our side until this job is done."

"Shit." Dani unbuttoned her outer shirt and dragged the pouch onto her lap. "Then let's just do this. Maybe she'll know what it is we're looking for. She worked with Hickman. Maybe he gave her some kind of clue."

"Let's not bring up Hickman, okay?" Choo-Choo shook his head. "If she didn't like him when she was sober, you should hear her with a few beers in her. She's called him everything but a pedophile. Says he's a coward and a traitor. Trust me, don't get her started."

"Thanks for the tip." For what felt like the hundredth time, Dani unpacked the materials, white pages first, then assorted objects. She held up the Tootsie Pop wrapper. "Would this hold a microfiche? How big is a microfiche?"

"Smaller than a regular fiche?" He took the wrapper from her and held it up to the light. "It could be teensy. Depending on who designed the tech, it could fit under your fingernail."

Dani held the Ho Ho wrapper up to the light as well, seeing nothing but printed letters through the shiny paper.

"You guys got the munchies or something?" Ev dropped down in her chair. "What's with the snacks?"

Choo-Choo nodded at Dani. They had no choice but to include Ev in their search. "We think the whole reason we're being chased is a file and that it's hidden somewhere in this stuff."

Ev squinted at Dani. "You think you've got the Widow File?"

"You know about that?"

"Of course I do. I work with Maureen, remember?" Her face flushed darker as she leaned in. "I'm the one they called, not you. I'm the one who needs to get that file back to them. Not you. That file is going to save Maureen's life and if you have it, you better believe it's mine." When Dani and Choo-Choo only stared open-mouthed at her rant, she dropped her head. "I'm sorry. It's just that I'm so worried about Maureen. I'm so worried this is all going to go wrong. I can't let her down. I can't. I owe her my whole life."

"Okay," Dani said softly, sliding over a stack of phone records. "You take these. Go through these lists and see if anything jumps out at you, any numbers you recognize, any dates or times that stand out to you."

"From Marcher's phone?" Ev's face regained its sour scowl. "What the hell am I going to learn from that?"

"You met Marcher, right? You've been to his lab. You've seen how he worked."

"Yeah, he was another freaking freeloader." Ev flipped through the pages without looking at them. "Came to this country from South America, like Mexico or someplace, probably illegal. He got a free ride to school and then spent the next ten years bashing the country that gave him everything."

Choo-Choo gave her a withering glance. "Was he from Argentina?"

"Yeah maybe. Argentina, Guatemala, something like that."

Dani pointed to the many receipts from the Argentinean steakhouse. "That might explain these. Maybe he was homesick?"

"Or maybe he was in collusion with some underground figures from Argentina. I don't think we're going to learn that from his dinner order. Let's try the photos."

Hickman had taken snapshots of the laboratory from several angles. Whole walls were covered in writing that only a scientist could decipher. "If that's the Widow File, we're going to need someone a lot smarter than me to read it," Dani said, thumbing through the photos. One picture showed a close-up of a worktable covered in party food. Little plates of nuts and what was probably fois gras on crackers and other party foods littered the surface. Around the edges, Dani could make out what looked like dollhouse furniture—tiny wire tables and chairs, as if a miniature café had been set up around the food.

"What was this party, Ev? And these decorations?"

Ev squinted at the picture and shrugged. "They were always celebrating something at Swan. Seemed like every time someone farted or didn't blow up the lab, out came the champagne and party food. Hickman loved it. His cover was an equipment salesman and he hung out in that lab a lot. I can't tell you how many times he reported in smashed after sitting around after hours with Marcher drinking champagne." She shook her head in disgust. "I can't stand the stuff. Tastes like perfume and feels like an ax in your head the next day."

"But what are these little chairs?"

Choo-Choo held the photo up for better light. "Oh, I had a girlfriend who used to do that."

Ev snorted. "You had a girlfriend? I thought you played for the other team."

He buried his previous look of disdain under a dry smile. "Teams shmeams. I never worried about what team I was on, Ev, as long as I got a chance at bat." He shifted in his seat, his body language cutting off the oblivious redhead. "She used to make whole little cafés out of the cork cages. Here," he reached for the caged cork on the table. "See these little wires? They're not all one piece. If you have the dexterity—to say nothing of the time and sobriety—you can unwrap those wires and make little sculptures. Obviously Marcher was so inclined."

He showed her the edges of the wire where the ends had been loosened and twisted into a heart on one side and an elaborate curlicue on the other. After being manhandled in the pouch for so long, however, the shapes had lost their precision and the wire cut into the base of the cork.

"Different champagnes have different kinds of wire," Choo-Choo explained. "Some are silver, some gold, some are even green. Simone used to make entire sets of chairs and tables and ottomans. She would insist we keep drinking until she had enough for a teeny tiny party."

Ev grunted. "This is fascinating. Really. What next? Barbie dolls?"

He ignored her. "And the little cork caps are unique to each brand as well. Simone liked White Star, so we had many nights of a full constellation. This cork," he looked at the small metal cap above the cork, "is Veuve Clicquot, a tasty little champagne. I always liked—"

"Did you say Veuve Clicquot?" Dani asked, leaning in.

"Yeah, probably just the yellow label, but still plenty drinkable. Why?"

Dani rubbed her hands over her face then reached for the cork, turning it to see the cork cap. "Veuve, that's French. For widow." She held up the cork to see the smiling face of a white-haired woman.

"Did you find it?" Ev lunged across the table but Dani whipped her arm back, the cork out of reach. "Give me that!"

"We don't even know what it is, Ev. This is a cork, not a nuclear warhead. We've got nothing to bargain with if we don't know exactly what we're dealing with." Ev lunged again and Choo-Choo caught her arm, twisting it behind her back at an ugly angle.

"Sit down, Evelyn." His voice was pure Choo-Choo, a sultry purr, but with an edge Dani had never heard before. "We are in this together. Stop being so grabby." He jerked her wrist harder until she sat back in her chair. "Are we going to play nice?"

"You do that again and I'll rip your head off."

He waved her off. "Save it for the finale."

Dani examined the cork. Champagne corks were bigger than regular wine corks but they were hardly spacious. She read the writing on the cork and checked the shaped wiring to see if she had missed anything in the scrollwork. "Nothing. I hope I'm not undoing some kind of high-tech monkey puzzle by unwrapping this, but here goes." She twisted the wire until the heart opened at the bottom, revealing gouges in the base of the cork. She worked carefully, loosening the wire around the base until the metal cork cap lifted slightly from the cork. Slipping the cage off, she set it on the table and used a fingernail to pry off the little metal cap. Underneath, cut into the surface of the cork, was a hole perfectly shaped to fit the tiny USB drive hidden there.

"I'll be damned," she said, picking the drive out of its bed. The hole had been cut with a precision she could appreciate, being familiar with jobs like this. "I didn't know they made drives this small. It's not much bigger than my thumbnail."

Choo-Choo held up his hand to prevent Ev from lunging once more. She made a sound that sounded an awful lot like a growl. "We've got it," she said. "Let's call them and make the exchange."

Dani tried to stay calm. "We still don't know what exactly we've got. This cork has gone through quite a bit today. We need to check to make sure the data on here is still intact. Or do you want to hand this over to the killers, have them find out it's empty, and watch them put a bullet between Maureen's eyes?"

"If you guys are stalling," Ev sounded much more sober than she had a second ago, "if you're trying to play an angle with me, you will die regretting it. Do I make myself clear?"

Choo-Choo jerked in his seat, as if he would grab her again, and Ev flinched. He smirked at her and turned back to Dani. "We need a computer. They have a computer." He nodded toward two couples huddled over a table in the corner arguing over something they had seen online. A laptop sat open and forgotten on the edge of the table. Ev saw it too. Before she could rise, Choo-Choo stopped her with a solid hand on her wrist. Dani wondered just how much that wristlock had hurt a moment ago, because Ev didn't seem to want to repeat it.

"I'll get it," Dani said. She made herself sound as mousy as possible to the drunk foursome, rambling out some story about needing to find out if her sister's flight was coming in and not having her phone number and other human communication shortcomings. The woman handed her the laptop after making her swear she wouldn't download or upload anything "risky." Dani almost laughed at that. "I promise," she said.

Back at the table, she plugged in the small drive. It held only one file but it was big. When she opened it, the computer stuttered under the command, finally bringing up a document over twenty-five pages long complete with photographs beside long columns of text. Dani found she couldn't focus on the faces or the text below them. Her eyes would not leave the silhouette of the bald eagle that sat between a badge and a banner that read CENTRAL INTELLIGENCE AGENCY. The only other word she saw was superimposed over every page: CLASSIFIED.

She heard a whistle of air leave Choo-Choo's slack mouth as the page populated itself with data. He read the names and he reached out to scroll down the page. "I know who that is. Him too. Him. He's dead." He muttered under his breath, speaking only to the computer. "Him, is that the guy who . . . ? Oh my God."

Ev tapped the side of the laptop. She'd moved in very close when they'd been distracted and now had the gun pointed at them. "Give that to me right now. This is what's going to keep Maureen alive. It's going to keep us all alive. Give it to me." Dani nodded and

Choo-Choo pulled the computer onto his lap. "What are you doing, Choo-Choo? Give it to me."

He huffed and gave her a long-suffering look. "Like this? If I give you this, we all die. This is a pigeon drive, Ev. Do you know what that is?" Ev shook her head, still scowling. "It's a relay drive. It's designed to automatically dump its data into whatever computer you plug it into. As of this moment, this drive is completely empty. Now unless you want to explain to those nice people that we're stealing their computer as a matter of national security, let me reload the drive." He started typing, not looking up as he spoke. "I'm assuming this classified notation means we don't want to share this with the entire world."

"Okay." Ev didn't sound wholly convinced. "But make sure you erase every trace of the drive. I'm calling this in. If you fuck this up, I swear I'll be the one who kills you."

He shooed her away with a flick of his long fingers and she stepped toward the door, pulling out her phone. Dani watched him type. "I've never heard of a pigeon drive before."

He still didn't look up. "That's because I just made it up. Ev is an idiot and this file is a nightmare. I recognize some of these names—these are political prisoners. Some were supposed to be at Guantánamo, some were supposed to be fugitives. I can't even imagine who some of these men are or what they're accused of."

"And so the CIA is looking for them?" she asked without hope.

"If anything Ev says is true and there are prisoners moving through Rasmund, I'm going to bet this is a list of those prisoners. And if it's called the Widow File, I'm guessing this isn't a rescue operation. The question is, are we working for the CIA or, equally terrifying, are we working for someone willing to steal from them?"

She could see Ev pacing on the sidewalk outside. "Whatever you're doing, you'd better hurry. She's not going to stay out there forever. What are you doing?"

"I don't suppose you have a thumb drive in any of your many bags of tricks? No? Next best thing. I'm hiding a copy of this in that woman's documents with our names and, hang on, what's your social?" Dani rattled off her social security number. "There's no way to include pictures of us but I'm telling her to take this to the police and media and anyone else."

"What makes you think she's going to do that?"

"Look at her, Dani. She's wearing brown socks with blue loafers. She's got a PBS tote bag and I'd bet anything she bought that hideous sweater in some fair-trade shop. Does anything about that say she's backing the Patriot Act?"

"Stereotypes! And she may never even find the file."

"I have a backup. I don't have a Facebook account, do you?"

"I know about eight people. No."

"Well then we'll do the next best thing. I've done screen shots, you know, taking pictures of what's on the screen, and loaded them as pictures on Twitter. I'm hash tagging every news source I can think of. I happen to have a large following on Twitter." When Dani said nothing, he nudged her shoulder. "Don't worry. I'll explain it later. Trust me when I say that it's going to be very, very difficult putting this genie back into the bottle. Let's just hope whoever gets this understands that you and I are the good guys. I really don't want to disappear."

He closed the program, removed the drive, and shut the laptop. Ev stood in the doorway, looking red and aggressive. She pointed to the door. Dani adjusted the repacked pouch underneath her heavy shirt and pulled on her purse. She felt as if she were girding for battle.

"Here we go."

CHAPTER THIRTEEN

Booker wandered southeast from Dupont Circle, not headed anywhere in particular. He didn't bother checking the time—judging by the emptiness of the streets he guessed it was somewhere after midnight. There was no point in going back to Dani's apartment. His skin prickled with anticipation—whatever was going to happen was going to happen soon. He might as well stay in motion. He wished he hadn't picked up his briefcase now, though. Whatever was going to happen would most likely require both hands. He needed to find somewhere to stash it.

He looked around to get his bearings and smiled. Directly across the street stood the National Geographic Society. Booker decided to take that as a positive sign. He jogged over to the wide shallow steps that rose toward the white square building, dark now except for the trim of lights around the exhibit windows. Low slabs of marble served as benches and Booker sat with his back to the street to open his case.

He took one gun, the SIG Sauer, the one with the most reliable action of all his guns. Something told him there would be plenty of guns in play tonight. There was no need to pack too many of his own. He could just help himself to those of anyone he killed. His knives, however, were another story. The one short blade with the finger hold sat warm and solid in a sheath at the small of his back.

He pulled another sheathed blade, long and serrated with a nasty hook at the end, and attached that to the waistband at the front of his pants. He liked his blades warm when he worked with them. A well-used piece of piano wire with caramel-colored oak handles he left coiled in the case along with the laptop containing the client's contact information. No trace of him would be found on the hard drives no matter how carefully someone searched them. He never used a laptop for more than one job. On the off chance that something went wrong tonight, whoever found the computer would have enough to ruin the client's life. Assuming the client was still alive. Considering the direction the plan was taking, that seemed unlikely.

He used a handkerchief to wipe off every surface inside and out. He was always careful to wear gloves but it never hurt to double check. Knives stowed on his person, Booker closed the case, locking in two guns, the laptop, and his garrote. The only thing he'd miss, he thought, was the wire weapon. It had been a part of some exciting jobs but this was no time for sentimentality. He had to travel light and be ready for anything. Stripping off his wool jacket, he draped it over the briefcase and shoved it under the bench. Since 9/11 D.C. was still jumpy about unattended baggage left in public places. If he didn't return to pick it up after tonight, he imagined the presence of the innocent-looking case would cause quite a stir in the morning. He thought Dani might like that the client's identity was unearthed here.

The earlier mist started to turn to something just shy of rain and Booker appreciated the fact that the chill didn't penetrate his skin. His early imbalance, his visceral reaction to stress, had faded. He felt like himself again, warm and light and free. When his phone buzzed in his pocket, he bit his lip in anticipation, not knowing what he wanted to hear more—sweet talk with Dani or word from the client that the plan was in motion.

He heard the latter. The client spoke in a wheezing whisper, rattling off his message quickly and hanging up before Booker could say a word: "They've got her. World War Two Memorial. Told me to stay at St. Regis. You've got to stop them."

Booker slid the phone back into his pocket and turned the corner onto Sixteenth Street. The St. Regis hotel was only a few blocks down the street and just past that was the White House, the Washington Monument, and the World War II Memorial. Without even knowing it, he had positioned himself perfectly to be part of the action. Another excellent sign.

The doorman at the St. Regis pulled the heavy brass door open for him with a flourish, his eyes momentarily raking over Booker's damp shirtsleeves. The doorman wore a long wool coat, a scarf, and a furry hat and he still looked cold. Booker smiled and stepped inside. The lights were low in the lobby, the chandeliers casting a glow over the wide marble floor. High-backed couches and low-slung armchairs clustered together in intimate groupings. Booker headed for the rear of the room. He knew the client. If he had been told to stay in the hotel, he would want to stay somewhere public.

It hadn't helped him though. Booker could tell before he even cleared the final sofa that the client was dead. Whoever had killed him had done a good job of covering it up. He looked like any old man dozing before a fireplace, the *Washington Times* open and draped across his chest. A glass of amber liquid with melting ice cubes left a wet ring on the end table. It looked perfectly serene but Booker knew a dead body when he saw one. Dead was dead. He didn't think anyone could ever mistake it for sleeping.

Without breaking stride, Booker continued down the lobby, veering to the right and making his way back out the door. Whoever had done this, whoever the client had inadvertently been working for, was now targeting Dani. Booker planned to put a stop to that.

X X X

"Give me the drive," Ev said as they headed down Massachusetts Avenue. Choo-Choo nodded and Dani handed over the tiny USB drive. "I can't believe this little thing brought on such a shit storm."

"Information is the ultimate weapon," Choo-Choo said, linking his arm in Dani's and pulling her close to his side. He kept himself bodily between her and Ev and Dani felt a wave of gratitude for her friend. She had seen more sides of Ev tonight than she had in the two years she'd worked with her; she'd seen more sides of the mercurial woman than she'd seen of almost everyone she'd worked with combined. Ev's behavior morphed from rage to apathy to depressed to sullen faster than she or Choo-Choo could keep track. Now, drive in hand and destination determined, she looked hard. She looked dangerous and Dani really hoped Ev was on their side.

"They let me talk to her," Ev said, her long legs covering ground quickly, forcing Dani to double-time alongside Choo-Choo. "She's not hurt, thank God, and she says they'll make the trade. She was glad we checked the drive. Good call on that. She said she was really proud of me, keeping both of you safe. She said I had surpassed her expectations." Choo-Choo squeezed Dani's arm against his side and Dani squeezed back. Ev was not getting any less frightening as she ranted.

"Where are we headed?" Dani asked, not that she had any choice but to follow.

"The Pacific side of the World War Two Memorial. It's a standard Stringer drop point. Kind of fitting tonight, don't you think?" Ev noticed their silence. "Heroes? People fighting for the American way?" Choo-Choo's eyes widened and Dani squeezed his arm. Ev dismissed them with a grunt. "We meet at the wall, under the American Samoa wreath. Maureen says we'll see them once we get there. I give her the drive, she passes it on, and we all walk away."

"You can't believe that, Ev." Dani couldn't hold her tongue. "They killed everyone we work with. They blew up our building. You think they're just going to let us walk away?"

Ev bared her teeth in an ugly grin. "No, I don't. That is, they won't until we don't give them a choice. Maureen gave me the code."

"The code?" Choo-Choo asked.

"Yep, the code we worked out in case something like this ever happened. She said in our line of work it was crucial to have a code in place in case a hostage situation occurred. It isn't unlikely, considering Maureen's position." Ev steered them through Scott Circle onto Sixteenth Street. Dani wished she'd worn fewer layers. This near-run had her sweating.

"She gave the signal that said she'll have people in place." Ev's breath showed no signs of struggling from their fast walk. "We're not alone out here. These sons of bitches are going to regret ever trying to fuck with us. Come on, let's pick up the pace."

By the time they made it to Lafayette Park, Dani's legs ached with fatigue and her eyes burned with the need to close them. The White House shimmered under the misted lights and from the corners of her eyes she saw flickers and flashes of light. Soft patches of fog lingered around bushes and trees and the rain made the black streets glossy when the occasional headlight shone on them. She clung to Choo-Choo, grateful for his solidity.

It took what felt like an hour to cross the pedestrian-only plaza, the Eisenhower Executive Office Building seeming to stretch on for miles. Turning the corner onto Seventeenth Street, she saw the Washington Monument glowing white and tall. It looked close but Dani knew it was an illusion. The *stomp-stomp-stomp* of their feet hypnotized her so that by the time they made it to the gentle sloping steps of the World War II Memorial, Dani had almost forgotten what they'd come for.

The memorial spread the length of a football field, and was ringed with tall columns etched with the names of states and U.S.

territories. Broad steps opened up in the center of the wall along which they walked and led down to a shallow fountain lit from below. Dani knew that if they went down the steps, they would be invisible from the street. She also knew that if they went down those steps, despite their easy shallow slope, she would never have the energy to walk back up. As it was, the soft gurgling of the fountain and the low, broad marble walls they stopped beside made her want to lie down, let the rain wash over her, and forget everything she had already pushed to the back of her mind.

"There's the van."

That snapped her out of it. Past the edge of the memorial, behind the column recognizing those veterans who had fought in the Pacific, a road snaked around a visitors' center and pulled to the curb sat a black, windowless van.

Choo-Choo whispered, "At least they're sticking to form."

Dani drew back. "I'm not getting into that van." Choo-Choo stood with her.

Ev marched several paces ahead before she caught what Dani had said and spun back. "What the hell do you mean you're not getting in? The hell you're not."

"The hell I am. You think I'm just going to climb into a black van with a CIA file? That's your plan, Ev? Don't you think you'd want to check and see if Mrs. O'Donnell is okay?"

"She told me to get us into the van."

"She told you?" Choo-Choo asked. "Or the people who took her told you?"

Ev scowled at him, whispering even though there was nobody in sight. "She told me. She told me the deal was made. Maureen told me to get into the van and she gave me the code that said the situation is being taken care of. She has a plan."

"You know what?" Dani pulled her arm free from Choo-Choo's and stomped to the corner where the marble walls of the memorial met in an L. She took a second to look over the wall, down at the long fountain, the lights playing off the bubbling water making her dizzy, and turned back to Ev. "I've spent the whole day running from other people's plans. I'm tired." She knew she sounded petulant and didn't care. Her legs and feet ached from exhaustion and the bags around her neck seemed to weigh a hundred pounds each. "I'm not taking another step until I see Mrs. O'Donnell and I get a guarantee that Choo-Choo and I walk away from this."

"You're in no position to demand anything!"

Dani hopped up onto the lower of the abutted walls and swung her feet. "Well, unless you're going to pull out your gun and shoot me right here, I'm not moving." At that moment, with the weight off her feet, Dani probably wouldn't have moved even if she had pulled out a gun. Choo-Choo smiled and strolled over to join her. The casualness of their refusal seemed to irritate Evelyn even more. She huffed and stomped her foot, then wheeled away on her own toward the van.

"If you two screw this up," she yelled back at them, "I swear I'll kill you. It must be nice to be so cavalry with someone else's life!"

Dani dropped her chin to her chest. "Cavalier." She heard Choo-Choo giggle. "The word you're looking for is 'cavalier.'"

Dani felt herself drawn into Choo-Choo's growing laughter. "Oh my God," he said softly, his hands over his face. "'Cavalry.' Oh my God. All this time I thought she was enigmatic. Turns out she was just stupid." They leaned against each other, shoulders shaking as nervous exhaustion turned into shuddering giggles for the second time that night. Dissociation, Dani thought, one of the long-term effects of stress. The laughter died out, bone weariness flooding back in, and the two leaned more heavily against each other.

Dani rubbed her eyes; even her knuckles ached in the cold. The rain and mist played tricks on her mind, shadows appearing to jump and dart while traces of white flickered on the edges of her vision.

She closed her eyes and leaned in to rest her head on Choo-Choo's shoulder—a mistake, she knew, because she could feel sleep rushing in. "What are we doing?"

"Fuck if I know," he answered. "Ev is insane but it doesn't mean she's wrong. I keep running it over and over in my head and I keep coming back to the same place. You got the job after applying to the Feds. Grandfather pulled strings with his government cronies to get me in. I think we work for the CIA. I think Rasmund is a front for the CIA."

"But that's illegal, isn't it?"

He patted her head where it rested against him. "Don't be as dumb as Ev. Most of what the CIA does is illegal. And maybe it's not even the CIA. Maybe it's the NSA or some other A that doesn't have letterhead or a tab in the Appropriations Committee binder. What difference does it make? Whoever it is, they've got the power to make people disappear." She knew that information should probably make her panic but Choo-Choo's shoulder was so warm and solid and it felt so good to close her eyes. "I bet Hickman found out what was going on downstairs. I bet he stole the file. He was a good man."

"You're a good man."

"So are you."

Dani giggled and dragged herself back up into sitting position. She ran her fingers through his rain-darkened hair, pushing it behind his ear. "You really are a good man. You could have left me a dozen times today. You didn't have to be involved. You could have run but you didn't. You stayed with me and you helped me."

"We helped each other. I guess that makes us real friends then, right?"

"I guess so."

He stared at her for a moment. "I hope this isn't the last day we get to enjoy it."

"We're about to find out." She nodded when she heard a car door slam. Ev headed back up the sidewalk toward them, Mrs. O'Donnell at her side. The older woman looked as regal and intimidating as ever, wrapped in a long black coat. Dani kept her voice low. "It looks like being kidnapped agrees with her." Choo-Choo made a noise of agreement and helped Dani jump down from the wall.

"I'm glad to see you two are okay," Mrs. O'Donnell said. "I should have known if anyone was going to make it out alive it would be you two. You're both very resourceful, aren't you?"

"Don't forget Ev," Dani said. "She made it out too. She's no slouch."

"Of course." Mrs. O'Donnell gave the redhead a tight smile and Ev smiled shyly, ducking her head. "Evelyn tells me you've seen the file. Did you make any copies?"

"No," they answered together.

"Evelyn also tells me you don't wish to get into the van. Is this true?"

"It is." Dani stood tall, though leaning against Choo-Choo to feel his support. "We'd like to leave. Just go away."

"It really isn't safe. The people who took me will look for you."

"We'll take our chances."

Mrs. O'Donnell nodded, her eyes toward the ground. When she looked up, she sighed. "Why does everything have to be so difficult? Evelyn, may I have your gun please?" Ev jumped at her name, hurrying to pull her weapon for the woman. Mrs. O'Donnell turned back to Dani and Choo-Choo. "I'm going to ask you again, did you copy the file?"

"I checked," Ev said. "There were no copies."

"You checked?" Mrs. O'Donnell rubbed her thumb over the younger woman's cheek. Ev tilted her head into the touch. "Sweet Evelyn, do you trust me?"

"Of course. With everything."

"I'm glad. Do you have a suppressor?" Ev shoved her hand into her pocket and pulled out a long, fat cylinder. Mrs. O'Donnell smiled at her and screwed the suppressor to the end of the gun. "Good girl. Now close your eyes."

Dani felt Choo-Choo lean forward as she did, not believing what they saw. Evelyn stood still, eyes closed, tilting toward the woman's touch, her face a picture of bliss. Mrs. O'Donnell's other black-gloved hand brought the pistol up under Ev's chin. Dani wanted to scream, to demand she stop, but couldn't make the words form. Even when the muzzle of the gun touched the soft skin under Ev's chin, the young woman didn't open her eyes. Dani closed her eyes at the spray of red that exploded from Ev's skull.

The body dropped backward, sprawled before Mrs. O'Donnell like a rug spreading itself on the pavement. Choo-Choo started to pull Dani to the side but Mrs. O'Donnell stopped them.

"Ah-ah-ah," she scolded, waving the gun in their direction. "None of that. I assure you, I am the least capable of the marksmen drawing down on you right now."

Dani stared at the horrible scene before her. "She loved you."

"I know. I loved her too. In my way. Evelyn was very loyal. That is a rare quality these days. Believe me, I appreciated it."

"So you shot her."

"I spared her."

"That was big of you," Choo-Choo said.

"Evelyn was many things," Mrs. O'Donnell continued, "but a genius wasn't one of them. She said she was certain you didn't copy the Widow File even though you saw it. I assume you understand what you saw?" When they said nothing, she nodded again. "Then I can also assume you did copy the file. I want that copy." She raised the gun toward them. "Where is it?"

Dani lifted her messenger bag from her shoulder, slipping the strap over her head and tossing the bag onto the ground. "Here."

Mrs. O'Donnell smiled. "Well now we know two things. One, you did copy the file, and two, we know one place it's not. Let's try this again."

"What are you going to do?" Choo-Choo asked. "You're going to kill us? Make us disappear? You really think you can make a dozen people who all work at the same place just disappear in one day and nobody is going to notice? I can see Ev—she made it pretty clear she doesn't have anyone—but I'm not some runaway junkie from nowhere." His voice grew stronger as he spoke and he stepped forward. "I am Sinclair Charbaneaux. My family doesn't slide under the radar, and they don't take payoffs. How are you going to make me disappear?"

Mrs. O'Donnell chuckled. "My, but you have a high opinion of yourself. What makes you think you haven't already disappeared? Have you seen your passport lately? Talked to anyone in your family? Hmm?" She watched him watch her. "Do you really think you got the job because you're a Charbaneaux? That got you the interview. You got the job because, like everyone you worked with, you are erasable.

"We took the liberty of intercepting communication with your family. You obviously didn't notice. Not quite the favorite son, eh? Even as we speak your family thinks you're in the Seychelles on a party yacht. You gave your notice weeks ago. Naturally, I phoned your grandfather myself to convey my concerns. It seems that since then you've sent quite a few disjointed e-mails and texts explaining your choices, your desires, and your complete unwillingness to follow in your family's footsteps."

Her smile was ugly. "Would you like to know what your father told me two days ago? It seems he's given up the search for you. He knows how elusive you can be when pursuing your pleasures. How did he put it? 'I don't want to find him with a needle in his arm and a dick up his ass.' That was the spirit of it at least."

Choo-Choo swayed where he stood. Dani could see the words hitting him like stones. "And you?" Mrs. O'Donnell smirked as Dani pulled Choo-Choo closer to her. "We had to search for someone to leave a trail with for you. Do you even have any family? All we had to do was break up with Ben by text, tell him you were leaving town and never wanted to hear from him again. He wanted to know if he could get his shirts back. You two really know how to knit a tight circle, don't you?"

"Why?" Dani asked. "Why are you doing this?"

"This?" Mrs. O'Donnell waved the gun. "This is the price of power, the price of justice. It's fitting that it happens here, at this memorial that honors those men and women who understood what it is to sacrifice, to make difficult moral choices for the higher good.

"The world is at war once again. The entire world, not just the United States." Mrs. O'Donnell's voice swelled with emotion. "There is no one front, no one enemy. We are facing men and women who are willing to strap bombs to their children and send them onto crowded buses and into busy cafés. And what are we told to do? We're told to fight with honor."

She jabbed the gun at them. "Let me tell you what honor gets you. Honor and justice get you smoldering embassies and planes shot out of the sky. Even as we speak there is an investigation into extraordinary rendition. They don't want us exporting our interrogations, yet God forbid we perform them domestically. People are horrified to find out that the civilized world still relies on torture to retrieve information to keep people safe. They seem to think the men we interrogate, men who were raised like animals in hovels, will respond to the threat of jail time. That we should give them backrubs and an education and a cup of warm cocoa and they'll roll over on their terrorist brothers and hand us the information we need to keep the world safe."

She drew herself up to her full, imposing height. "It doesn't work that way."

"Wow," Choo-Choo said, clapping slowly. "That's quite a speech. Been practicing?"

"You *would* sneer at it, you silly, useless boy. You're a parasite, a gluttonous eavesdropper who contributes nothing to the world. But I defend you anyway."

"By killing me?"

She closed her eyes as if overwhelmed by the enormity of his stupidity. "*I* am not killing you. You are being killed by Hickman and the Oversight Committee and the investigators and the weak-minded who insist we keep them safe but insist we hide the deeds. Your death comes at the hands of terrified children hiding under the covers and pretending there is no monster underneath the bed."

She looked toward the Washington Monument. "Do you think I want to do this? Do you think I relish having to erase a decade of my work? I've given my life to build Rasmund and now I have to oversee the eradication of every nut and bolt."

"And person," Dani said.

"Yes, and every person. All of it because Hickman stuck his nose in where it didn't belong and what he found scared him. He was a coward and now all my work is being erased."

Choo-Choo gave a derisive snort. "I notice you're not being erased."

"No, I'm not." Mrs. O'Donnell smiled. "And I'm not done fighting. They can force me to erase my work but they cannot erase my cause."

"You're the third person today," Dani said, stepping forward, "who has said they're going to kill me. The third today. That's got to be a record, right? Do you know what makes Evelyn better than any of you? Poor sad crazy Evelyn? At least when she said she was going to kill me, she took credit for it. She owned it. She didn't pass it off as some holy obligation coming from God himself. She was willing to pull the trigger and willing to own it. She didn't need all this moral rationalizing pseudo-patriotic bullshit. You are nothing but bullshit."

Mrs. O'Donnell put the gun in her pocket. "And you are nothing but fallout." She raised her hand, her finger pointed to the sky. With a flick of her wrist, she dropped her hand, her finger pointing at Dani and Choo-Choo. A second later, two shots rang out.

X X X

Booker watched the van arrive. Just once he wished people like this would show up in a lemon yellow convertible or a beaten-up Impala, but no, the black panel van seemed to be standard issue for villains. Nobody stepped from the vehicle so Booker made himself comfortable on the curb in the shadows around yet another statue. He peered up at the wet bronze face—John Paul Jones. Water gurgled from bizarre-looking sea creatures at the statue's feet. Funny, Booker thought, that they put in a water feature for a sea admiral when they could have just turned the statue around and given the man an eternal view of the Tidal Basin. Still it wasn't a shabby spot for a Scot to be memorialized. The Washington Monument shone white and huge a few hundred yards to his right; straight ahead and less than half that distance, the World War II Memorial glowed yellow and somber.

It was a nice spot for a clandestine meeting, a place he would have picked himself for a hit. The wide open spaces, the broad pass of Independence Avenue behind him leading away from the Mall gave the illusion of safety but the lights of the many memorials played strange tricks bouncing off the wet pavement. Low wisps of fog hung close to the trees and manicured shrubs. An unchecked imagination could make a person see figures darting through the night.

Booker's imagination stayed put. He kept his focus on the black van parked less than fifty feet from where he sat. The streetlights made the moisture sparkle on the glossy paint job. The shadows could swallow him before anyone could step foot from the vehicle.

He didn't know how much later he saw the trio arrive onto the broad walkway of the World War II Memorial. Interesting, he thought, watching the redhead charging ahead and Dani walking after her, arm in arm with the tall blond man. He had seen that man before. Booker rarely forgot a face. It didn't matter now. Now he just wondered which one, if either of them, Dani could or did trust.

They argued and Booker smiled at the stubborn stomp of Dani's little foot. She looked mighty out there holding her ground in the light of the memorial. The other two towered over her but Dani seemed to him the hardest force at play. He wanted to cheer for her. The redhead apparently lost the argument, because she walked off toward the van alone. The passenger window rolled down and she leaned in to talk with whomever sat inside. Booker watched Dani and the blond for a moment, swallowing down a flare of jealousy when he saw her rest her head on his shoulder. He indulged himself with one quick image of her head on his own shoulder, of Dani finding her comfort with him. Nothing to be done about it now.

The door to the van opened and Booker perked up. Maybe now he would finally get to see who was pulling the strings, who had the power to silence the news and silence the client. When the tall, black-clad figure stepped out, Booker let his head fall back.

"You have got to be shitting me," he whispered to the sky. Mrs. O'Donnell? That iron bitch was the principal? He'd seen her tied to the chair in the van, her imperious posture and snotty expression looking down on him. He'd wanted to slap her just because he could, but the client had held his hand. Now he knew why. The whole kidnapping bit had been for show to get her off-site and into the driver's seat. He'd been played. Unbelievable. He wished he'd slapped her when he had the chance.

He watched the two women walk into the pool of light and he knew what was going to go down. Four people stood together at the memorial, only one was going to walk away. What he didn't know was how many other figures were in play. Would Mrs. O'Donnell shoot them all herself? It didn't seem likely. Not that she didn't seem capable of murder. The woman looked like she'd bathe in the blood of kittens given the chance, but three people were difficult for one person to kill without some serious firepower. He'd bet she'd brought along a shooter.

He had to admire Mrs. O'Donnell's approach. She started by dropping the redhead to the ground in a cloud of blood. That certainly got their attention. He tried to imagine what Dani must be feeling, industrious, clever Dani who probably kept her head down and did her job and cashed her check and never worried about things like climbing the ladder and impressing her boss. Now that the boss turned out to be the boogeyman, would she panic? Or would she get pissed? He bet she'd say something funny either way.

Mrs. O'Donnell's voice echoed off the marble walls but Booker didn't bother listening to her ramble. Villains and their speeches. They always loved the sound of their own voices. Instead he kept an eye on the van. Sure enough, once Mrs. O'Donnell had really hit her stride, he saw a man, all in black, slip from the van and pad quickly across the street toward the statue where Booker sat hidden. If the man in black's attention hadn't been so focused on his boss, he might have seen the figure in the shadows as he passed. Booker was smiling at the close call when a sliver of light fell across the shooter's face, and then he groaned inwardly.

R. Mrs. O'Donnell's sniper was the client's obnoxious assistant, his "internal security consultant." Booker had never picked up a clue. At that moment he knew that as soon as he finished this job,

Booker was taking a vacation. His instincts clearly needed a break. This job had been a disaster since the get-go.

Booker rose from the curb, pulling the damp seat of his trousers away from his skin. He could see his breath in the mist but felt warm and comfortable. Staying in the shadows, he followed the sniper to his position on the Washington Memorial side of Seventeenth Street, directly across from Dani and company. Pretty nervy, he thought, striking a hit in such a public location.

R stood in a shooter's stance, his attention on the targets in his sight. Booker watched him for a moment, wishing he would have the chance to see R's face when he realized it was Booker who killed him. But Mrs. O'Donnell raised her hand and R tensed and Booker knew he had to strike. Sliding the serrated blade out of its sheath, he slipped up behind R, ready to move his hand between the shooter's left arm and his chin. With a simple flick, the blade would slice from jugular to jugular and blood would explode. But R was fast and got a shot off before the blade hit home, a second shot going wild as Booker leapt back from the blood spray.

Booker swore.

Dani had screamed.

CHAPTER FOURTEEN

The marble exploded behind Dani and half a second later her thigh erupted in pain. Before she could register the wound from the ricochet, another shot fired, this one hitting Choo-Choo square in the chest as he lunged to cover her. The force of the bullet threw him backward and for one horrible second he lay balanced over the low wall of the memorial, blood blossoming across the front of his shirt, his eyes wide with terror. Gravity and momentum won, throwing his body over the wall and down onto the level below. Dani screamed, jumping up to try to catch him or save him or touch him, but the wound in her leg screamed louder and she fell to one knee.

Mrs. O'Donnell screamed too, although hers was a scream of anger and impatience. "Shoot her! What are you waiting for? Finish the job!"

Dani crab-walked back against the wall, keeping her head beneath the ledge as if this would somehow make her invisible. Blood poured from the hole in her leg, making her slide as she scrambled to put distance between herself and her screaming former boss. When the yelling stopped, Dani listened for a sound from Choo-Choo but heard only the rush of the fountain and her own panicked breathing. Mrs. O'Donnell had turned from her, looking toward the lawn of the Washington Monument, and Dani stared, trying to see what she watched for.

It was Tom. Dani knew him from the set of his shoulders and the shape of his head. His white shirtsleeves had become transparent in the rain and his dark hair clung to his forehead but she knew him. He looked just as he had looked outside the hotel—warm and comfortable despite the icy air, despite the purpose he was bending himself to. Dani had to squint to be sure but from where she sat, it looked like he was smiling at her.

"Well, well, well," Mrs. O'Donnell said. "If it isn't the freelancer. Trying to score a little overtime pay, Mr. Booker? Because I must say that you—"

Booker fired without breaking stride, the bullet hitting her in the center of the forehead. "Shut up," he said as her body collapsed in a heap. "God almighty, does she ever shut up?" He stopped less than twenty feet from where Dani huddled. "How badly are you hurt?"

Dani blinked several times, her thoughts refusing to line up in any orderly fashion. She managed to get to her feet, pressing her fist into the wound. "I think I'm supposed to say it's just a flesh wound."

He laughed, his smile bright in darkness. "People say it's only a flesh wound when it's someone else's flesh that got wounded." He turned to stare at Mrs. O'Donnell's body. "So who are they? Or should I say, who are you? CIA? NSA? Homeland Security?"

"I don't know," Dani said truthfully, sliding herself sideways. "I haven't really found out. I don't think any of the answers is better than another."

Booker shook his head, muttering something to himself. He pulled out a handkerchief, wiped down the gun, and tossed it onto Mrs. O'Donnell's body. The action should have reassured her—Booker was throwing down his weapon—but the resignation in his posture set off alarms in her mind.

She had a bad leg and a very short head start, but everything in Dani's body told her to run.

XXX

Booker threw the gun onto Mrs. O'Donnell's body. They'd never trace it back to him. There was no point in carrying it anymore. Gunshots on the Mall tended to make the police nervous. He was running out of time. The last bits of this job were going to have to be done by hand. The thought of killing Dani with a gun seemed vulgar and cold, in any event. He wanted to feel the blade sink into her flesh. He wanted to see her eyes when she died. He owed her that.

When he looked back and saw her limping into the shadows, he had to smile again. That took guts. From what he could see, the wound on her thigh was messy. That she could run at all told him it had missed the major infrastructure of the leg, but still, it probably hurt like hell. Never let it be said Dani Britton lacked grit, he thought. He called out to her.

"Dani, stop. Don't do this to yourself. I get it. You're tough. It doesn't have to be like this." It really didn't, but as he set off at a casual stroll after her, he had to admit that he was more than a little glad it was like this.

She was headed toward the Tidal Basin where the sidewalks were dark and hidden from traffic. It would have been a smart play if the weather was warm and the trees and bushes in bloom. There might have been a place to hide or groups of tourists strolling in the warm night air to seek help from. This time of year, however, the branches were bare and the sidewalks deserted. With her injured leg, she wouldn't get far and when he caught up with her, he would have her to himself. Booker bit his lip and smiled.

XXX

Even as she ran Dani knew she was screwed. If she'd run the other direction, she might have seen a cop or gotten to the street, but

209

running the other direction would have put her closer to Tom. She would have had to step over Ev's bloody body.

Who was she kidding? She'd run the direction she'd run because that was the direction she'd been facing and her only thought was to go forward. Forward meant down to the Tidal Basin and the long, open sidewalk.

She bit her lip against the shrieking pain of her leg. Her boot felt like it was full of pudding as blood soaked into her sock, and her jeans stuck to her in the most revolting way. She barreled lopsided and off rhythm toward the stone wall around the water. Tom shouted something but she couldn't hear him. She could only hear her heartbeat in her ears and the *thump-slide thump-slide* of her gait.

The wall around the basin gave her something to lean on, speeding up her pace. She wouldn't say it made her optimistic but the increase in distance held despair slightly further at bay.

The mist had turned to full-blown rain. Her clothes weighed a ton. If she had any hope of keeping up this pace or any pace, she had to shed some of the weight. The wet woolen outer shirt clung to her as she peeled it off and Dani nearly lost her balance as she wrestled the clinging beast from her wrists. Images of falling on her face, her hands bound neatly behind her in her stupid shirt, made panic rise up in her chest until she finally freed herself from the garment, flinging it behind her. Maybe Tom would trip on it.

X X X

Tom wiped R's blood from the serrated knife on his pants leg as he trotted along the basin wall. The hooked blade was his second favorite weapon, the first being the smaller knife at his back. He debated which one to use. The serrated blade ended things quickly and really he did owe Dani as much mercy as he could summon. Yet he was drawn to that little blade, the one he called Nugget, which required skill and proximity. It made a mess and worked best in the closest of quarters. It wasn't a coward's knife.

Something black lay heaped on the sidewalk and Booker slowed to study it. He crouched down beside it and poked at it with the hooked tip of the blade. A shirt. It could have been anyone's—D.C. had no shortage of homeless people, or a jogger or any of the tourists who had strolled this sidewalk when the sun had been up could have dropped it—but Booker decided it was Dani's, that she had peeled it off as she ran. She'd been wearing a shirt like this, something two times too big for her.

He tried to dam the thought before it got to him but failed. He kept forgetting how small Dani was. If she hit five feet, he'd give her a nickel. He kept seeing those little boots in her closet and how low the clothing bar had been set. She'd even installed a second, lower peephole in her apartment door. It didn't make him pity her. Far from it. Booker didn't know if he was even capable of pity anymore. He'd kill a frail old woman just as quickly as a strapping young buck. No, what he admired in Dani was the contrast between her petite frame and her mighty presence. That was the only word he could find to describe her—mighty. She'd eluded him, ducked him, lied to him, smiled at him, and talked to him, really talked to him. He wished he could call her right now. He wished he could get his thoughts straight, because even as he didn't want to kill her, he also knew that he looked forward to it.

X X X

The small elation of confidence she'd felt when she'd hit the wall dissolved further with every step she took. Dani knew she was hitting a different wall altogether. She didn't know how much blood she was losing. She told herself that if it had been a femoral artery she'd be dead already but that didn't comfort her much. She felt cold to the bone, not the cold that came from the rain or the night air but a cold that came from shock and loss and operating at a deficit of supplies. She couldn't keep this up. She couldn't keep running but the dark and the rain made focusing difficult. A few pathways rose up from the sidewalk but from where she stood, the enormity of propelling her body up the slope seemed insurmountable.

Maybe Tom had given up. The dwindling rational voice in her brain screamed "NoNoNo" but the rest of her rejoiced at the thought, clinging to any possibility that meant stopping this marathon, closing the eyes, laying the body down. She should never have entertained the thought, because her legs mutinied and her hands joined in, grabbing at the wall and hauling her into one of the shallow look-out alcoves peppering the wall around the Tidal Basin. Less than three feet deep and six feet wide and open to the sidewalk, the alcove had waist-high metal fencing that let visitors peer down into the icy water of the man-made reservoir. Dani would have been hard-pressed to find a worse hiding place short of just lying down in the middle of the sidewalk. But it seemed she was no longer the master of her own body. The arms and legs and cold toes and bleeding fingers commandeered the decision and Dani found herself crouched in the corner of the alcove, her head resting on a lower rung, her bleeding leg straight out before her. The buckle of the Rasmund pouch strap dug into her side where she pressed against the wall. She started to pull the damned thing off and got only as far as pulling her shoulder free. The pouch rested in her lap, the strap around her neck.

In the unfunniest of ways, it was funny. She'd started this whole nightmare in a crouch. She'd crouched in front of Hickman when she'd heard gunshots and seen him dead. She'd spent the day scrabbling and crouching and hiding until she was running and sliding and jumping off of roofs. She'd been shot. She'd hidden in a beanbag chair. She'd had a bologna sandwich just like the ones her dad would make her. She wished she'd kissed Joey from Big Wong's. She wished she'd kissed Choo-Choo. She doubted there was going to be much more jumping and sliding tonight. At least she didn't feel cold anymore.

X X X

Booker stopped and listened. He didn't hear any footsteps. The soft sound of traffic floated in from a distance but he no longer heard the irregular beat of Dani's footsteps.

Was she hurt? Worry stabbed at his gut. He didn't want to think of Dani fallen down or unconscious. He knew what he was going to do to her would hurt but he would make that hurt better, he would make it mean something. Dani didn't deserve to die alone and cold, hit by a car or bleeding out from a bullet.

Or was she hiding? Had she found a lead pipe or a two-by-four and decided to lie in wait for him? Did she have a plan even now, injured and exhausted, shocked beyond reason? The idea of stepping from a shadow and seeing Dani coiled and bloody, her messy hair and bright eyes waiting to attack, thrilled Booker in a way that surprised him. He felt that same rush of blood he'd felt upon entering her apartment. It felt sexual and spiritual and primitive and scintillating all at the same time. More than a little bit, he hoped he'd get the chance to wrestle a weapon from her.

He saw her boot first.

The little round toe of it peeked from the edge of one of the fenced viewing alcoves around the basin. Booker froze, waiting, but the boot didn't move. He risked another step, leaning forward to peer around the edge. Her right leg, the injured one, sprawled out before her, her left leg was bent and falling to the side. Dani looked too pale as she lay with her head back against the fencing, her mouth open, her eyes closed.

Booker's breath caught in his throat. She wasn't dead. She couldn't be dead. But she could be close.

"Dani?"

XXX

She was in the cubby behind her father's seat. She could feel the rumble of the road in her skull where it rested against the metal. She was warm and he was talking to someone and she didn't want to open her eyes. "Dani?" her father called to her. She didn't want to open her eyes but she wanted to see her father. "Dani? Come on. Wake up."

She peeled one eye open, then the other, blinking hard to bring them into focus. A wide, pale face smiled at her, pretty blue eyes with long lashes and deep wrinkles in the corner. Chapped lips smiling at her. Not her father—he had brown eyes like hers. This was . . .

"Oh shit!"

Dani banged her head on the fence, throwing herself backward where there was nowhere to go. The sudden rush of panic gave her strength to get her feet under her, hardly aware of the pain shooting up her right leg. Her heels slipped in the wetness and her hands grabbed at the stone and the railing to lift her up and away from the face, the man, Tom, the killer, who held his hands up, still smiling, letting her get up on her feet.

"I'm sorry," he said. "I didn't mean to scare you."

"Are you going to kill me?"

He sighed and scratched his head. "Dani . . ."

"Oh, oh." She started to cry. "Don't. Don't. Don't do this."

"If there was any other way—"

"Don't. Don't. You don't have to do this."

XXX

214

He couldn't bear to see her cry. He didn't want her to cry.

Crying usually enraged him. Too often, begging elicited savagery from Booker, but this time was different. This time it hurt him.

He'd run her to ground. He'd pushed her too far and rather than feel pride in his prowess, he felt loss at breaking such a creature. All he could think to do was crowd up against her, to hide her tears in his body. He pressed in close, wrapping his arms around her waist and lifting her up against the fencing. The wind off the water behind her blew her hair in a wild cloud around her head. She pushed at his shoulders but with no leverage she couldn't budge him. Her hands burned where they touched the bunched muscles in his arms.

"Dani. If there was any other way . . ."

"There is. There is. You don't have to. You don't have to do this."

"I have to. I have to."

Their words poured over each other, their breaths mingling in the warm wet privacy between them. She trembled and jumped against him and he slid his left thigh between her knees, lifting her up on his leg, forcing her to lean on him. His fingers dug into the waistband of her jeans, finding the belt loops and dragging her closer to him.

"If there was any other way, Dani, I would save you. I would." He couldn't bear it any longer. He would use the serrated blade. He would end this now and hold her until it was over. He would hold her as long as he could. He ground his hips against her to hold her in place and heard her cry as his hand slipped between them. The knife slid from the sheath and with a whispered "I'm sorry," he pushed the blade into her stomach.

The blade bounced back, twisting from his grip and nicking his hand before clattering to the ground.

"Son of a bitch," he muttered.

X X X

Dani felt as if she'd been punched. Cold air rushed in when he drew back swearing.

His wide eyes stared down at her stomach where the blade had tried and failed to puncture the Rasmund pouch. The stunned look on his face and the loosening of his grip gave Dani the chance to shove hard with both hands, pushing him back far enough to get a knee up between them. It was a brief victory because Tom responded with a backhand that snapped her face to the side, cracking her teeth together. She couldn't hear anything but a ringing in her ear but she felt him jerk her higher onto the fence. The top bar pressed painfully into her lower back.

He jammed himself hard between her legs, forcing the air from her lungs. He chanted her name over and over in a low growl that sounded angry and relentless and something else she didn't want to think of as she felt what she prayed was another knife hilt pressing against her through his pants. She felt his teeth and lips and tongue at the side of her neck and Dani thought she might be screaming even though she couldn't hear anything but hard harsh breaths.

She forced herself to go still. "Tom, please."

He stopped pressing forward but kept his lips against her neck. "Dani."

"You don't have to do this. Nobody needs to know about you."

"They're going to be here soon. They're going to be everywhere. If it had been anyone but the government, Dani. If it had been anyone—the mob, Wal-Mart, anyone. But the CIA? They never stop. They'll never stop."

"They won't know about you."

"You'll know about me. They'll know what you know."

"I won't tell."

He pulled back and pressed his forehead to hers. "You won't have a choice."

Tears filled her eyes. "You have a choice."

X X X

He had no choice. He knew he had to hurry. Police would be flooding the area any minute. They would never stop looking for him and nobody, not even Dani, was worth going into a cage.

"Listen to me, Dani." He stroked his thumb along her chin. "It's better this way. It is. If they take us, they'll put us in the deepest darkest prison cells they can find. They'll put us both in cages. You can't live in a cage. You can't. You wouldn't."

"I don't want to die."

"I know." He did. Such a simple sentiment, one that he'd heard a hundred times in his career, but hearing it from Dani broke his heart. She should live. They should both live but the unholy truth was that only one of them could. He shifted his grip on her, lifting so her bottom rested on one of the rungs, her uninjured leg able to brace itself on the lowest rung. She took the position, her bad leg straight but not bearing her weight anymore. Her elbows hooked over the top rung. It didn't look very comfortable but he could see her relax.

"Why don't you just run?"

He smiled. "I'm going to. I'll get away. Don't worry." He slid his hands up her collarbone, under the blue strap of the bag around her neck. He felt her pulse hammering hot beneath his thumbs and he couldn't help but groan at the way her pupils widened. She knew what he was going to do.

X X X

She knew what he was going to do and she couldn't believe she had to stand there and let it happen. His soft hands and muscular arms were going to strangle her, crush her throat until she couldn't breathe. She would crumple broken onto the ground like Ev and Mrs. O'Donnell.

Fuck that.

Before she could think it through, she grabbed the strap of the Rasmund pouch and whipped it like a jump rope out from behind her head and over and behind Tom's. Using every ounce of strength she had, she pushed off the fence twisting her body to the right, jerking Tom by the neck. She roared as she lunged and Tom faltered one step, then two. He started to drop to his knee into the corner of the alcove and Dani knew she had to get over his back to clear the alcove and reach the open sidewalk. She pushed herself up and over his dropping shoulder, her arms rigid as they shoved the pouch down and away.

She could see the space opening up before her. She felt him moving and felt herself getting distance from the fence. Fractions of seconds inched by as she forced her body to press past the muscular form pinning her in place and she was getting there. She was moving him. She twisted to the left, her arms straining to the right and she felt the balance shifting in her favor. Then she felt agony. A howl ripped from her throat as her body constricted to escape the pain that erupted from every cell in her body. She didn't even understand it as pain. She didn't know where she felt it. It was an agony as pure as anything in the universe and it threw her back against the fencing.

X X X

Booker punched the bullet hole in her leg. He ground his knuckle into the sloppy wet hole until he felt her skin giving way beneath his hand. He pushed and twisted and heard her wail as her back arched and her muscles tensed. He shoved his shoulder hard against her chest, knocking the air from her lungs and silencing her scream. He pressed himself hard against her, every inch of his torso fitting against hers until he had her bent backward over the black water behind her.

"Are you going to kill me, Dani? Huh? You going to be the sledgehammer?"

He knew she couldn't hear him, her body struggling to adjust to the trauma he'd inflicted on her leg. Her eyes rolled, whites showing bright and wide around her brown irises, and her mouth worked in a wordless cry. He watched her face, watched her blink rapidly, watched her mind come back to her body and he saw the moment she saw him. It was beautiful.

"Dani, Dani, Dani. You are perfect. Do you know that? Perfect. You want to kill me? Tell me the truth. Do you want to kill me?"

She stared at him, her mouth open, her teeth white in the dark.

"Yes."

He grinned. "Do it." He pulled her up so she could stabilize herself on the railing. When he was certain she wouldn't collapse, he held her with one hand and with the other, he looped the strap of the pouch around his neck once more. He then took both of her hands from the railing and pressed them until they closed around either side of the strap. He felt the loop tighten slightly as the strap took the weight of her adjusted balance.

When she'd settled in place, he reached behind him and pulled Nugget, the little silver knife, out from the small of his back. He held it up for her to see.

"Who do you think is faster, Dani? Huh? Come on, pull."

She bowed her head.

X X X

She knew what came next. Tension drained from her neck and shoulders and for the first time in her life, Dani understood why they called surrender sweet. It felt sweet. It felt inevitable. She knew what came next was going to hurt probably more than all of the hurt so far combined. But it was inevitable.

219

She raised her head to look at Tom. It occurred to her that she knew a lot of very good-looking men and the absurdity of the realization made her smile. Tom smiled back. That knife looked unpleasant so she decided to look at his face instead. He really did have beautiful eyes. They glistened with tears and she had to lean forward to hear what he said.

"If there was any other way, Dani, I would have saved you."

She smiled and raised her right hand to his face. He kept repeating himself even when she pressed her thumb against his warm lips.

"Shh," she said, sliding her left hand along the muscles in his chest, moving underneath the pouch strap, until her fingers played in the soft damp curls at his back of his head. "It's okay." His eyes widened in surprise and he leaned into her touch. She tucked the rough strap of the Rasmund pouch into the crook of her elbow and closed her eyes. "You are going to save me."

She threw herself backwards into the darkness of the Tidal Basin.

X X X

If the pain in her leg had been an explosion, what happened in her shoulder was a supernova. She heard ripping and crunching as Tom's head slammed into the railing, dragged down by the weight of her falling body caught in the unbreakable strap. The impact ripped her shoulder from its socket and she barely got her right hand up and onto the strap. Her body slammed into the stone wall of the basin, banging her head and scraping her skin.

Above it all, she felt the familiar sensation of her mind separating her thoughts into manageable compartments. She knew she felt pain even as she knew her brain would not allow her to experience it in its fullness. Cotton batting separated her from her howling shoulder and the waterfall of her leg. She spun from the strap by her weakening fingers and she noticed the strap had stopped moving.

She couldn't remember why but she knew that was a very good thing.

Thoughts came fast and moved through without sticking. Was the water cold? It was dirty. Her pinkie had slipped. Her boots were heavy. Were those geese? Bright light flooded the scene and the water below her became choppy. She was blind and a loud blender hovered over her head. Not a blender, a helicopter, and it shouted at her. It sounded like "Hitches for lease. Who's got to poop?" but she was pretty sure that wasn't what they said. Her ring finger slipped and her middle finger ached, the strap rolling in her grip. She wondered how far down the water was. The white light moved and she could see the glowing yellow lights of the dome across the water.

"Jefferson," she said. Jefferson was her favorite president.

She was unconscious before her head broke the water.

CHAPTER FIFTEEN

Three months later

Her leg ached. She knew she should have gotten out and stretched before this but it felt so good to be back behind the wheel.

Rain poured over the windshield. Without the wipers on she couldn't see the white eagle on the emblem on the side of the building. Not the Central Intelligence Agency emblem. She hoped she'd never see that again. This was the post office. She watched the man in uniform unlock the door, opening the station for the day.

She rubbed the scar through her jeans. The wound had gotten infected badly and she'd gone through several rounds of antibiotics and painful injections. Her shoulder had required two operations. She still didn't know where she'd been treated. It was a hospital of some sort but one with no windows, plenty of cameras, and numerous heavily armed guards. It was the type of hospital where interrogations interrupted sleep night after night until days and nights ran together in a wash of drugs and pain.

Tom had been right. Or whatever his name was. She would have sold him out. Even if she had felt some kind of loyalty to him, she never would have been able to hold out against the onslaught of intimidation and interrogation. Pain meds were withheld, sleep interrupted, and a bewildering barrage of faces and badges and weapons and rankings marched before her. She'd have told them anything they wanted to know. She had told them things they couldn't possibly have been interested in. More than a few times, she wished she'd died at the Tidal Basin.

They didn't tell her much. She still didn't know which agency she had supposedly been working for or who had been behind the hit. She didn't know who had hired Tom and she didn't care. Through the haze of drugs and fear, she'd heard nothing but strings of letters and "chief director of this" and "deputy director of that." At one point she'd overheard someone talking about the NEA. The National Endowment for the Arts? The National Education Association? She'd wondered if maybe that was where the woman whose laptop they'd borrowed had worked. It made more sense than thinking teachers and ballerinas were interrogating her. It didn't matter. Nobody answered her anyway.

She'd been there at least a month when they'd let her know that Choo-Choo had survived. She'd begged a thousand times to see him and on a thousand and one they led her to his room. The bullet had shattered ribs, collapsed his lung, nicked a vertebra, and caused massive internal hemorrhaging. He'd barely pulled through. The marine guard stood over her as she sat on the edge of his bed and wrapped her good hand around his long fingers.

He blinked several times until he could focus on her and he smiled. "Hi."

"Hi." She nodded toward the IV bag. ""Good drugs?"

"I've had better." He laughed and winced at the pain it caused.

She'd wanted to see him so badly and now she couldn't think of anything to say. When she'd learned he had survived, she'd felt herself come back to life. He was the only other person who knew what she knew, who knew their innocence of the crimes committed under Rasmund's roof. His hair lay greasy and lank against his skull

223

and his once beautiful skin looked rough and broken. She didn't imagine she looked much better.

He licked his dry lips. "It seems like the interrogations are slowing down."

"Maybe they believe us. Maybe they'll let us go soon."

He squeezed her fingers. "Where will you go?"

"Probably back to Oklahoma. You?"

"They're encouraging me to stick to the story that Mrs. O'Donnell told Grandfather. Once I'm fully recovered they want to help me perform the prodigal son's return."

"Are you going to?"

"They're very persuasive." He sighed and stared up at the ceiling. "I'll do my penance. It certainly isn't the first time I've done the walk of shame back into the bosom of my family. Maybe I'll go to our place on Martha's Vineyard. You know, buy some pants with whales on them and pretend to love to sail." Dani watched him stare at nothing. She saw the hard line of his lips and the thought occurred to her that Choo-Choo might decide to kill himself.

They hadn't been allowed to see each other much after that. Twice they'd passed on the way to physical therapy and once they'd stood outside the shower room together but there really wasn't much they could say. Every word was recorded and not subtly. Guards watched every move they made. The nurses had even applied body monitors to read her reaction when they told her that Tom— Booker, they called him—had survived his injuries. They'd watched her eyes and listened to her pulse rate when they informed her he was being detained and treated in the same facility. She didn't know what they wanted to see or if her lack of reaction worked in her favor or against it. She had told them she hoped they would keep him away from her but not much else. Maybe it was the drugs but Dani's idea of "enemy" felt kind of blurry in that place.

She had no way to measure the time at the time, but six weeks later a trio of men with briefcases had come into her room and taken her statement. She'd told them everything she knew, which amounted to very little. One of the men had mentioned an investigation but nobody answered her questions regarding its progress. Two weeks after that the same men reappeared with a thick binder of pages covered in dense type. They told her to read it, understand it, and sign where marked. She'd started reading, wanting to be certain she wasn't being pressured to sign a confession, but after sixty pages of impenetrable government doublespeak, she'd begun to sign. It took her two hours to sign and initial the three hundred-plus page document and all she really understood of it was that it guaranteed her silence on the matter of Rasmund until the world came to an end. She didn't need to read what the consequences might be.

The next day she got a change of clothes, five thousand dollars cash, and a ride in a windowless van to her apartment. She also got her car keys. When they'd slid the door open beside her old maroon Honda, she'd cried for the first time in weeks. The van had pulled away while she stood weeping in the street.

Whoever had searched her apartment had been more than thorough. Wall panels had been pulled down, floorboards pulled up, bedding and cushions shredded. They'd even dumped out her mustard, horseradish, and all of her cereal boxes. There were flies everywhere.

"Slovenly fuckers," she muttered, and then said it louder in case the place was bugged.

She didn't pack much. After all that time in a hospital gown, Dani could hardly remember what she used to wear. She'd grabbed a duffel and thrown in some jeans and shirts, underwear, bras and socks, and a couple pairs of shoes. She almost left the hideous shawl/poncho thing her Aunt Penny had made her, but relented, shoving it into the bag. They were going to wind up burying her in that monstrosity. She didn't bother with toiletries. Everything felt tainted.

She had only one photo of her with her father and it still sat on her nightstand. She opened the frame and slipped the picture out. If they were going to bug anything, that frame would be it.

Finally she headed back to the kitchen. Every drawer had been upended; every pamphlet and note she'd had on her refrigerator taken down. All that remained was her collection of magnets.

Every summer when she'd ridden in the truck with her father, they'd picked up a magnet at each city they stopped in. There was a flat rubber magnet of an alligator from the Everglades, a slice of wood with a river cut into it from white-water country in West Virginia. The Las Vegas magnet had a big pair of dice and a poker chip, and a glittery pink cowboy boot danced on a banner for Houston. She'd collected dozens of magnets over the years and they were the only things she valued as much as her car. Holding the bag against the refrigerator, she swept the collection into the bag on top of her clothes. She tossed the apartment key onto the counter and didn't bother to lock the door behind her.

They'd seized her bank account and canceled her credit cards. Even though she'd been in no position to complain, she'd had to work hard to keep her mouth shut. Typical government move. They didn't know who exactly was guilty or what role she had played in it. They didn't care that their own people had put the plan in motion and that she'd been shot and injured by one of their own agents, however rogue. They told her that the money, her paycheck, had been obtained illegally and was therefore now the property of the United States government. They had made it clear that the five thousand dollars was purely a courtesy, and a generous one, and she wouldn't be receiving another dime in compensation. It seemed the powers that be considered five thousand dollars the golden ticket to rebuild a life. Maybe they thought the cost of living was cheaper in Oklahoma. She certainly couldn't stay in D.C. Maybe they figured she would be too busy fighting to make ends meet to think about whether justice had been served.

She didn't know where she was going. She sure as hell wasn't going back to Oklahoma. She'd said that for the agents bugging the rooms. Maybe she'd head to Florida. Dani liked warm weather and Florida was about as un-Oklahoma as she could think of. There was one stop she knew she had to make and she'd driven all night through West Virginia to get there, despite her injured leg and stiff shoulder begging for a break.

The rain let up enough to read the sign she'd parked in front of—the Lexington, Kentucky, Central Post Office. This was her third time in Lexington, her second at this location. Dani grabbed the duffel on the floor of the passenger side and hauled it up onto the seat. She fished around until she found the wide clay magnet painted green with a black horse running behind a white fence. In raised letters, chipped from banging around inside the bag, were the words LEXINGTON, KENTUCKY—THE BLUEGRASS STATE.

X X X

The last thing Dani had done before she'd left Oklahoma five years ago was to implement another little trick her father had taught her. She stopped by the bar where she'd worked. She'd high-fived and made her good-byes and then ducked behind the bar to the big cardboard box that served as the lost-and-found collection point. It had always amazed her, the things people left behind—cell phones, wallets, IDs, even an upper dental plate. It seemed a lot of folks came through Flat Road, Oklahoma, but few came through twice. She flipped through the items until she found something she thought she could use—a driver's license belonging to one Tenna Rene Hardy of Lawrence, Kansas. The woman in the picture was taller than Dani but had the same black hair. As her father would have said, "A man on horseback would never know the difference." She'd pocketed the ID and pulled away, headed for D.C.

Her last stop on the way to her new life had been in Lexington, Kentucky, where she now parked. She'd gone into the post office with the fake ID, a handful of cash, and a breathless story about needing a large post office box to send her mail to while she went on a Christian mission trip spreading the Good Word to the poor souls in Africa. The clerk had listened to her politely, taken her money, and explained to her the rules for renewing the box as needed.

Every year since, Dani sent a money order to the Lexington post office to renew her post office box. That wasn't all she sent to Lexington. Twice a year, at Christmas and her father's birthday, Dani would go through her stashes of cash and count out five thousand dollars. She'd stuff this into a padded envelope and mail it to Tenna Rene Hardy in Lexington, Kentucky. She never sent the packages from the same mailbox twice; she never put a return address, although she often scribbled silly little notes like "Ho Ho Ho!" and "Mama says howdy!!!" Her plan had been to take a trip this spring, collect her five years' worth of mail, and find a new hiding place for it. Needless to say, she'd missed Christmas this year.

Dani groaned at the stiffness in her leg as she rose from the car. She fished a plastic bag from beneath her seat and grabbed the little clay magnet. She'd been eleven when her father had given this to her. He'd taken her to Keeneland and let her see the horses run. Dani ran her fingers over the running horse.

Using her car key, she pried the black magnet strip off the back. It broke away easily along the same lines she had glued it on five years before. Beneath the magnet, in a little crater in the clay, sat the post office box key. Dani limped inside and opened box 551. Nine padded envelopes sat scattered in the bottom of the drawer. Forty-five thousand dollars in cash wasn't enough to live on forever, but it was a damned sight more than the U.S. government had seen fit to provide. It was enough to get a good running start to somewhere.

Before the madness had taken her, Emmaline Britton had told her daughter that it was better to be careful than clever. Pulling back onto the highway with nothing but a bag of clothes, her car, and a bundle of untraceable cash, Dani Britton thought it might be better still to be both.

ACKNOWLEDGMENTS

If this book makes any sense at all, the credit goes to my development editor, David Downing. You are much nicer than East Coast deer. Thanks as always to Terry Goodman for being patient with me and to Christine Witthohn for always having my back. Jacque and the team at Thomas & Mercer never fail to impress with their enthusiasm, friendliness, and professionalism. I'm in good hands.

Big sloppy kisses to my entire family—blood and otherwise. A special kiss to my niece Lucia Redling, who kept me motivated during the first escape scene.

I'd be more of a wild-eyed mess than I already am without the fierce friendship of the Book Thugs. I am beholden to you.

And finally a special thank you to the raccoon that kept breaking into my house and wound up giving me the idea for the file's hiding place. For that, I won't kick you out of my chimney.

ABOUT THE AUTHOR

JESSICA ST. JAMES

A fifteen-year veteran of morning radio and an avid traveler, S.G. Redling lives in West Virginia.